MONSTERS

ALSO BY DAVID A. ROBERTSON

THE RECKONER BOOK TWO

MONSTERS

DAVID A. ROBERTSON

**HIGHWATER
PRESS**

**Canada Council
for the Arts**

We acknowledge the support of the Canada Council for the Arts, which last year invested $153 million to bring the arts to Canadians throughout the country.

Nous remercions le Conseil des arts du Canada de son soutien. L'an dernier, le Conseil a investi 153 million de dollars pour mettre de l'art dans la vie des Canadiennes et des Canadiens de tout le pays.

HighWater Press gratefully acknowledges the financial support of the Province of Manitoba through the Department of Sport, Culture & Heritage and the Manitoba Book Publishing Tax Credit, and the Government of Canada through the Canada Book Fund (CBF), for our publishing activities.

HighWater Press is an imprint of Portage & Main Press.
Printed and bound in Canada by Friesens
Design by Relish New Brand Experience
Cover Art by Peter Diamond

Library and Archives Canada Cataloguing in Publication

Robertson, David, 1977-, author

    Monsters / David A. Robertson.

(The reckoner ; 2)

ISBN 978-1-55379-748-7 (softcover)

    I. Title. II. Series: Robertson, David, 1977- . Reckoner ; 2

PS8585.O32115M66 2018   jC813'.6   C2017-907839-9

24 23 22 21 20 19 18   1 2 3 4 5

Also issued in electronic format:
ISBN: 978-1-55379-760-9 (ePUB)
ISBN: 978-1-55379-761-6 (PDF)

HIGHWATER PRESS

www.highwaterpress.com
Winnipeg, Manitoba
Treaty 1 Territory and homeland of the Métis Nation

TO ANYBODY LIVING WITH THEIR OWN MONSTERS,
BIG AND SMALL. I HAVE THEM TOO.

PROLOGUE

HOURS AFTER VICTOR HAD ENTERED BLACKWOOD FOREST, he hadn't yet caught any game. Not a moose, not a muskrat. And it wasn't ineptitude—Victor had always been a successful hunter—but he hadn't even seen game. Old tracks led nowhere. New tracks were impossible to locate. He'd meandered through the entire area he'd frequented since he was a child, and stopped only for a bagged lunch.

Crack.

Victor took a quick breath, and peered through the darkness, towards the sound. It was faint, but in the quiet of the woods, unmistakable. He walked silently in the same direction, expertly navigating over twigs and roots and fallen branches. He saw a clearing in the distance.

Crack.

He waded through the black as though he were a part of it. Rifle raised, letting the muzzle guide him. Close to the clearing, he crouched down, squinted his eyes, and tried to make out a mound in the middle of the open space, where the cracking sounds originated. But he couldn't figure out what it was. It just looked like a big pile of blackness.

He moved forward methodically, patiently, inch by inch. It happened this way. The hunt. It had happened this way since he was a little boy.

Crack.

Louder. Crisper—and something else: Breathing. A low, almost indistinguishable growling, coming from behind the mound. An animal that had found better luck than Victor. He repositioned his rifle.

The smell. It thrust into his nostrils. Flesh. Tinny blood. Death. Feet away, Victor saw what the mound really was: a collection of dead animals—carcasses, stacked one on top of the other. Moose. Muskrats. Prairie chickens. No wonder he hadn't seen any game. A pile this wide, this high. He moved around it, inch by inch, methodically, patiently. He tried to think of what animal would do this. What animal would kill all this game? And keep it like this?

Crack. Snap. Rip.

The sound of bones breaking, flesh and tendons tearing. The source: a dark figure, squatting on two legs, working away at a large bone. In front of the figure lay another carcass. Victor could make it out in the clearing, with the northern lights shining overhead. Two legs. Two arms. Well, one and a half arms. The dark thing had the other half in its mouth.

"Upayokwitigo," Victor breathed out, low enough that the creature didn't hear him, too intent on eating its prey.

He backed away, sliding each foot along the ground. Methodically. Patiently.

Snap!

A small twig under Victor's foot. He gasped.

The thing raised its head.

Victor fell backwards. He scrambled on his elbows and heels until his back hit a bush.

The thing moaned. It moved towards him.

"Awas! Awas!" Victor yelled.

It neared him. Growling. Hissing. It moved like water on its hands and feet.

"Move," he whispered to himself.

It was at his feet now. He felt its saliva drip against his legs. The creature reached forward.

Victor clutched at the ground and dug his fingers into the dirt.

"Awas," he whimpered. "Awas."

The creature's head jerked backward, then forward, and then it screamed.

Victor pushed back with his heels—into the bush, through the bush. The thing lunged at him and swiped wildly with one of its hands. He felt a rush of wind as it missed him by a hair. Victor scrambled to his feet, turned, and ran. He didn't look back, even as the awful screams burst his eardrums. He shot his rifle into the air as he ran, again and again, trying to scare it away. He ran hard and fast for what felt like hours until he burst out of Blackwood's tree line towards the only building that was lighted.

The Fish.

1

X MARKS THE SPOT

COLE COULDN'T REMEMBER A TIME WHEN Wounded Sky First Nation offered this brand of quiet. Not when he was a child, and not since he had returned to the community after ten years away. If he were to believe Choch, it was the calm before the storm. Cole was waiting for the storm, but it hadn't come. Yes, he had used his remaining anti-anxiety pills over the past week, but not because he'd encountered any stormy incidents like murder or a flu epidemic. Rather, he'd taken a pill upon his return to Ashley's trailer, for his friend's wake. The memory of Ashley being shot right in front of him had appeared, thick and fresh. He'd taken his last pill during the gathering for Alex, as guilt reared its head at Cole's inability to save her, and as her brother, Michael, sent a barrage of glares in his direction. Deserved glares, Cole had thought, not only because he was the last person to see her alive, but also because Alex had kissed him, and Michael knew it.

Deserved, but still not easy to take.

Cole hoped the stillness of the community was the quiet *after* the storm, not before. A collective sigh. A long breath out. Choch had been quiet, too. Cole hadn't heard from the spirit being since they'd met at the ruins, when he'd given Cole textbooks instead of a ticket home— and when he'd told Cole that school started Monday in Wounded Sky. This was the first clear direction the spirit being had ever provided. Of course, the calm—the non-spirit-being-related peace—could've simply been that it was early in the morning. Cole shrugged, as though involved in a deep conversation with somebody other than himself. A boy could dream, right?

Cole had a hockey stick resting against his shoulder, and a pair of skates fastened onto the stick, bouncing against his back with every step. He'd borrowed the hockey equipment from Brady, who had become something like his counselor, with Elder Mariah still recovering from the sickness at the clinic, and had remained something like his landlord as Cole continued to sleep at Brady's place. The skates fit about right, although there remained a legitimate concern as to whether they'd remain intact. Brady hadn't worn them for years, long enough that they had trouble finding them in his closet. "This is like an archaeological dig," Cole joked while they searched. The bigger problem? Brady was left-handed and Cole wasn't, never mind the fact that the stick was made of wood.

Cole knew where to find another stick, with the right curve for him, too. And another set of newer skates that may have fit better. But Cole couldn't bring himself to use Ashley's equipment, or to ask Brady if it would be okay, or to go back to the trailer. So, he made his way to the arena with Brady's skates and stick, and he didn't much care if the skates fit or if the stick had the wrong curve.

The sun began to rise over Blackwood Forest and the lights were on in the community hall. Cole felt drawn to it. Over the last week he kept an eye out for anything strange, a clue as to why he'd been told to stay here even though he'd stopped the murder spree and cured the virus. An influx of staff from Mihko Laboratories had definitely caught his attention. They were mostly at the clinic—descending upon it after those afflicted by the illness had become healthy (thanks to Cole's blood). But they were around the community, too—at the Fish, the mall, and the community hall, where they'd been sleeping and where the lights were on right now.

Cole took a slight detour. School didn't start for a while, and he wasn't in a rush. A security guard met him immediately upon his arrival at the community hall's front doors, and not one of Reynold's employees, either. No RMS—Reynold McCabe Security—anywhere on the man's clothing.

"Can I help you?" The man's warm greeting belied his presentation, dressed all in black and his body hard and sharp like he'd just come from working out. Like all he did was guard things and lift weights.

Cole tried to look over the man's considerable shoulders, but each try was thwarted as the guard tilted his body to obscure Cole's view. "I was just…" he started blankly, more concerned with assessing what he saw. But there wasn't much to assess. From his vantage point, all he could see were cots. Some of them were made crisply, and with precision. Others were still occupied: human-shaped mounds under blankets.

"You were just what?" the guard prompted.

"I'm just…" Cole moved Brady's hockey stick to his other shoulder and noticed the guard flinch "…wondering why you need to guard the hall? I can see why there's guards at the clinic and facility, I guess."

The guard looked around as though worried about company, and then he breathed in, and out, deeply. "You're Cole Harper, right?"

"Right." It failed to surprise Cole anymore when a stranger recognized him.

"Right," the guard nodded, "so you know what it's like to…" he searched for the right words "…lack trust."

Cole shrugged. "Sure."

"Yeah, you get it. So, Mihko, they have a history here…I'm sure you know that, Cole."

"You mean that huge lab accident that killed my dad? That history?"

"*That* history, yeah. So, they're not really popular here, and neither are you, right?"

"I'm slightly more popular now, if you haven't heard," Cole grumbled.

"Well, *they* haven't had any public meltdowns or anything since they've come. So, we'll call it even, how about that?"

"I guess there was the clinic…" Cole grimaced at the memory of the community turning on him, turning into an angry shouting mob and blaming him for the deaths and murders only because he'd come back to the community "…and the quarry." *The quarry.* Yet another reason for Michael to glare at him. Cole had knocked Michael out right after he'd found out Cole had walked Alex home and Alex had kissed him.

"They're trying to build trust," the guard said, "coming here to help after all that's happened. The murders, the sickness..."

"Yeah, I'm kind of more popular because I *stopped* those murders."

"...but until they have that trust, if they need guys like me to make sure they can help without interruption or interference, well..." the guard half-grinned.

"What are they worried about? Somebody's going to come and do something in their sleep? Do you think we practise, like, guerilla warfare or something?"

"They had pitchforks out for *you*, didn't they?"

"That was different, and I didn't cause a huge, like, epidemic chemical leak or whatever the hell happened down there at the facility!"

"That's kind of my point, bud."

"Nobody would've done anything to me, and nobody's going to do anything to them, so what's the deal?"

Cole moved towards the front door, but the guard pushed him back, one hand to Cole's chest. "Kid, I'm losing my patience."

"Anybody in *my* community is perfectly entitled to ask questions of our guests," Reynold McCabe said from behind Cole. "You'd do well to humour the boy."

Cole's heart skipped a beat. Choch, the friendly neighbourhood spirit being, typically was the one to appear out of nowhere. The last time Reynold McCabe snuck up like this, he'd held a gun to Cole's head, accused him of murdering Maggie and, by extension, Alex and Ashley. Reynold had knocked Cole on the back of the head and had him arrested for murder. Cole didn't turn around, but he watched the guard's face reluctantly soften. Then, Reynold stepped around Cole and faced him and the guard, shifting glances from one to the other.

"That clear?" Reynold asked.

"Yes," the guard said through his teeth, "crystal."

Reynold looked disheveled. Cole had only ever seen him completely put together—slick hair tied back into a braid, ironed shirts, sport coats, and crisp new jeans. *Weird*. Now his hair was loose, uncombed, and falling over his shoulders like broken cobwebs. His shirt and pants were scrubbed with dirt and covered in grass stains. He smelled, too. Like an old, neglected hockey bag. Sweat and mould. Reynold must've noticed Cole giving him a good inspection because he buttoned up his shirt quickly and tied his hair back into a ponytail.

"You okay, Mr. McCabe?" Cole asked him.

"I'm fine, Cole, although I appreciate your concern. That's how it should be here. We should be concerned for each other." Reynold kept working at his pony tail, smoothing it back as best he could. Cole and the guard waited, and watched, and both of them exchanged curious glances about the acting Chief of Wounded Sky First Nation. Reynold continued: "Anything that happened in the past, happened for the same reason, you understand."

"I understand, sure," Cole said.

"Now," Reynold looked at the guard, and Cole watched as the big hulk of a man seemed to shrink before Cole's eyes, "there won't be any more problems, will there?"

"No, sir," the guard said.

Cole looked back and forth between the guard and Reynold. Each time he looked at Reynold, he looked him over, head to foot, and everything about this exchange made Cole want to leave *now*. Forget whatever weird stuff was going on in the hall. It had nothing on this.

"Good," Reynold said after both men had not said anything for an uncomfortably long silence, just stared at each other. "Cole," Reynold nodded.

"Mr. McCabe," Cole echoed the same goodbye.

Reynold tucked his dress shirt into his pants, then walked away like this had been a typical exchange.

Cole kept standing there, but now it was supremely awkward. No eye contact with the guard either. He almost felt bad for the guy—who'd gone from authoritative to meek in no time. A couple of seconds passed before the guard cleared his throat. "So you're going skating this morning or…"

"Right, yeah." Cole lifted the stick for a moment, and then rested it back against his shoulder.

"Maybe you should do that, then."

"Yeah, maybe I should."

Cole tried to shake off the last several minutes as he continued on his way to the X. He felt that if he thought about it too much, Choch might pop into his head. Moments like this were the perfect mental conditions for Choch. *Oh, CB's confused about something? Weirded out? Let me make that worse.* But Choch remained silent, as he had been. Silent and, well, just plain absent. He hadn't been working at the Fish, being the world's worst and most annoying server and making up food specials that didn't exist. Jayne, his half-burning ghost companion, hadn't been around either. He stopped short of calling either of them and walked alone with only his thoughts to keep him company.

Cole stopped out in front of the rink where he dropped his anxiety medication last week. He crouched down and sifted his fingers through the dirt, as though the pills might still be there. Bits of grass and small pebbles fooled him for a split second, but none were his tiny white tablets. The crisp, cool rain Wounded Sky's autumn season offered had long since dissolved the pills. Cole stood up and hovered over the same spot, looking down, imagining himself from a week ago, kneeling in front of the pills, contemplating whether to gather them up or not. He hadn't been desperate enough then.

The lobby was silent and devoid of the familiar litter. No popcorn kernels. No spilled and sticky soft drinks. No drink lids, straws, or candy wrappers. While the quiet was nice, the cleanliness seemed wrong, like it wasn't a hockey rink lobby without the snacks half in mouths and half on the floor. For the last two Saturdays the hockey game had been cancelled. Cole had heard these were the first Saturdays without a hockey game for as long as anybody could remember.

Snap!

A hockey puck hitting the boards grabbed Cole's attention. He walked across the lobby and pushed the doors open to find Tristan skating by himself on the far side of the ice. Tristan had a bunch of pucks lined up and was shooting them. Cole could hardly see each puck make its way from Tristan's stick to the net.

"Whoa," Cole whispered to himself. As strong as he was, he'd never be able to shoot a puck that hard. More than just muscles, shooting took balance, skill, and coordination (and also, for Cole, a right-handed stick). He'd been prepared to suck when he decided to go to the X this morning because he didn't expect anybody to be there. It would be just him and the ice. Now, he had a mind to turn around and leave. Looking like an idiot in front of Tristan had not been in the plan.

But he had run away enough. So he sat down, unnoticed, in the front row of stands and put on skates for the first time in ten years. Cole felt seven years old. He had trouble, as he did then, putting the skates on. He manoeuvred his feet to sneak them inside the boot, jiggled them, and pounded his heel into the rubber mat—all things that his mom and dad used to do. When he finally got them on, he tied the laces tight. His dad used to say, "The skates fit when you can't feel your toes." Cole pulled the laces so hard that his knuckles turned white, got them as tight as he could.

Cole stood up. The skates felt like high heels. His ankles bent from side to side, and he couldn't find his balance. He clutched Brady's stick in his hands and used it as a cane from the stands to the gate. Tristan still hadn't noticed him. Cole stood at the gate for a moment, his breath fogging up the glass, and he watched Tristan take a few more shots before unlatching the gate and pulling it open. The clack of the latch thrusting down, and the squeal of the gate opening caused Tristan to stop mid-shot. He turned around just as Cole stepped onto the ice, in time to see him almost fall right on his ass, saved only by a desperate reach for the boards.

Tristan skated over as Cole attempted to steady himself without the help of the boards, and wondered if Brady's skates were super dull, if he hadn't tied them tight enough, or if he'd really gotten that bad.

Tristan snowed his pants with an aggressive hockey stop. "What are you doing here?" He tapped Cole's stick with his own. Judging by Tristan's face, it wasn't a playful tap.

"Skating?" Cole tried not to sound sarcastic.

Tristan looked down at Cole's skates, moving back and forth as he tried to keep his balance. "How's that working out for you?"

Cole shrugged. "It's not like riding a bike."

"This is the last place I expected to see you, Harper."

"It's probably the last place I thought I'd be, too. But, you know, if I'm going to be here, I figured I might as well do as the Romans do, right?"

"The what?"

"When in Rome?"

Tristan shoved Cole, hand to upper chest. Cole's back slammed against the glass. He barely kept his balance.

"You know where I *thought* I'd see you?"

"No." Cole pushed himself off the boards even as Tristan skated closer to him, the toes of his skates pushed up against the toes of Cole's.

"At Maggie's wake. That's where." Tristan's eyes started to well up. "I know you went to Alex's. I know you went to Ashley's. But Maggie's? AWOL." He wiped at his eyes before any tears could fall.

Cole didn't know what to say. He knew he should've gone. He'd run out of meds by then, and he didn't want to risk having another panic attack. Tristan didn't need to hear that and he wouldn't have wanted to hear it. It was selfish. "It was just, I don't know...one too many. I'm sorry."

Tristan lunged forward, put his forearm against Cole's throat, and pressed him against the glass. The tears were back then, and they fell freely. "That must've been really goddamn inconvenient for you."

Tristan had trouble getting the words out, trying not to sob. Cole could hear little hiccups when he talked. Cole tried to say something, but he had trouble speaking, too. His problem, however, was Tristan's forearm pressed against his neck.

"I can't believe Maggie would go and get murdered like that and make things so hard on you."

Cole tried not to slip into an even worse position. He turned one foot sideways so that the blade was stuck against the ice.

"Not so tough without your friends around, are you?"

Cole tried to choke out some words, but he failed. Finally, he reached his hand around Tristan's forearm and pulled it down, away from his neck. He caught his breath. "I…just don't want to…hurt any-body else."

"I'm right here. Take a shot."

Cole shook his head in response. He could have knocked Tristan all the way across the ice. But where had hurting Mark got him? Or Michael? More scrutiny, more unwanted attention, suspicion. He slipped out of Tristan's grasp and held himself up against the opened gate to prevent a nasty fall.

"What, you're just going to leave?" Tristan wiped the tears away from his eyes, from his cheeks. He cleared his throat and stiffened his face.

"Yeah, I'm just going to leave." Cole stepped off the ice. "I'm sorry about Maggie. I should've come. You're right."

"Yeah, well…" Tristan sounded unprepared to deal with Cole's admission. A long silence followed before he continued "…just don't bother coming back here when I'm around, okay?"

"Don't worry," Cole said as he sat down on the front row and started to untie Brady's skates, "I won't."

Tristan slammed the gate shut. Cole watched as he skated to the other end of the rink, and took a slapshot in stride. The puck clanged off the post, and the sound reverberated through the rink. Cole was quite certain he wouldn't come back here to skate, even with Tristan absent.

He checked the time on his phone. Time for school. The first day back since classes had been cancelled following all the chaos.

Cole pulled off his skates and slipped them back onto Brady's hockey stick. He stood up and shook his head at the thought he'd had last night, that getting back on the ice would help him fit in. School was the important thing, he decided. Fit in there? Golden. And after his encounter with Tristan, it could only get better from here.

2

MR. 87%

COLE HAD BEEN AT HIS ASSIGNED LOCKER for an uncomfortably long time, fumbling to get the lock open, hitting each of the three numbers as precisely as he could, attempt after attempt. His frustration rose each time he tugged the lock and was met with resistance. Finally, Cole looked around to ensure the coast was clear, and then he broke the lock open. He didn't have anything worth stealing anyway.

"Hey, Cole."

A jolt ran though his body. He still had the broken lock in his hand. He shoved it into his pocket.

"Stuck around in this shithole, hey?" Lucy—Cole was eighty-seven percent certain that was her name—leaned against the locker next to his. "Thought you'd be long gone after what went down."

Cole opened his locker, but he didn't actually put anything inside it. "I didn't really have a choice." He stood there, staring at the empty metal space until the locker began to shut and he had to move out of the way. Lucy closed the locker and leaned a bit closer to him.

"Speak up, boy. I can hardly hear you."

Boy, Cole repeated in his head. At least it didn't have *city* attached to the front. "I said I had to stay." Cole backed away a step. She looked him over, and he did the same. He tried to remember her. He had a certainty about her name now. She'd been almost too perfectly pretty before, and had remained pretty. Soft, like she'd been drawn with pastels. Soft, but somehow hard. In how she carried herself, how she talked. She'd taken to wearing blue contact lenses now. They looked Photoshopped.

"I would've left if I were you, Cole." She hugged her books against her chest and slid one leg up, resting a heel against the bottom of his locker. "Would've gotten right the hell out of here."

"Like I said, I didn't really have a choice, so..." Cole looked around for help, but all the faces passing by weren't showing the interest that Lucy was. Not a flirty interest, really, although Cole wasn't sure what that would feel like. He'd never engaged that much with kids, girls in particular, back in Winnipeg. He'd stuck mostly to Joe and the rest of his basketball teammates.

"I've gotta tell you, it's pretty goddamn refreshing that you're, like, this awkward, quiet kid. Doing what you did, being a big 'hero' and all," she air-quoted when she said the word *hero*, "you could have the run of the place."

"I'm just trying to stay out of the way," Cole said.

"Do your time, that sort of shit?" Lucy said.

"Yeah."

"Or is it," she pushed off from the locker with her foot, and got close enough to Cole that he had a vision of an anti-anxiety pill, "just me?"

Cole tried to even his breath out. "Wh-why would it be you?"

"Because you're pretty good at shouting at crowds."

"Only when they shout first."

She got closer. He tried to back away farther, but the stream of kids heading to first class was an impenetrable wall. "Can you—"

"It's because of my dad, though, really."

"Your dad?" Cole still had no memories of Lucy.

"You serious right now? *My dad.*"

"Ummm..." Cole was trying to collect his thoughts, but they were like shards of glass scattered across a floor "...I'm serious, it's just that..."

"Oh shit, you *really* don't know." She put her hand on his shoulder. "I just figured since I remember you, that you'd remember me. Or do you think I'm not memorable or something?"

"No, you are," Cole said, "I just didn't remember who your dad was...is..."

She squeezed his shoulder, then finally let go. "Well, now you do. Calm down, us McCabes don't bite. Much."

"Lucy McCabe," he breathed.

"Lucy McCabe," she mimicked with a whisper, like she was telling a ghost story.

"I knew that."

"Ha, okaaaaay," she raised a sarcastic thumb. "So, going to math?"

"Math?" Choch had given Cole textbooks, but not a class schedule. But if Lucy had math, would he, too? She'd been a grade behind.

"First class," she said.

"I uhhh..." he saw Brady and Eva at their lockers, just a few down from his, putting their backpacks in, getting their textbooks out. His nerves calmed instantly. "Excuse me, Lucy. Sorry." He motioned towards his friends.

"Right, the other members of the Bloodhound Gang, got it." Lucy backed off. "See you around, Cole."

When she was gone, Cole took a breath and approached Eva and Brady.

"What was that all about?" Brady asked.

"You saw and you didn't do anything?" Cole asked. "I was literally on my heels."

"You're a big boy, Cole," Eva said.

"Some of these things, you're going to have to figure out for yourself, my friend, okay?" Brady said.

"Yeah, I guess," Cole said, and wanted to drop it. He felt like Eva, and in particular Brady, wanted him to drop it, but added, "She's just *there*, you know?"

"The point is, if you're sticking around Wounded Sky," Brady said, "and both Eva and I are glad to have you, don't get me wrong, you're going to have to deal with some things without us."

"I know, I'm sorry. I feel totally useless sometimes," Cole said.

"You know you're not useless," Eva said in a motherly tone, "just pick and choose, right? Murderer on the loose, ask Eva and Brady, absolutely. Lucy McCabe being a space invader, not so much." She made hand gestures as she weighed the options and the obvious answers she'd presented.

"That's the other thing," Cole said. "I didn't remember that *he* was her dad."

"She's a totally different kind of tough than Reynold is," Brady said. "But still, tough. Like, intimidating."

"You think they're different?" Eva said to Brady. "She walks around like Queen Everything. How's that not the same?"

Brady shrugged. "Point taken."

"At the very least, she likes attention as much as her dad," Eva said, "that's all I'm saying."

"Anyway," Cole said, "I won't bug you guys for *everything*. Sorry."

"Oh, Cole, you can bug us. Don't get mopey," Brady said.

"We kind of like having you around," Eva said, "especially now, after…"

They all stopped talking for a moment, reflecting on the silence that Eva had left. The calm again. The calm that wasn't the calm. Finally, Brady held up his math textbook. "Shall we?"

"I was going to ask if you could at least help me get to class." Cole laughed sheepishly.

"Yes, my friend, we can at least do that." Brady patted him on the shoulder.

"How's the class so big?" Cole asked upon entering the room and noting that nearly all the desks were occupied.

"It's an amalgamated class," Eva explained. "We go to class with the Elevens."

"Which is generally a hoot," Brady said.

"Right." For a moment, Cole had forgotten most of the kids their age had died. It made sense, then, why Lucy had known about math class. Lucy was beside one empty desk, and Pam, whom Cole had seen working at the X his first night back in the community, was on the other side. Cole thought about sitting there—he felt it would've been a good "face your fears" moment—to show Eva and Brady that he could do something without them. But one look from Lucy and he decided otherwise. Not on the first day. The only other empty desk was encircled, almost protectively, by Eva and Brady, now taking their seats. Cole guessed it had belonged to Ashley. Even though Michael was already sitting behind Ashley's desk, Cole decided to sit there.

"Hey," he said to Michael, pulling the chair away from the desk and sending a nails-against-chalkboard sound through the classroom.

Michael nodded with a subtle eye roll that Cole caught.

Cole sat down, placed his textbook on top of the desk, and tried to bury himself within its pages. He could feel Brady watching—Eva, too. And most everybody else. Cole half-turned towards Brady and whispered, "I don't think I should've sat here. Should I move?"

"No," Brady whispered back, "it's okay. Ashley would want you to sit there."

"For real? Yeah?"

"Yes, for real."

"It's disrespectful," Michael said under his breath, but Cole heard it as though Michael had shouted it.

"Mike." Eva tried not to sound exasperated, but she still did. Michael's attitude towards Cole had been consistent since the quarry and the revelations about Cole and Alex. Eva had been patient with him, and with the tension between the two of them, but it seemed that patience was wearing thin. "Ashley's boyfriend should be the one to say whether it's respectful or not. Right?"

"Yeah," Michael said. "Right."

The bell rang for class to start, but the math teacher wasn't there yet. The quiet that met Cole when he'd entered the classroom fell away as the minutes wore on. Everyone broke off to conduct their own conversations, one impossible to discern from the next, even with Cole's keen sense of hearing. Over the chatter, the awkwardness between him and Michael became too much to handle, and he wasn't sure how long he could go with Michael's eyes burning into the back of his head. Cole turned around to face him.

"I never really said sorry about your head." Cole pointed to the back of his own head, as though Michael wouldn't remember that Cole had knocked him out. "Sorry, man."

Michael shrugged. "Whatever. I came at you, so..."

"Is that..." Cole looked around the room as he tried to figure out exactly how to verbalize his thoughts. Finally, he just said it. "Is that why things have been weird? I mean, I know things have been messed up anyway, but I'm talking between us."

Michael took forever to say something. Cole's mind flashed to when he went to the clinic yesterday. He'd wanted to track down Dr. Captain, Michael's mom, to ask if she had any anti-anxiety meds, you know, laying around. The guard posted at the front door wouldn't let him inside the building because he didn't have family there. There were strict rules for visitors, the guard had said. That guard hadn't been an RMS employee, either. Cole wished that he'd busted in and found one. Just one. Finally, with a big, drawn-out sigh, Michael said, "Look, Cole, I don't have a list of 'why things have been weird between us' or anything, but I could make one. Fast. And it'd be really long."

"Would the top of the list be that I walked home with Alex?"

"Of course that's part of it. Come on. You kissed—"

"She kissed me." Cole interjected, but did it really matter? And was it even right to interrupt Michael in the first place?

"*And* you were the last person she saw."

"I just didn't want her to walk home alone, Mike. That's it. I didn't... I wanted her to be safe. I'm sorry." How stupid. How stupid to say that, even if it were true. Because she hadn't been safe. She'd been murdered. But what else could he have done? Gone inside the house? And then what would Michael have thought? Her blood would've been on Cole. Literally. Just like Ashley's blood, and Maggie's. All of this went through his head, but Cole only added "I'm sorry" again.

There were never enough sorrys.

If Michael wanted to say anything more about Alex, he didn't. Instead, he gathered himself, and shook his head as though he'd nodded off and was trying to wake himself up. He went on to what must've been item number two on the why-things-are-weird-with-Cole list: "I don't like that Eva's been spending so much time with you."

"*And* Brady. We're just friends. All of us."

"At Alex's wake, she's off talking to you about whatever, and I'm just standing there on my own. It was my sister's wake, Cole."

"I know it was, Mike. I felt bad about being there, because everything that went down, and she was just trying to make me feel better about it. That's all."

"I needed Eva with me. That's the point. It wasn't about you."

Cole didn't know what to say. He thought about it, maybe for too long. He scanned the room, counting students. Seventeen.

"Do you remember after the vigil at the clinic? When I chased after you?" Michael asked.

"Yeah, I said we were friends. We both did," Cole said.

"Right, yeah. *Friends.* So if we're friends, why are you doing all of this to me? Why'd you do that with Alex? Why are you trying to take Eva away?"

"I'm not trying to take anything from you, man," Cole said, "I—"

The classroom door opened and the math teacher, Mr. Dumas, walked in. He fumbled with some papers on his desk, pushed some out of the way, and straightened others out by stacking them together and knocking them against the desktop. Eventually, he looked up and smiled at nobody in particular. "Morning, everybody."

Mr. Dumas walked to the front of the class. Cole wasn't sure if he was waiting for a collective "Good morning, Mr. Dumas" or not, but he paused as though expecting *something* anyway. When nothing came, he added "welcome back" to his salutation.

Then he met eyes with Cole, and to Cole's chagrin, Mr. Dumas saw fit to create a greeting, special for him. "Let's all welcome back Cole Harper to Wounded Sky First Nation High School."

Cole's new classmates provided some polite applause. Mr. Dumas kept going. "Mr. Harper, I have to say, everybody here owes you a debt of gratitude."

Mr. Dumas fell silent. The classroom, too. It became apparent that he wanted Cole to say a few words.

So, Cole said, "I just want everything to get back to normal, Mr. Dumas."

Mr. Dumas didn't hide his disappointment that Cole hadn't stood on a chair and given some epic speech about his heroism. Cole wanted to be thought of positively in the community, but he didn't have any desire to get into public speaking. Mr. Dumas adjusted his glasses. "Yes, well. Let's pick up where we left off. I know it feels like forever ago, but we were just getting into algebra."

Mr. Dumas walked over to the whiteboard, ignoring the collective groan, and scrawled a question on it.

"Now, can anybody solve this problem? How about no homework for whoever can do it? You've got five minutes."

Cole looked through his backpack, rummaging through the textbooks Choch had given him one by one, and realized that he'd not been given any paper (or pencils, for that matter). He sat up straight to find Pam placing one piece of paper and one pen on his desk.

Cole smiled. "Thanks."

"All good," she said.

Cole watched as she shimmied between two chairs and sat down at her desk. She exuded *something* from her cute button nose to her chin-length black hair to some kind of code written on her forearm to her white Chuck Taylors with notes scrawled all over them with black marker.

"Hey. Psst."

Cole swivelled around. Eva raised her eyebrows and motioned to his piece of paper, then the time on her phone—a nudge to do the math problem. Cole gave her a thumbs up and reviewed the question on the whiteboard. He read it over a few times, then got to work. He was still done before anybody else. He looked around the class, but he tried not to look at Pam again because he didn't want to feel creepy.

"Cole. Wanna give it a shot?" Mr. Dumas had an erasable marker in hand. He extended it towards Cole, who, in turn, made a mental note to take *way* more time to answer questions in the future. Refusing to go up, however, seemed like a bad choice.

Do nothing to make people look at you the way they did before.

Cole stood slowly, and walked just as slowly to the whiteboard. He accepted the marker and wrote his answer underneath the question Mr. Dumas had given.

Cole placed the marker down. The sound was louder than it should've been. He stepped back to allow Mr. Dumas to review the answer.

"You got it."

Cole nodded sheepishly. He half-expected more applause, like clapping for him was mandatory after catching the killer. Lucy sized him up, coming at him with her eyes, which was as intimidating as when she'd come at him physically before class. Pam raised one eyebrow, like The Rock. Cole didn't know whether she was impressed or just being sarcastic. Eva and Brady looked unimpressed, like, *so what*, they'd seen him do way harder things than solve a math equation. Mike burrowed into Cole's soul with a look of hatred. It gave Cole a chill, and he looked away. He walked to his desk, head down, but he felt Mike's eyes on him the entire time.

Making things right with him was a problem Cole didn't know how to solve.

3

VITAMINS

"DIDN'T THEY GIVE YOU A LOCK?" Brady asked Cole when all four of them, Eva, Brady, Cole, and a subdued Michael—but at least not a glaring Michael—arrived at their cluster of lockers after first period.

Cole cupped the broken lock in his pocket in case it made a bulge. "I guess not."

"Kids'll steal your stuff," Michael said.

Eva nodded in agreement. "They will."

"I don't really have any stuff to steal," Cole said.

"Suit yourself," Brady said, "but, I have to tell you, there's a black market up here for textbooks. It's pretty scary, actually."

"Right," Cole laughed.

"Hey, you guys want to head over to the clinic?" Eva asked.

"Don't we have second period?" Cole asked.

"No, there's a spare," Brady said, "didn't you get a schedule?"

"Not yet," Cole said, "going to school here was kind of a last-minute thing."

"Clearly, since, you know," Brady waved his hand up and down, putting Cole's wardrobe on display. It wasn't Cole's wardrobe; it was Brady's.

"Is he at least paying you rent?" Michael grumbled to Brady, but everybody pretended not to hear.

"I wouldn't mind seeing my kókom quick," Brady said.

"*Trying* to see your kókom," Michael corrected.

"Trying to, yeah," Eva agreed. "Visiting hours have gotten strange."

"They wouldn't even let me in yesterday because I didn't have family there," Cole said.

"My kókom's your family," Brady gave Cole a pat on the shoulder. "I'll get you in."

Cole shrugged. "Worth a shot. Sure." And if Dr. Captain was there, he'd see if she had a small supply of pills that could get him through the next however-long-he-would-be-here.

"And then we just have lunch, so there's no rush," Eva pointed out.

"After lunch is…" Cole prompted.

"Gym," Brady sighed.

"Okay, so we can't miss that," Cole said, "especially if there's a basketball court."

"I mean there *is*—" Eva started.

"But it's crap," Michael interjected.

"Excuse Mr. Grump over here," Eva said, elbowing Michael in the side, who then brushed her arm away.

"Hey, if there's a hoop and any kind of ball, I'm good." *Anything*, Cole thought, to wash away this morning's experience.

The basketball talk had led to a conversation about Cole's team in the city, which Cole kind of enjoyed, even though lately every conversation seemed merely a distraction, for him and for everybody else. So they didn't have to talk about sickness or death. So, for Cole, there were fleeting moments where he didn't see Ashley's face, or Alex's, or Maggie's. Or Scott, the one who had killed them.

When the clinic was visible, the basketball talk ended abruptly.

"You know what I want to know, now that Mihko is back?" Eva asked.

"What they're doing here?" Brady said.

"What they *did* here," Eva said.

"And what they had to do with…everything," Cole said.

"Right," Eva said. "It'd be awesome to know why I was a lab rat."

"Couldn't have been harmful, at least," Michael said. "You never noticed anything anyway if they were experimenting on you."

"That's the point," Eva said. "I never even knew anything was happening, that they were, I don't know, pumping something into my body?"

"Vitamins," Cole said.

"What?" Brady asked.

Cole hadn't noticed saying anything out loud, but obviously he did. "Vitamins," he repeated. "I thought I was getting vitamins, from my dad. Maybe you did, too."

Eva looked trapped in thought. She looked around, her eyes darting here and there, her mind working. She shook her head. "I don't remember…"

"Maybe it wasn't," Cole shrugged.

"You can't just say that, and then say it wasn't," Michael said.

"My dad was doing something different," Cole said. "That's what I mean."

"Different how?" Brady asked. "He worked for them, didn't he?"

"Yeah, but what he did on me was, like…" Cole tried to remember the wording in the file on him, wording that had been different from the files on all the other kids, including Eva. "…unauthorized." That was the best word he could come up with.

"And it worked," Eva said.

"Yeah," Cole said. "It worked for some people. Some people, not so much. Like Chief Crate."

"Cole, he died the night you got back, you couldn't have done anything about that."

"What about all the others?" Cole said, and he meant more than just the ones who'd fallen ill. He meant everybody who had died, everybody he hadn't been able to save.

"He's right," Michael said.

"Shut up, Mike," Eva said.

"Why are you always on his side!?"

"Because you're wrong, that's why!"

"Hey!" Brady said. "Stop it. We're supposed to be in this together, okay?"

"Why, because we all know Cole has mutant blood?" Michael said.

"Because we still have stuff to figure out," Eva said.

"Cole, where *are* those files?" Brady asked.

"I don't know. They disappeared, so…"

"Well we should find them," Eva said.

Yeah, if Jayne ever bothered to show up I could ask her, Cole thought. "Yeah, we should try," he said.

"I'm going to ask my dad about vitamins, I guess," Eva shrugged. "It's a start, right?"

"Let's see if we can even get in first," Cole said. He was relieved, at least, to see a different guard at the clinic's front doors. This guard could still try to keep him out for the same reason, but at least he wouldn't know that Cole had been here yesterday.

"Family you're seeing?" the guard asked when the group got to the doors.

"I'm going to see her dad," Michael said, pointing to Eva.

"Is he a relative?" the guard asked.

"Hey, we're all cousins, right?" Brady said in an attempt at humour.

The guard didn't bite. He just kept looking at Michael, waiting for an answer.

"No, but—"

"Sorry, no admittance unless you have family," the guard said, echoing the exact words the other guard had recited to Cole yesterday.

"Mike, just tell them you're seeing your mom, man," Cole whispered.

"She's not working right now," Michael said to him. "They put her on leave."

"On what?" Cole imagined the pills he'd wanted dissolving into thin air. "Why would they put the only doctor on leave?"

"She said they wanted to give her a break, so they made her take time off," Michael said. "They've got other doctors here anyway."

But none that would help me out, Cole thought. Now what was he going to do? Maybe see Scott. Ask him about the files, about why he'd really killed his friends, and try to get Scott to say more than, "That's classified," like he'd said at the camp. But Cole figured that would be nearly impossible, not just to get Scott to talk, but to get in to see him at all. If a guard was at the front door, there would definitely be a guard outside of Scott's room. And Scott might not even be conscious to begin with. On the weekend, Cole had heard he was still in a coma from the beating he took from Cole—and the gunshot from Eva.

"You?" the guard asked Cole.

"Oh, uhhh," Cole scrambled to pull his thoughts back to the task at hand, "my Auntie. Mariah Apatagan."

The guard looked Cole over carefully. "The old lady?"

"That's right," Cole said. "*The Elder.*"

"He's actually my cousin, for real," Brady piped in. "Elder Mariah's my kókom."

"And kókom means?" the guard asked.

"Grandmother," Eva said with an eye roll. "Honestly, if you people are going to come into our community, eat at our restaurant, sleep in our community hall, shop at our grocery store, keep us from seeing family or *friends*, and do whatever the hell your doctors are doing inside here, you should at least learn some basic Cree."

"Grandmother, aunt, check," the guard said to Brady and Cole respectively. "And what about you, sunshine?" he said to Eva.

"My dad, Wayne Kirkness." Eva looked like she was holding in a sharp response. Her lips had disappeared into her mouth.

The guard looked at the clipboard he had, nodding his head. "Alright, go on in. Except you," the guard said to Michael, "you'll have to wait outside."

"Really? What's the big deal?" Cole asked, mostly in an attempt to score some points with Michael.

"Sorry, kids, I've got my rules," the guard said.

"It's fine. I'll just wait," Michael said to the group.

"You sure?" Eva asked, at which Michael nodded.

Before he turned to leave, he shot Cole a look, one that indicated that Cole had not scored points at all. Cole was spending time with Eva, again, without him.

Inside, they split up. Brady went to see Elder Mariah, and Eva and Cole went to check in on Wayne. At the very least, Cole wanted to hear the vitamin question Eva planned to ask. Without the files, without his own father to ask, it was probably the best—the only—productive thing to do. They found Wayne awake and sitting up in bed when Cole and Eva entered the room. ·

"Hey, Dad." Eva sat down beside the bed.

"Hi, Mr. Kirkness." Cole stood at the foot of the bed to give Eva and her dad some space.

"Hey, kids." Wayne put his pocketbook down to give them his full attention. Cole looked him over. This was the first time he'd seen Wayne since the night Scott shot Wayne in the stomach. For a second, Cole pictured Eva's dad in his arms, bleeding all over Cole as he carried the man to the clinic. Wayne looked a million times better now. That night he had looked white, cold, and perilously close to death.

"How are you feeling?" Eva asked.

Wayne patted a bulge under his hospital gown where his stomach was. "Oh, you know, fine. A lot less sore today. I'll live," and then Wayne looked at Cole, "thanks to you."

"Mr. Kirkness," Cole said, "you were shot *because* of me, remember? You'd be fine if it weren't for me."

"Yeah, and Eva would be dead," Wayne said. "Not being shot and her being dead is *not* fine. I'll take the bullet any day of the week and twice on Sundays. So, you did save me."

"Twice on Sundays." Eva imitated him sweetly. "Dad, you sound like an old man."

"You saved me from a life without my daughter," Wayne said. "Thank you for that if nothing else."

"You know," Cole met eyes with Eva, "Eva actually saved *my* life, Mr. Kirkness."

"Oh God, Cole, would you just let my dad thank you so we can move on?"

"You're welcome," Cole said with a bow, at which they all laughed until Wayne held his stomach and grimaced.

"Dad," Eva leaned forward and put her hands on his forearm, "are you okay? Should I call somebody?"

Wayne laughed. "You could, but they wouldn't be here for a week."

"Why?" Cole asked. "Isn't that their job?"

"They're far more concerned with the people who magically recovered from the flu," Wayne said. "I'm chopped liver."

"That was weird, everybody suddenly recovering like that." Eva gave Cole a knowing look.

"Super weird," Cole agreed.

"Anyway, it doesn't matter," Wayne said. "All I have to do is get better, then hopefully I can leave. I could probably leave right now and nobody would notice."

"Except for the guard at the front door," Eva said.

"We could do it like in the movies, only reversed," Cole said. "We could dress Mr. Kirkness up like a janitor or something, and then *leave* with him. Poof. Done." Eva and her dad had stone faces. They didn't know what he was talking about. "Like in *The Fugitive?* When Harrison Ford dresses up like a janitor and goes *into* the hospital…"

Eva shook her head and ignored Cole. "How much longer do you think you'll be in here anyway, Dad?"

"I've no idea. Nobody says anything to me. But if I can't laugh, I probably can't go home yet," Wayne said.

"Maybe if they actually paid attention to you," Cole said.

"What kind of attention are they giving the patients anyway?" Eva asked.

Wayne shrugged, which also made him wince. "I just see doctors wheeling them back and forth every now and then. It's funny, though…" Wayne paused for a moment, thoughtfully "…we keep talking about how they've recovered, but they don't look all that better to me."

"They look sicker?" Eva asked.

"Kind of," he said. "Not the same sick, but not well? I'm not a doctor."

"Why would they be sick at all?" Cole wondered out loud.

"Okay dad, can I ask you a question?" Eva asked firmly.

"Of course," he said.

"It's important."

"Yes, I know that look on your face."

"When I was seven, did you ever give me something from Mihko?" she asked.

"What? Give you what from Mihko?"

"Like medicine, or vitamins? Something? Maybe you didn't even know what they were, maybe…"

"Eva, I would never—"

"Visiting hours are…over." A guard at the door sounded out of breath.

Cole checked his phone. "It's not even eleven-thirty, what are you talking about?"

"We just got here," Eva said.

"Your father requested medical attention," the guard said.

"I *thought* about requesting medical attention," Wayne clarified.

"And you're not a doctor, man," Cole said. "What are you going to do, intimidate his pain away?"

"A doctor is on the way, and you two have to leave." The guard stepped sideways to give Cole and Eva room to clear out.

"We were talking," Wayne said, sounding desperate to find out what Eva had been getting at. Cole knew the feeling, and by the looks of her, so did Eva.

"Dad, this is bullsh—"

"Get out. Now!" the guard demanded.

MONSTERS

"Just go," Wayne said. "I'll text you, okay? We can talk about this later." He picked up the book and smiled to try and relax his daughter and Cole. Himself, too. But both kids could tell it was forced. "These Harlequin romances can wear an old man out."

"I'll text you," Eva promised, and they left.

They were escorted by the guard all the way through the clinic to the front doors. When they got there, they found Brady along with a few other visitors complaining to each other.

"You, too?" Cole asked Brady on the way out.

Brady snapped his fingers. "Like that. Barely got a chance to say hi to her."

"How'd she look?" Cole asked, remembering what Wayne had said. He hadn't been sick with the flu, but Brady's kókom had.

"Tired," Brady said.

"Tired like she was still sick or…"

"Like she almost died," Brady said sharply, and then he sighed sharply, too. "Sorry, Cole, I didn't mean to snap. It's just…I wanted to see her."

Michael checked his phone as they approached him. "You were in there for like, five minutes. Why'd they kick everybody out?"

"Don't ask," Eva said, "because we have no idea."

"They wanted to shut us up," Cole said. "We were onto something."

"What, with the vitamins?" Eva asked.

"Why not? You think that was a coincidence?"

"I don't know." Eva breathed heavily. "Are we supposed to think they had, what, the room bugged or something?"

"They run secret experiments on kids, so why not bug a room?"

Brady held his stomach. "Maybe we can discuss conspiracy theories over lunch at the Fish."

"There's time now anyway," Eva said.

"That's the spot for conspiracy theories," Michael said.

"Oh," Cole said, trying to get into the conversation with Michael, "you mean Victor?"

"Victor and the beast," Eva said. "It's crap."

"It's *not* crap," Brady said.

"Yeah, that's like a Mistapew sighting—" Michael started.

"Mistapew…Big Foot?" Cole said.

"—like that video on the internet from Norway House a few years ago," Michael said. "*That* was just somebody in a Chewbacca suit. What Victor saw? Some dude acting crazy in the woods."

"Cole, tell me I'm not alone here. You believe the stories, right?" Brady asked.

Cole nodded.

"I don't care who says they saw it," Eva said. "There's no such thing."

"But it's not just Victor. More than one person has seen it," Brady said.

"So more than one person has seen somebody acting crazy in the woods," Michael said. "Simple."

"Somebody has the time to do that?" Cole asked. "Run around and act crazy?"

"You can't just fake-act like Upayokwitigo," Brady said.

"Upayok…" Cole tried to repeat what Brady had said.

Eva explained, "It means *He Who Lives Alone* in Cree. Nobody will ever actually say wit—"

"Shut it, Eve," Brady said.

"I didn't say anything!"

"You did with your eyes!"

"Why won't anybody say it?" Cole asked.

"I don't know," Brady said. "It's a curse, you know? It's like if somebody sees a black cat cross the road, they won't drive down that road."

"It's a *superstition*," Eva said.

"Can we just go for lunch and ignore Victor?" Michael asked, and took Eva's hand firmly. He glanced at Cole. Cole noticed. It was time for them to be alone. He nodded at Michael, conceding.

"You guys go on," Cole said. "I brought a lunch."

4

EASY, TIGER

THE MORE COLE WALKED AROUND THE SCHOOL, the more he realized that the high school wasn't simply reminiscent of the elementary school, it was the exact same layout. He knew where all the bathrooms were. Where the janitor's closet was. The office. The gym.

He'd forsaken time at the Fish, time with his friends, for what his therapist called "exposure therapy." She would've been proud to see him do it. She used to tell him that if something seemed too big for him, too impossible, then he needed to face it. He *had* to face it. And if he did, the big impossibility would seem smaller. *Possible*, even. Cole felt like a seven-year-old again, walking around the school.

One moment, it felt easy, remembering how he used to hide in his locker then jump out to scare the crap out of Brady, Eva, or Ashley. Or escape into the furnace room with his friends and pretend that they'd travelled to another world.

The next moment, he heard screams. He felt heat. He saw fire. The chaos he remembered became the chaos in his body. In his tumbling heartbeat. In his shaking limbs. In his clammy skin.

"So, do you solve complex math problems on blackboards when nobody else is around, or what?"

Cole jumped.

He'd been bracing himself against the wall, distracted by the bad memories, wrapped up in trying to use his calm breathing. Pam snuck up without him noticing at all.

"Whoa, easy, tiger." She put her hand against his back to keep him from falling on her.

He steadied himself with her help and turned around so that they were face to face. "Huh?"

"I said, have you ever taken a job as a janitor at a college just so you could solve complex math problems in secret because you're, and I quote, 'wicked smaht.'"

"Oh, *Good Will Hunting*. Got it."

"Nice one. I've been waiting to meet another movie nerd."

Cole laughed, but it came out all wrong, probably because his heart was still racing. "Yeah, I do all the…math, m-mostly at MIT, just without the…the monologues." He could hardly string a few words together. *Keep it short*, he thought.

"And therapists? Have a shitload of them lined up so you can screw around with them?"

"Got that c-covered. Only one, though."

"Yeah? Interesting." Pam grabbed his arm to keep him steady. She walked him down the hallway, forcing him to continue his tour of the high school.

"Psychiatrist…back in the city. Not s-so interesting."

"Anxiety, right?"

"How did you—"

"I'm psychic." She put two fingers to her temple and looked to be concentrating really hard, but, just as fast she said, "No, I'm kidding, it's just ridiculously obvious. What happened?"

"Being here, it's so…much like the ele-elementary school, I…" Cole desperately tried to stay in the moment, so he didn't seem like a total loser, but he didn't do so well. He started to feel worse. "It just r-reminds me of…"

"Hey, say no more. I get it." Pam stopped them in their tracks. She grabbed Cole's waist, and turned him towards her. She nodded sharply. "Are you okay, really? Can I do something? Maybe give you some more movie trivia?"

"I'll be fine. It'll…pass."

"Maybe you should go lie down for a bit. You're talking like you're freezing cold, Harper."

"Yeah, maybe."

"Do you know where the nurse's office is? I could totally walk you there." She re-fastened her arm around his.

"Some hero...right? Can't even h-handle...first day of school." Cole struggled to keep his knees from buckling, and to not let her see how shaky his entire body was.

"The best heroes are flawed, Harper. Come on, if you're really a nerd you would know that from all the comics." She tugged him in the direction of the nurse's office.

"No, I know the way." Cole had embarrassed himself enough. If he had to use the wall to get there, he'd do it.

If she were disappointed that he didn't invite her to walk with him to the nurse's office, she didn't show it.

"Cool, see you in gym," she said, like they'd just passed each other in the hallway.

Cole took a seat on one of the wooden chairs in the nurse's office. He put his head between his legs and tried to breathe the way he'd been taught to breathe, but he failed miserably at it. Pam had been right: it *did* feel like he was cold. Naked, outside, in the middle of winter. He couldn't catch his breath, let alone breathe in for five seconds, out for seven seconds. The nurse's office reminded him of Alex, ten years ago, when Cole brought her to the nurse at the elementary school. She was hunched over while the nurse applied peroxide and then bandaged her scrape. She held Cole's hand, squeezing it with each sting of the peroxide. Alex had recounted this moment to him the night she was murdered.

Cole started to see black spots in his vision.

"Just a minute."

Cole heard a chair roll across the floor.

"It...it's f-fine."

It was. He knew it was. Each time he felt like this a little voice in his head told him that he was going to die, but he hadn't died yet.

"Cole?"

He still had his head between his knees. He looked up to find Dr. Captain standing in front of him.

"Dr. Captain?" Cole said with the same intonation Dr. Captain had used.

"Oh, dear." She rushed over to the sink, filled a small paper cup with water, and brought it over to him. Cole took it, and sipped it. She checked his pulse, felt his heartbeat, and watched the seconds tick on the clock on the wall. "One forty-four," she whispered to herself.

"Is that b-bad?"

"You're fine. We just need to calm you down." She moved to the side and put a hand on his shoulder.

Cole took another sip of water. He tried to take a deep breath in through his nose, and managed two seconds worth of inhalation. Three seconds of exhalation. "What…what are you d-doing here?"

"Volunteering." Dr. Captain sighed. "I needed…*need*…to keep busy."

"Mike said you were on leave." Cole leaned forward. "Shouldn't that m-mean that you're…you're resting?"

"*They* told me it'd be good for me, with everything that's happened," she said. "Alex. Everything."

"Makes sense d-doesn't it?" *Four seconds in, five seconds out,* Cole thought. His heart was evening out a bit. He guessed his heart rate was about one twenty-two.

Dr. Captain shrugged. "I need to work. Work is my distraction. If I didn't have it…"

"Yeah, I know about distractions, Dr. Captain."

"Plus, usually that's a choice you're given, not something you're told to do. They don't know the people here. I do."

Cole took a deep breath, held it, and breathed out. His vision was fine now. "We were just at the clinic. They kicked us out. *Everybody* who was there. It was so weird."

"Why would they do that?"

"I don't think they want us around. Us kids. We—" Cole hesitated.

"Is this about what happened with the flu? Your blood?"

"It could be."

"Cole, I want you to know that I never told them about what happened, okay? Have any of you?"

"Not that I know of." Cole breathed again. In. Out. "I don't know, maybe it's just our imaginations. But, I mean, I was there the other day looking for you. They wouldn't even let me in the door. My whole life is one big question mark."

Dr. Captain knelt down and took a good look at Cole. "You weren't feeling well when you came to look for me? Did you have another panic attack?"

"I was...worried about having one," Cole said.

"Have you been having a lot of them?" Dr. Captain took Cole's wrist, watched the clock, and counted. "One-twelve. Better."

"I've been *having* them."

She grabbed a blood pressure metre from across the room, secured the Velcro strap around his arm, and started pumping the little black ball. "Any different from the city?"

"It kind of comes in waves. Anxiety. More now than before, yeah."

"I can't say I blame you with what you've been through." She watched his blood pressure reading intently. "And you were coming to see me because..." she unstrapped it. She didn't seem concerned.

"I take medication when it gets bad. Anti-anxiety meds. I didn't have many when I got here, and then I spilled most of them on the ground last week. I was just hoping that maybe—"

"I'd be able to get some for you."

"Yeah." Cole looked down, as though he had something to be ashamed about. But she lifted his chin up. She smiled.

"More people than you think are going through what you are, Cole."

"I feel like, last week, I needed them so much. Then I thought I was doing pretty good, mostly, for me, and today it's like I'm back at square one."

"You don't need to explain yourself." Dr. Captain pulled up a chair and sat in front of him. "I don't have meds, though. I do at the clinic, but I can't get in there."

"Not even for a second?" Cole asked. "That sounds like more than just being on leave."

Dr. Captain slapped her knees softly, then rubbed her hands against them. She leaned forward, elbows against thighs. "I want to know what's going on in there, too. Sounds like we both do. Especially now that they've kicked people out suddenly."

"Well can't you, like, go there at night? Do you still have a key?"

"There are always guards now, and they took away my key. So, no. I think…" but she didn't finish her thought.

"You think?"

"I don't want to cause you more anxiety. You've done enough."

"I know that I haven't," Cole said. "It's why I'm still here." But the whole *doing* thing, the reason why he was here, remained a mystery. He thought of Choch, and that he'd actually like to see the spirit being. Even his messed up, vague clues were better than silence. The silence wasn't as nice now as it was this morning. He should've gone to the Fish. Maybe, today, Choch would've been there, after what had happened at the clinic. Maybe—

"Cole," Dr. Captain said.

"Huh?"

"I lost you there for a second. You okay?"

"Yeah, sorry. Just thinking. What were we…?"

"You were saying that you're still here for something, that you hadn't done enough. Personally, I think that's a bit of an understatement. But—"

"This is my life," Cole said. "My therapist says I'll always have anxiety."

"Yes, and manage it, and avoid getting involved in things like this."

"No, not avoid. That's the worst thing to do. Anxiety tells me I can't do stuff all the time. I'm never supposed to listen to it. Dr. Captain, I've been stabbed, I've been choked, I've been shot at, I've seen my friends—" Cole paused. He skipped over the part where Dr. Captain's daughter died. "I've handled it before and I'll keep handling it. Pills or not. Just tell me what I can do. Tell me what I'm *supposed* to do."

Dr. Captain stood up. She put out her hand and helped Cole up, too. She looked deep into his eyes, trying to determine, Cole felt, if he could really handle it.

Finally, she said, "Those files you were talking about. Do you still have them?"

"No," Cole lamented, "but I want to find them. You think they'll help?"

"I think they're all we have. I think it's a start."

5

GYM CLASS HERO

JAYNE'S ABSENCE WAS ALMOST MORE PROBLEMATIC than Choch's. She failed to appear after Cole had called her on several occasions over the last week. He'd finally gone looking for her where he thought she might be—the ruins, the cemetery—but not the most obvious place: the camp. It was the last place he'd seen Jayne, and where Scott had hid while murdering Cole's friends. It was where Cole found the files in the first place, and where Scott stabbed him in the heart. Cole didn't think he'd be able to go there without his heart exploding, his palms soaking with sweat, his body shaking, the world spinning out of control. But what were the other options? If anybody knew where the files were, it was Jayne. After all, he left her at the camp specifically to keep an eye on them.

"Cole." Brady knocked him gently on the shoulder. "*Friend.* You in there?"

Cole shook his head, as though he could shake out his thoughts. He tried to ignore them instead. "Yeah, sorry."

They were in the boys' change room. Brady was in his gym clothes, but Cole had no reason to go into the change room himself. He didn't have any shorts or tank tops or sneakers. He'd only come with Brady because he'd been disappointed with the gym and couldn't stand to look at it. The floors were worn out, and there were no inflated basketballs (and no pump to fill them with). One of the rims had been ripped down, too.

"You could've borrowed something from me, again, you know," Brady said on the way out of the change room. He looked Cole over.

"I mean, if you don't want to wear my clothes anymore, we really have to hit up the mall and find something for you." Brady opened the door and they walked onto the hardwood. "Something without a majestic wolf on it."

"I guess," Cole said.

"But if you find something with a majestic coyote, *definitely* pick that one up before it's gone!" Choch called out. He jogged over to them. Cole looked around desperately, making sure he wasn't hallucinating—because what the hell was Choch doing here?

"You don't see many coyotes up here, Mr. Chochinov," Brady said.

"Oh," Choch said, slapping Brady on the shoulder, "I've seen at least one."

"What are you doing here?" Cole still felt confused. After going AWOL for so long, why did Choch decide to show up during gym class?

"Brady, my dear, two-spirited friend, would you please tell Cole what I'm doing here?"

"You're the gym teacher?" Brady answered what seemed painfully obvious, at least to him.

"I'm the gym teacher," Choch said proudly and, for added effect, he tweeted the whistle that was hanging around his neck.

"I'm *sorry?*" Cole held Choch back. "Could you give us a minute?" he asked Brady.

"Uhh, sure." Brady nodded, then he continued onto the gym floor towards Eva and Michael.

With Brady a safe distance away, Cole put both hands on Choch's shoulders and looked him dead in the eyes. "What do you think you're doing? You just abandon me, and now you're going to teach Phys Ed?"

"I'm the gym teacher. What?" Choch repeated innocently. He removed Cole's hands from his shoulders. "And you've always indicated to me that you'd appreciate some space, so I gave you space."

"Yeah, but…" Cole switched gears. "Since when are you the gym teacher?"

"Ohhh," Choch looked around thoughtfully and blew a gust of air out of his mouth, "since *forever*, really. Ask the kids, they'll tell you."

"They'll tell me what you've *made* them know," Cole said.

"Kids *are* impressionable, aren't they?"

"How long, in real life, have you been the gym teacher?"

"Since…today? I suppose, if we're being specific."

"*Why?*"

"In my defense, CB," Choch put his hands up, "the food is good at the Fish, but one can grow tired of, you know…" Choch paused thoughtfully "…well, I'm not a pescetarian is what I'm saying. Needed a change."

"A pesce-what?"

"Cole, pescetarianism is the practice of following a diet that includes fish, or other seafood, but not the flesh of other animals. I got that from Wikipedia."

"You just gave me textbooks and f—"

"Ah! No swearing. A certain author's editor advised him not to use the F-word in the sequel."

"A certain…*what?*"

"Just don't swear, okay?" Choch said quickly.

Cole tried to find his calm. "You just gave me textbooks and kissed off."

"Much better, but very eighties. I think that's a Violent Femmes song, maybe?" Choch shrugged. "Anyway, here, I can keep a watchful eye. You have gym…" Choch paused to think. "I don't have the schedule, but you have gym relatively often."

"I'll skip class." Cole wanted the quiet back again. He needed Jayne, not more of this crap. He'd forgotten, in Choch's absence, how infuriating the spirit being could be.

"And not come to a place where you can play basketball? *Please.* Unrealistic. Especially with your experience this morning, am I right?"

"The balls aren't even…there's no way to inflate them!"

Students were watching them now. Both Cole and Choch noticed, and lowered their voices.

"I'll inflate a ball for you," Choch sung.

Cole stood there, silent, and looked over the spirit being, with his Wounded Sky High School sweater, whistle, matching sweat pants, and perfectly white sneakers. Ridiculous, as usual. At least he wasn't wearing a suit. Cole sighed. "Could you at least try to be less annoying or something? Difficult? Whatever?"

"What do we say?" Choch straightened up, raised three fingers, switched it two, and then back to three, "I can never remember how many fingers Scouts hold up. Or is it Cubs? Anyway, we'll do our best, dob-dob-dob. You dyb-dyb-dyb. Do your best. That's all I ask."

"Fine. I kind of wanted to ask you some things about—"

"Great!" Choch stuffed his whistle into his mouth and blew it, and the shrill tweet echoed through the gym. "Okay, everybody find a partner! We're going to be working on our lacrosse skills today."

Choch left the students to pair up while he went to grab equipment from the storage room. Cole watched in disbelief as Choch walked all the way across the gym, and by the time he looked away most of the pairings had been made. Notably, Eva and Brady were already together—Cole's first and second and only choices. He suspected this to be a common occurrence, and looked around for somebody else to buddy with. Michael, whom Cole might've asked just to generate some more good will, had partnered with Lucy.

"Hey."

Cole felt a tap on his shoulder and found Pam standing behind him.

"Found your footing?"

"Yeah, Dr. Captain talked me down, I guess," Cole said. "And you."

"Wanna be my partner?" Pam asked.

"Sure." Cole might've felt good—*acceptance!*—but a quick glance showed that they were the only two single students left.

"The good thing is, if you have another spell, you can just use your lacrosse stick for support."

"Convenient."

"I'm practical. What can I say?"

Cole and Pam found an open spot on the gym floor.

"Hold on a moment, kids!" Choch emerged from the storage room, his arms full of lacrosse sticks and balls. Cole and Pam stopped. "I was hoping to get Mr. Harper here paired up with Mr. Captain. No offense dear, I just think they'd match up better together. For the drill." Choch called across the gym in Michael's direction. "Mr. Captain, you're going to pair up with CB over here, please." Cole read Michael's lips, which didn't take much skill, while Choch instructed Lucy to join up with Pam.

"Match up better?" Cole whispered to Choch. Pam and Michael switched places, both of them looking none-too-pleased with their new partners. "I know you haven't talked to me, but you know what's been going on. Michael and I?"

"You literally just thought getting paired with Michael would generate some good—"

"I know what I *thought*, but now that it's happening I don't want to."

"You do sound whiney sometimes, CB. Anyway, *friends close, enemies closer*, am I right?" Choch said.

"He's *not* my enemy."

"But he's not quite your friend, either."

"You suck."

Oh, what Cole would have given for an inflated basketball. Racket sports were not his thing. He held the lacrosse stick in his hands, placed firmly against his palm scars, and gave it a long look. It was a racket sport, wasn't it? There was a handle, and netting. What else would it be? He twirled it around, back and forth.

"Let's go, Cole." Michael was about fifteen feet away from him, the lacrosse stick cocked back, ball in the net, ready to launch.

"Is lacrosse a racket sport?" Cole asked.

"What?"

"I was just wondering if it was a racket sport or not."

"I don't…" Michael pursed his lips and breathed out through his nose. "…look, I'm not giving you a history lesson, okay? And stop talking like we're still friends."

"I thought we were getting along this morning," Cole said, then quietly added, "a bit."

"I was being civil for Eva, that's it."

"Eva told you to be nice to me?" Cole shot a look at Eva, who was either ignoring him and Michael or so into passing the lacrosse ball with Brady that she hadn't heard them talking.

"Can we just get this over with?" Michael asked.

Cole nodded. "Sure, fine."

Michael whipped the ball at Cole's head. Cole ducked out of the way.

"What the f@#&?" Cole glared at Michael, and then retrieved the ball as it bounced off the wall behind him.

(*Sorry, dear readers, CB will get used to the whole no-swearing thing. The book's still suitable for middle years. Promise.*)

"You're supposed to catch it with your *stick*, not your head," Michael said.

"I know we're not seeing eye-to-eye or whatever, but we don't have to do it like this."

"I just threw you the ball, Cole. Get over it."

"I thought Eva told you to be nice to me." Cole no longer felt annoyed at Eva for giving Michael that direction. He wanted Michael to listen to her.

"What can I say? She'll forgive me."

Cole sighed and tossed the ball at Michael. It lobbed through the air. Michael caught it, then twirled it back and forth in the net like it was second nature. "You're actually awesome at that," Cole said reluctantly.

Michael threw the ball at Cole again, harder than the last time. This time, Cole caught it with his right hand. He didn't even flinch. "*Dude*, fricking stop!" Cole walked over to Michael, and dropped the ball into his hand.

"How the hell did you do that?" Michael asked.

Cole felt dumb for catching the ball. Could he not have just ducked, like the first time? What would he do next? Dunk the basketball in front of everybody? He walked away from Michael, shaking his head. To others, he looked mad at Michael, but really, he was mad at himself. There were more important things going on (he *thought*, anyway) than carrying on some stupid fight with Michael. Especially over a girl. Cole lifted his lacrosse stick. "Can we just play? Please?"

Michael tossed his racket to the ground. "You're not a hero; you're a freak." He walked across the gym, jumped up onto the stage, and sat beside his bag.

Cole didn't move. He stayed there, standing, with his racket up, like he expected Michael to produce a ball from his gym bag and throw it to him from across the gym. He saw everybody looking at him and Michael. He didn't know what else to do. He couldn't go to the change room. He didn't have anything to change into.

"Cole Harper!" Choch blew his whistle for good measure as he walked over to Cole. "I don't tolerate tomfoolery in my class. Give me ten man-makers *now*."

"What?" Now Cole threw his stick down. "That's bullsh@t, Mike started it!"

"*That's bull*crap, *Mike started it,*" Choch mimicked Cole in a baby voice. "Make it twenty! And stop swearing!"

"What the heck are you doing?" Cole shout-whispered. "I thought you were here to watch over me."

"I'm trying to keep up appearances. Just go with it," Choch whispered, looking positively delighted with himself. "Thirty! That's enough of your lip, Harper!"

After that, Choch added a wink.

"You know I don't get tired." Cole walked over to the baseline.

"Oh you will, Harper. You will." *CB, sorry that I'm in your brain, but did that not sound* exactly *like Yoda in Empire Strikes Back? I know you can't get tired, but I've just been* dying *to say something like that.*

Cole thought, *stick to Jedi mind tricks,* and then he stood there waiting. "Well? I know you want to—"

Choch blew his whistle.

"—there you go."

Cole took off running to the free-throw line and back. Centre line and back. Opposite free-throw line, back. Opposite baseline, back.

Twenty-nine more to go. Eventually, kids started tossing their lacrosse balls around again. But not Michael. He sat there on the stage, staring at Cole. During each man-maker, all the way from thirty down to one, Cole tried his best not to look at his former friend.

6

THEY

"SO, LET ME GET THIS STRAIGHT. THERE'S REALLY NO SPECIAL?" Cole had been studying the menu as if for a final exam. Rebecca stood at the edge of the table chewing a piece of gum, shaking her head, and tapping her foot. "And there's never *been* a special?"

"Cole, you ask that every time we come here, lately." Eva lowered Cole's menu and gave him a stern look. "Just order."

"And Choch has never—"

"Worked here!" Brady said. "He's been the gym teacher for a hundred years. Stop being ridiculous."

Cole placed the menu on the table. He didn't know why he kept asking about Choch. He knew what the answer would be. He just wanted confirmation, he supposed. And part of him wanted somebody to recognize *something*, a meal special, or to recall a memory of Choch in his uniform—so he'd know Choch wasn't in complete control. As early as yesterday, Brady and Eva remembered that Choch had worked here, and they just figured he'd gone on vacation or something. Today? *Poof!* Choch was the gym teacher, end of story.

"So are you going to order, or…" Rebecca looked like she was about to stab her pencil right through the order pad.

"*Yes*," Eva said. She and Brady had already ordered.

"Alright, I'll get the fish and chips." Cole handed Rebecca the menu. "Sorry."

Rebecca didn't respond. She scrawled down Cole's order, stuffed the menus under her arm, and left in a huff.

"I've got to say, my friend," Brady said, "I'm glad you're back and everything, you saved my kókom, but that was incredibly painful."

"Seconded," Eva said.

"Do you think your kókom looked…tired…this morning just because she'd been sick?" Cole asked.

"That's what I thought," Brady said, "and, when you think about it, she's an Elder, too. So, being that sick, I guess it takes longer to recover."

"But she looked so good the week she got better, even last week," Eva said. "I thought they might let her go."

"Yeah, me too," Brady conceded.

"Have they let anybody go?" Cole asked.

"Not sure," Eva said.

"Anyway, they'd let me know if something was wrong," Brady said, "if she was more than just tired. Right?"

"Of course," Eva said as she scrolled through her phone messages. "My dad hasn't texted me back."

"Sleeping, or…" Cole said.

Eva looked at him matter-of-fact. "My dad doesn't sleep. Come on."

"They kicked everybody out and now they've taken away phone privileges?" Brady asked.

"Looks like it," Eva said.

"See? We *did* set something off over there," Cole said. "We need to find out what's going on.

"And it's not going to help asking my dad about vitamins," Eva said. "It has to be in those files. We've got to track them down."

"Agreed," Cole said.

"I was totally chomping at the bit for some more sleuthing," Brady said, but he sounded sarcastic. "I thought we were done with all of this."

"We're not," Cole said.

"Okay, so where do we start?" Eva asked.

"The last place I saw it, it was at the camp," Cole said.

"The camp," Brady stated. "The camp, out in Blackwood Forest. Just to clarify. With the…you know."

Their silence spoke volumes. They might've all been thinking about other possible starting points—Cole certainly was—but there weren't any.

"In case you guys don't know what I'm getting at," Brady said after a while, "every single person who's seen that thing has seen it in the woods, at night." He continued very slowly. "At *night*, which it is right now, and *in the woods*, which is where you're talking about going."

"I guess whether it's Upayokwitigo or not," Eva said, "it was probably still something, and Victor's saying it even chased him."

"Like, full-on chased?" Cole asked.

"That's what he says," Eva pointed at Victor, who was sitting alone in a booth. "Go and ask him."

"Cole, this thing, let me try to help you understand what we're considering here. It'll start eating animals, okay? It'll clean out traps, hunt, whatever. Then, when animals can't fill its hunger, it will start turning to bigger game."

"Humans," Cole said.

"And the hungrier it gets, the worse it becomes. I mean, these things end up being giants. Like, huge skeletal monsters. With, by the way, a heart of ice."

"But humans at first," Eva said.

"That's right," Brady said. "That thing could be walking around us right now, okay? Possessed, and super dangerous. And, not to be repetitive, it is also in the woods. *At night.*"

Cole looked Victor over, then Brady, then Eva, assessing whether he'd be going out into the woods alone—or with what Lucy had called "The Bloodhound Gang."

"So you don't want to go?" Cole stated the obvious.

"I'd prefer not to die," Brady said.

"I thought you wanted to sleuth again," Eva said, managing a smirk.

"I was thinking more of the non-life-threatening kind of sleuthing," Brady said.

"Well I think the dangerous sort is the best kind of sleuthing," Eva slammed her hand on the table. "I'm in."

"You're just saying that because you don't believe there's anything out there!" Brady said.

"Brady," Cole said. "It's us three, man. It's gotta be."

"Ugh!" Brady looked like he wanted to tear the hairs out of his tidy braid, but Cole knew that look on his face.

Brady was in, too.

The clearing was empty. The tent had been removed, and the fire pit that had once housed ashes and empty cans of beans was gone, leaving behind only a discoloured area in the dirt.

"Not so much as a footprint," Eva said after she'd thoroughly circled the area.

"It's like somebody took a rake and combed the whole place over," Cole said.

"Scott talked about *they* when we were here, remember that?" Eva asked, kneeling right where the tent had been erected.

"Yeah," Cole said.

"So, *they* cleaned up after him?" Brady asked. "Covering Scott's tracks or…"

Cole stood over the place he'd been stabbed, over a patch of dried blood. *They* hadn't cleaned up everything. Eva stood beside Cole and put a hand on his shoulder.

"Who else would've?" she asked.

Cole pried his eyes away from his own dried blood. "The RCMP?"

Eva almost belly laughed. "You mean Jerry? That's hilarious. Even if he *had* thought to clean up the camp, it wouldn't have looked like this."

"And besides, we would've heard about it, if they'd actually done that and found the files and everything else," Brady said.

"True," Cole said, "but we should check it out anyway."

By now, they were all standing in the middle of the clearing, looking around, looking at each other.

"Let's get back to who *they* could even be. Scott said he was getting paid a ton of money, right?" Eva asked.

"Yeah, and it would have to be somebody who'd cover up that they'd killed kids." Cole turned away from the group. He started pacing back and forth, looking over the area, looking out into the woods.

"So they have a ton of money and they have no conscience," Brady stated.

"What needs to be covered up? They have a disease, they wanted the cure…but Scott tried to kill *me*, too," Cole said.

"Okay, wait, let's just start where we need to start," Eva said. "We're getting way ahead of ourselves. Dad always says to start small, and then work your way up. We can't go ass-backwards, we'll never figure it out."

"So what's next, then?" Brady asked. "The files aren't here."

They had all started pacing over every inch of the camp, ruining the work *they* had done to clean the place up.

"If the RCMP doesn't have the files, which they probably won't, I don't know. The clinic?" Cole said.

"Which is guarded," Brady said.

"Maybe Michael can somehow get keys or something from his mom?" Eva said. "Steal them, then put them back?"

"No, Dr. Captain doesn't have keys. She told me," Cole said, "plus I doubt Michael would help if I'm involved unless he listens to Eva and is actually nice to me." Cole had been waiting to bring that up. Now seemed like a bad time, but when would there be a good time?

"Pardon me?" Eva said.

"You told him to be nice to me! You don't tell your boyfriend to be nice to your best friend, that's so lame! I feel like some pathetic loser."

"I was just looking out for you."

"Well, you can stop. I need to fix things with Michael on my own."

"If I didn't look out for you, you'd be dead, or have you forgotten the knife to your heart?"

"That's different!"

"Why? They're both because I care about you."

"Still here," Brady interjected, but both Cole and Eva ignored him.

Cole and Eva were face to face now. They'd almost collapsed into each other.

"If you cared about me, you'd…"

"I'd what?"

What? Cole didn't know what he wanted to say there. Maybe, that if she cared about him, she'd be with him, not Michael? Was that what really upset him about this? He didn't feel like some pathetic loser, he *was* a pathetic loser. "You'd just stay out of it!"

"Cole…" Eva backed off.

Cole turned away and walked to the edge of the clearing. He looked out across the woods, into the darkness. That's when he saw a dim light in the distance.

"Do you guys see that?" Cole pointed at it.

Brady and Eva came over and looked in that direction.

Eva shook her head.

Brady said, "No. What do you see?"

"Nothing, sorry." Cole looked at Eva for effect. "You know what, I just need to get some air. I'll be a minute."

"Cole," Eva repeated. "Don't…"

"Don't what?" Cole was already walking out of the clearing.

"Don't go out into the woods alone like that." Brady said.

"I'll be fine," Cole said. "You guys stay together."

Cole made his way towards the light. Soon, he could see the source. Jayne was glowing like embers in a dying campfire.

"Jayney," Cole said when he got to her. "Why're you so sad?"

She was sitting, knees hugged to her chest, rocking back and forth, humming a song he didn't know. "Nothing."

"What're you doing out here? I've been looking all over for you."

Jayne managed a smile. It was the first fake smile that Cole had ever seen from her.

"What's going on?" Cole sat down beside her. From here, unable to see the dim light Jayne gave off, Eva and Brady couldn't see Cole, either. But he kept his voice down anyway.

Out here, the smallest sounds were screams.

"Choch made me come." Jayne stopped rocking and let go of her knees. She leaned against Cole's shoulder with her non-burning side.

"I was worried about you," Cole said.

"Sorry, Coley. I've been hiding, mostly."

"Hiding?" Cole asked. Jayne got even dimmer. He felt the chill of the woods, even with her beside him. Her voice was shaking, like she couldn't even feel her own heat. "From what?"

Jayne didn't answer.

"Jayney? What are you hiding from? You can tell me, you're safe."

"Promise?" Jayne looked up at him with puppy-dog eyes. She had tears coming out of her good eye and steam coming out the other.

"Remember what you said? You're 'vincible' right? You know that, silly-billy," he said.

Jayne thought about it.

"Cole!" Eva shouted from the distance. "Come back! Please! I'm sorry!"

"Yeah, Cole. It's really, really creepy out here," Brady said.

"Jayney..." Cole prompted.

"The boogeyman," Jayne blurted out. "I'm hiding from the boogeyman."

Cole rubbed his face. "The boogeyman? Are you sure?"

"I saw him, Coley! I wouldn't lie to you, you know that!" Jayne's fire brightened fast. Cole could see almost the whole forest around him, and Eva and Brady impatiently looking in his direction. Brady kept shining the flashlight from his phone into the dark, trying to spot Cole.

"Okay." Cole moved away from Jayne. He could feel the heat through his clothes, against his skin. "Okay, I'm sorry. Alright?"

Jayne took some deep breaths, just like Cole would've done. As she did, her flames evened out.

"When did you see the boogeyman?"

"Right after the last time I seen you." Her flames went dimmer than he'd ever seen them. They were almost out.

Extinguished.

"You mean…" Cole started.

"Right there." Jayne pointed directly where Eva and Brady stood. "He took your papers."

"Papers? The files?"

"Yeah."

"Have you seen him again, Jayney?"

"Yeah, *that's why I'm hiding.*"

"Where have you seen him?"

"Everywhere."

7

ASSEMBLY

COLE CHECKED THE TIME. 7:40 A.M. He tiptoed expertly (very few floor-board creaks) to Brady's bedroom. He turned the handle as quietly as he could and eased the door open. Brady was fast asleep, his legs sprawled out across the mattress, covers kicked off and half on the floor, half stuck under his legs. His hair covered his face. Too cute, and sleeping too well to wake him. A good night's sleep was rare for him since Ashley was murdered. Cole crept across the room and went through Brady's drawers until he found a pair of sweats and a black tank top. With them firmly in hand, Cole backed away from the dresser and towards the bedroom door.

"You're welcome."

"Oh." Cole felt like handing the clothes back to Brady. "Sorry."

Brady sat up in bed and pushed the hair away from his eyes. "I said you could borrow my clothes. Anything of mine is yours. Seriously."

"I just didn't want to wake you."

"Cole. Stop it. It's. All. Good."

Cole nodded. "Thanks, man." He straightened up.

"No worries," Brady said. "No more hockey, I guess?"

"I think early morning basketball will suit me more than early morning run-into-Tristan-and-get-strangled."

"I'm sorry, what?"

"Do you think people will ever accept me here? Like, that it'll just feel normal?"

"What's normal? You know?"

Cole sat down beside Brady. "In another decade, say?"

"You're sticking around that long? You *really* should've packed better."

"What can I do to change that? Can I do more than I am now?"

Brady pushed his hair away, trying to blink himself more awake. "It'll never be normal, my friend. That ship has sailed. What happened, it happened. We can't change the past."

"But the future…"

"Cole," Brady breathed sharply, but kept his voice measured, "a good start is acting normal yourself. So just, you know, play basketball."

Cole sat there, quiet. He thought about it—really thought about it. Finally, he stood up. "Shitty thing is I'll be using a volleyball, but whatever."

"At least you have a volleyball." Brady fell backwards and sprawled out again. He closed his eyes.

Cole started to leave, but then he stopped and slapped his hand against the door frame. "By the way, you're, like, the best pretend sleeper I've ever seen."

"I get it from my kókom," Brady said with his eyes still closed. "We see and hear *everything*, Cole."

"Right…well, thanks." Cole held up the sweats and tank top, in an apologetic gesture, but Brady couldn't see it.

Cole pushed open the gym doors, and he had to look around more than once to make sure he'd gone to the right school, the right gym, and hadn't entered some sort of weird portal. The hardwood floors had been freshly waxed and there was a cart full of inflated basketballs beside the court. On the floor beside the cart, there was a present wrapped in bright red and white paper with a silver glittery bow on top. Cole picked it up, held it by his ear, and like he was five years old, he shook it. Something rattled around. Something big, but not altogether hard. He sat down on the floor, cross-legged, and tore the paper off to reveal a shoebox. He lifted the lid and found a brand new pair of basketballs shoes, simple black. Sleek. The exact style he liked. He took off his outdoor shoes and slipped on the new pair of kicks. He looked around, all over the gym.

"Is this for me?!"

Nobody answered.

They were a perfect fit. He tied the laces nice and tight, and then he stood up and ran in place. They felt amazing—like he was running on air.

He scanned the gym again.

"Hello?"

Cole took a basketball from the top shelf of the cart like he was stealing it. He rolled it around between his hands, feeling the composite leather, the grooves. He bounced it several times, then took it to centre court. After one more bounce he took off running towards the hoop. He jumped two feet past the free throw line, cocked the basketball behind his head with both hands, and then slammed it through the hoop.

"Holy shit, Harper."

Cole wheeled around. Pam was standing at the doors to the gym, a clipboard gripped between her chest and forearm. He was frozen. He couldn't have moved if he wanted to.

"I was—"

"Weighing your options between the NBA and solving murders?"

"I've been wor—working on my vertical. Back in Winnipeg."

Pam walked across the gym floor and stopped right in front of Cole. She took the ball from him. "You could've saved yourself a thousand-dollar plane ride and jumped to Wounded Sky." She shot the ball with both hands. It clanged off the rim.

"Just drills. That's all." Cole couldn't look her in the eye. Instead, he looked at the storage room door, at the gym doors, at the stage, at the blue mats. He pictured himself hitting his head against them for his stupidity. "What're you doing here so early?"

Pam rolled her eyes. "Look, I don't want to ruin the surprise…"

"But…"

Pam stared at the basketball shoes Cole had on. "I guess you kind of ruined it yourself, though."

"Oh, I just found them. I thought—"

"You saw a present in the middle of the gym and thought, *hey, this must be for me?*" Pam chuckled. "You city folk are entitled."

Cole might've lost it if Pam hadn't winked right after.

"Sorry, was that the surprise?" he asked.

"All of it is."

"Like, everything?"

"Yep," she said. "The balls, the fixed rim, the floor, the *shoes…* somebody likes you."

"Somebody-like-*who* somebody?" Cole asked.

"I will say that I wasn't totally against it." Pam hugged the clipboard to her chest again. She looked down to the floor. "Alex was my best friend."

The silence between Cole and Pam resonated in the empty gym. Eventually, Pam looked up to find Cole looking at her, half smiling, half frowning. His eyes apologized for something he'd thought over and over again since Alex's murder—that he should've saved her. Somehow. Some way.

"Ummm…" Pam was the first to talk. "Joe, your friend from Winnipeg, told me your shoe size, what kind you liked."

"He'd know. Joe. How many times did he say 'dude' to you?"

"Dude? Oh, about five million times. 'Dude you're going to get Cole some new kicks? Awesome, dude. Listen, dude, I'm, like, size eleven. He's my size, dude. Dude, dude, dude.' It went something like that. And then I told them, and *voilà.*"

They laughed, and then they got caught in another silence.

"Who's *them?*" The question felt accentuated after the silence.

"Huh? Oh, sorry. Mihko."

"The laboratory people? With the doctors and guards and—"

"Mihko. Correct."

"Weird." The word *them* kept repeating in his head. *Them. They. Them. They.* Cole shook his head at the thought. Why would they do something like this for him, and at the same time, try to kill him, his friends?

"Super weird," Pam chuckled. "Anyway, there's an assembly this morning. For you. They were going to present it all to you. It's a big to-do."

"An assembly?"

"Surprise! You look like you're going to shit yourself, Harper."

"That obvious?"

"You suddenly look like you did yesterday."

He felt like he did yesterday, too.

"Anyway," Pam said, "I came to start setting up. Didn't think you'd be in here already, dunking like Spider-Man to embarrass Flash Thompson. Y'know."

"That's the shitty *Spider-Man.*"

"That's the shitty *Spider-Man*, but the only one where he dunks a basketball."

Cole looked around the gym. He imagined it filled with teachers, students, parents—dignitaries, even? Reynold McCabe. His heart felt like it was going to pound out of his chest and start bouncing all over the newly waxed floor. The imagined crowd *did* scare the shit out of him. He didn't want to consider how it would feel when the real one showed up.

The change room was the safest place to be. Cole had been sitting in it for half an hour. He was leaning forward, staring at the floor, counting the little blue speckles embedded in the grey tiles. Three hundred ninety-seven so far. He would've been happy to hide there all day, counting speckles and pretending to be curious about how many there were, and naming clusters of them as though they were constellations. He could hear footsteps entering the gym. They'd started coming in about ten minutes ago. It sounded like a stampede.

"Why can't you just get over this?" Cole whispered to himself, but he knew better. You didn't just "get over" anxiety. His therapist had told him as much. It was something you managed, by doing things the right way. By not letting it hold you back. Exercising. Eating right. And yes, taking a pill every now and then when you felt like you really needed it. "But this is something you'll always have to live with, Cole," she'd said within the confines of her office, over the hum of the A/C unit sticking out of the window behind him, the one that he listened to when he didn't want to hear what she had to say. Things like how when he was sixty years old he'd still have anxiety, and still have to live with it. Diet. Exercise. Perseverance. The occasional pill. Counting speckles.

"Imagine that it's a person," she'd said.

"I imagine that it's a…a beast or something," he'd said.

"It can be, if you let it," she'd said. "It's sitting on your shoulder, whispering into your ear, and it's hungry. Every time you listen to what it's whispering to you, it grows. It keeps growing until it's not sitting on your shoulder anymore, but you're wearing it like clothing."

"But if you don't feed it…" Cole started. If he didn't listen to those whispers, it would shrink. It would shrink so small that he might not even hear it whispering sometimes.

"Right," she'd said. "If you don't feed it."

Last week, at times, it had shrunk. Yesterday it had grown. Now it was a bit bigger, the whispers getting louder.

"What do you have to do?" he'd asked.

It was exactly what he'd done at the memorial, when he didn't feel like he had the strength to even stand. He had to get up and let all those people honour him, like they'd planned to do. He reached under the bench and pulled out the new shoes they bought him. He nodded to himself.

"Okay," he said. "Okay, fine. You win."

Cole put the shoes on the bench beside Brady's gym clothes, and gave the floor one last look. He stopped at four hundred eighteen speckles and three constellations. The last one, speckles in the shape of a moose's asshole, he dubbed "Chochinov Minor." He'd managed to laugh at that, easing his anxiety momentarily. Cole added that to the list his therapist had given him. Diet, exercise, etc., etc., and humour. He stood up with a deep breath, walked across the change room, and opened the door.

Considering the high school had a relatively small student body, the gym looked packed. At least, it did to Cole. As soon as he opened the door from the change room, he could see an ocean of faces. Most of them were looking right at him. At least most of the faces were friendly. Only Michael, sitting beside Eva and Brady, didn't look friendly. By contrast, Eva smiled when she saw Cole. A *let's-put-shit-behind-us* smile. Hesitant. Hopeful. Brady waved Cole over and pointed to an empty seat he'd saved for him.

"Hey, Harper."

Pam had an empty seat beside her as well, right at the front of the gym. Presumably, this, too, was for him. The Guest of Honour. He looked towards his friends, smiled at them apologetically, and walked over to Pam. There was no way he was going to make things worse by sitting near Eva when Michael was right there. He'd already gone out with her into the woods last night without him.

"Thanks for coming out," Pam said when he sat down beside her.

"I wouldn't want to make you look bad," Cole said.

He glimpsed at her clipboard, the one she'd had earlier in the morning. He could see an agenda clipped onto it with speaking notes.

"So you were setting up the assembly, now it looks like you're emceeing it...what else do you do?"

"I get bored," Pam said. "I need to do stuff."

"Like?"

"Like, I don't know, do some IT stuff. You know, computers."

"I've heard of them, yeah." Cole turned towards her. He touched his knee against her thigh by accident, and moved it away. "So—what about computers?"

"Nerdy stuff. Typical IT nerd activities. I never see the sun, and when I'm not helping kids with panic attacks I'm playing Fornite."

Cole laughed. Pam kept a straight face.

"Seriously," Cole said.

Pam shrugged. "Just keep the website up to date, not that anybody goes on it. You can't even get internet if you're, like, one hundred yards away from the centre of Wounded Sky. Troubleshoot when staff's got email problems. So, that's, abooouuut…every minute."

"Cool."

"Yeah. So, for *this*, I'm just calling up Anna, then Reynold, then somebody from Mihko."

"Anna? Anna Crate?"

"Yep. I wasn't going to at first, because I hate McCabe, but when I pictured how mad he might be after what happened yesterday, I totally couldn't resist."

"What happened yesterday?"

"Harper, you *have* to get on our group text." Pam held out her phone and shook it in the air. "If you're staying, you just have to. It's like the Wounded Sky First Nation play-by-play."

Cole just sat there with a dumb look on his face.

"Right, so, get this: Anna announced that she was running in Chief Crate's place." Pam clapped her hands once, delighted at the trouble this was going to cause.

"Really?"

"Check it out." Pam pointed at the front of the gym, where, standing beside some teachers and the principal, sure enough, was Anna Crate. "And it didn't even matter that you were late showing up, because Reynold's not even *here* yet. He's probably so pissed." Pam sported a huge smile.

"When's the election again?" Cole asked.

"Sunday," Pam said, "and I think Reynold is royally screwed. I mean, some people are going to vote for him, of course, but everybody who was going to vote for Chief Crate is going to vote for Anna. *Everybody.*"

"And I thought presidential elections were dramatic."

"Well, McCabe's also not a guy you want with the nuclear codes, I'll tell you that."

Cole sized up Anna while he, and the entire crowd of kids, waited. She looked as likeable as Chief Crate: kind, approachable, a person you could sit down and talk with about anything. Case in point: Choch was standing with her, talking her up, having the absolute time of his life. Cole wondered what they were talking about. Normally, he'd be able to hear from that far away, but the drone of restless students keeping themselves entertained prevented him from eavesdropping. It was either that, or Choch was shutting him out.

A moment later, Reynold walked into the gym with Lucy at his side. He gave Lucy a kiss on the cheek, which she begrudgingly accepted. She nodded at Cole on her way to the crowd. Reynold stood there until Lucy had taken her seat, assessing the room, and then walked across the front of the stage, chest puffed out and chin up, trying to look as confident as possible.

"Well, I'm up," Pam said.

"Good luck," Cole said.

She got up, clipboard in hand, walked to the front of the stage, and tapped the microphone a couple of times to make sure it was on. The loud knocking sound that echoed through the gymnasium speakers served to quiet down the assembly, which was in a buzz since Reynold's arrival.

"Morning, Wounded Sky-ians!" Pam kept a straight face the entire time. "You know, I was going to start off by asking if you'd heard any big news lately, but that would've been way too obvious for an icebreaker."

The crowd was silent for a moment. Then, as though one student was gauging from another what they could, or should, find amusing, the odd laugh and clap sprinkled through the gym. Pam carried on, undeterred.

"Totally unrelated, not sure if any of you have heard this, but there's an election this Sunday that actually means something now."

No laughs, but rather a large round of applause. Chants of "Ah-na! Ah-na!" broke out.

"But I digress," Pam said. "We're here this morning to honour Cole Harper…"

Even bigger applause than for Anna Crate? Cole blushed with disbelief. He tried to keep looking forward, and not at all the students cheering for him.

"...yeah," Pam said, responding to the applause. "Once again, Harper has saved lives in our community, so..."

"We love you, Cole!" a voice blurted out from the crowd.

"...we just wanted to be as fickle as possible and tell him we love him, even though a week and a half ago most of us wanted to kick him out of our community."

No applause. More like murmurs that Choch might've described as, "WTF, as the kids say nowadays." Cole looked over to see Choch's reaction, because he was sure that the spirit being would love this, but Choch was nowhere to be found.

"We are so much like sports fans here it is totally crazy." Pam, for the first time, held up her clipboard and looked at her notes. It was either that, or she was looking at her schedule to see if she could fit detention in between her IT work, event planning, emceeing, and canteen shifts at the X. "With that, I'd like to call up Anna Crate."

Anna came up to the mic and gave Pam a hug. The crowd roared. Cole cheered, too. She stood at the mic for an eternity, looking at once humble and appreciative, until the applause died.

"Tansi. Kininaskomitin for the warm welcome, but this morning is not about me." Anna looked at Cole. "This morning is about Cole Harper. I know my husband would've been so proud of you, for what you've done for Wounded Sky once again, Cole. I am honoured to give you my thanks on behalf of Chief Crate, and I want you to know that you are welcome here for—"

"But Mihko isn't!" a kid shouted from the crowd.

"Now, now," Anna said in response, "I know we all have questions, and those questions are valid. There will be a time for those questions to be answered. But this morning is not that time. They have done a good thing for Cole, and I appreciate their gesture, as we all should. Cole, what I want to say is simply this: welcome home. Ekosi."

Anna left the stage to give Cole a hug, and say another thanks to him over the crowd, which was at its loudest during their brief embrace.

This sat in stark contrast to the subdued applause that accompanied Reynold to the stage after Pam had provided him with a succinct welcome devoid of any irreverent humour.

Cole expected Reynold to look like a tea kettle. A *Looney Tunes*-level tea kettle. Whistling. Boiling over. An unmistakable shade of red. But he didn't. He looked calm, straddling the delicate line between confident and cocky.

"Good morning. It is an honour to be here with you. Thank you to Mrs. Crate for her warm words, and, most importantly, to Mihko Laboratories for their very generous donation to not only Cole Harper, but to Wounded Sky High School itself. I have never seen the gym look like this, I can tell you that. I, for one, welcome them here with open arms, just as I do you, Cole."

"Yeah because they're paying you a ton of cash!" a student called out.

"They are infusing our entire community, our businesses, with much-needed revenue. And let's not forget that they are here to help. They came here during an intense time of need."

"Still late to the party!"

"The flu was already cured!"

Reynold continued on as though he couldn't hear the catcalls. "They'll help us figure out exactly what happened. Now. If I may continue with Wounded Sky's very own hero." Reynold looked directly at Cole. "As much as I know he hates hearing it. He's a humble young man, and we should be very proud to have him as one of us, whether he is here physically, or not..."

"A hero you arrested, McCabe!" a voice called out from the back.

"Cole..." Reynold took the mic off the stand and walked over to Cole so he was standing over him, looking down at him, "the gift you've been given is on behalf of all of us. Ekosani."

"Ekosani," Cole said to Reynold.

Pam went to take the mic from Reynold, but he ignored her and walked back onto the stage. "If I may, I'd now like to call up Cameron Xavier, Head of Mihko Laboratories, who has taken time from the busy work he has over at the clinic to be here this morning. Cameron?"

A short, pale man came onto the stage and met Reynold at the mic. Reynold gave Cameron a big hug, and they exchanged a few words away from the mic, both wearing enormous grins. Cole strained to hear what they were saying, but the odd collection of boos and applause and chatter made it impossible. After Cameron and Reynold gave each other another man-hug, Reynold passed Cameron the mic.

"Hello, Wounded Sky High School!" Cameron said as though it was a pep rally, but when nobody responded he cleared his throat and spoke at a normal, appropriately restrained level. "On behalf of Mihko Laboratories, I would like to say how honoured we were to provide this small token of our appreciation to Cole for what he's done for your community. Of course, we were here many years ago, and while I understand more difficulties have befallen…"

"Murders, asshat!"

"…your home," Cameron continued, "I am glad to be back here under better circumstances, thanks to this young man we are celebrating today. Mr. Harper, I hope this small gift…"

"Why don't you give him some of the money you're giving *Chief* Reynold!"

"…helps you feel even more at home. Eko…Ekosani."

Pam hopped up to the stage amidst dead silence and took the mic from Cameron. She hit the mic twice. "Is this thing on? Kidding. Thank you, Mr. Xavier. Eh-co-zan-nee," she said very slowly. "Alright, the moment you've all been waiting for, fellow classmates. Please give a hand for Cole Harper!"

Cole had been dreading this. He tried not to turtle, to crumple to his knees and cover his head with his arms like he was in a plane going down. *It wants you to crumple, so you get on that stage, Cole,* he told himself. He stood up and met Pam centre stage. She handed him the microphone, and then leaned in and said, "Uh oh, you're not looking so hot."

"I-I'll be okay." He walked to the middle of the stage to chants of, "Har-per! Har-per! Har-per!" and nobody laughed when he tried more than once to place the microphone onto the stand. His hands were shaking feverishly. *Just be fast, get off the stage, and don't be an idiot.* He closed his eyes and said a little prayer, then opened them.

There were SO. MANY. PEOPLE. He took one very deep breath.

"Uhhh, hey," Cole started. "Thanks everybody. Thanks to Mihko Laboratories for the gift. Gifts. I, uhhh, I think that, y'know, playing basketball helps, I guess, feel normal. Just helps me to relax." *They don't need your life story, Cole.* "So, it really means a lot. The longer I'm here, the more it feels like home again. We always, y'know, did things to support each other. I think Brady and Eva should be up here, too. I would've been lost without them. Literally." The gym was dead quiet. Cole wondered if he was sucking that badly, or if people were actually listening to what he had to say. "I just wish something like this wasn't… I wish that…"

Oh god, don't cry. Please, don't cry.

"It's okay, Cole!" Eva? Was that Eva? Even after their fight? Cole had been too busy looking down at his shoe laces, trying to will tears back into his tear ducts.

"Harper!"

"Love ya, bud!"

Cole looked up, let out a shaky breath. A tear fell. Curved down his cheek. He could feel it hang from his chin. "I just wish none of this happened. I think…I know I would've stayed anyway." Cole nodded, forced a smile. "Ekosani. Really."

The crowd erupted into applause. A few kids got up from their seats in the back row, followed by more ahead of them, and still more ahead of them, until it turned into a standing ovation. Cole waved to the side, to the front, to the other side, at nobody in particular, and awkwardly kept waving, waiting for the applause to die down. But it didn't, not for a long time. Eventually he just walked forward a few steps and sat down at the edge of the stage. He watched, and listened, and damn-it if a smile didn't find its way onto his face.

8

THE THING

AFTER THE APPLAUSE HAD DIED DOWN, as students left the gym, Cole sat there, still. He watched the room slowly empty, tired, as he always was when coming down from an anxiety attack. It had taken everything out of him, all his energy and strength. He managed to give a few fist-bumps to kids, a few high-fives, shake Anna Crate's hand, and nod to Reynold, who had only nodded as well.

Cole decided to skip his next class to wander the halls again—this time, hopefully, minus the panic attack. Or maybe he'd stay here, and use the new shoes, the newly waxed floor, the replaced rim, the inflated balls. He had earned this. He sat there and waited, willing the students to move a bit quicker, and the gym to be empty. He could picture his black shoes on the bench in the change room, calling his name, their new shoe smell ready to be soiled by his smelly feet. But the beautiful moment Cole imagined was put off when Dr. Captain came up to him, navigating her way through the swarm.

"Cole, hi. Congratulations," she said.

"Thanks," he said. "I hope I didn't sound like too much of an idiot."

"You sounded fine."

"I'll take your word for it. I've already blocked it out. I was thinking more about not collapsing than what was coming out of my mouth."

"Public speaking is hard for most people," she assured him.

"I thought death and taxes were what people feared most," he said.

"No, those are inevitabilities. That's different from fear. Public speaking, well, people fear *that* more than death."

Cole thought about that in the context of what he'd learned about death, and what happened after. *Jayne. The northern lights.* He had to agree with Dr. Captain. Public speaking was definitely scarier. "I guess so."

"You've been through scarier things," Dr. Captain said.

"I would rather face Scott again than speak in front of the whole school. And I literally almost died, so…"

"So there you go."

"There you go." Cole repeated.

Dr. Captain was beating around the bush. Cole watched Brady and Eva approach as though their ears were burning. They stopped several feet away. Eva told Brady she'd see him in class. They hugged, then Brady left. Eva stayed and waited, presumably for Dr. Captain to leave. Cole suddenly wanted Dr. Captain to get to the point.

"You should've asked…what was his name?" Cole asked.

"Xavier. Cameron."

"Right. You should've asked Xavier to give you your job back while he was here."

"It would be better if I had some ammunition if I did that." She paused. "Did you find the files?"

"No, sorry. I went out to Scott's camp last night looking—"

"Out into the woods, at night? I didn't expect that you'd do that, Cole. People have been seeing—"

"Hey, I was more scared a few minutes ago, right? Public speaking…death…it was no sweat."

"That's perceived fear, Cole, not actual danger."

"Anyway, I didn't find them. There was nothing there." Cole pictured the folder. He remembered pulling it out of Scott's backpack, looking through it, and the shock of what he found inside. All the kids in his class: the ones that died in the fire, the ones that died by Scott's hand, the ones that were under threat. The experiments that had been run on them. The big green stamp on his file. *Successful.* Had they all been given pills like Cole had? Had his just been different? Did the other kids' parents administer the "vitamins?" If not, then who did? Eva hadn't remembered vitamins. Then he thought about the flu, and

Wayne telling him and Eva that patients looked sick. Why? "I'll find them. If you can decipher what's in them, maybe…" Cole trailed off.

"So somebody took them?" Dr. Captain said.

"I guess so." Cole wasn't about to tell Dr. Captain that, according to Jayne, the boogeyman took the files. "They didn't disappear into thin air, so I'll just keep searching. They'll turn up. They have to turn up."

"Any ideas *where*?"

"No good ones. I was going to stop by the RCMP office, see if they cleaned the camp out, along with the files. But it feels like a stretch."

Cole looked at Eva again. She seemed impatient. Dr. Captain saw Cole looking at her. She looked back and forth, from Cole to Eva and pushed herself away from the stage. "You'll let me know if…"

"Yeah, I'll let you know."

When Dr. Captain left the gym with a smattering of Cole's high school contemporaries, Eva took her place, standing right where Dr. Captain was. But then she hopped up onto the stage and sat beside Cole.

"What's with the silent treatment? Is it about last night?"

He looked at his hands, interlocked and resting between his thighs, his scars hidden. She was direct, he'd give her that.

"I'm sorry for last night," he said, "I was being a jerk, and you were just trying to make life easier for me."

"Maybe you were right, too, though," she said. "It's like I was saying yesterday morning, me and Brady. Some things you can handle on your own, right?"

Cole nodded. "But I wasn't trying to give you the silent treatment, it was more that I had to sit at the front, for this…" Cole indicated the whole gym with a sweeping gesture that required both arms "…*thing*."

"You looked me off," Eva chuckled, "you *know* you looked me off."

"Can you imagine if I had to, like, get from where you guys were sitting, to the stage, when I was called up? I would've died halfway there. My heart was just…" Cole hit his palm against his chest rapidly.

Eva and Cole were the last people in the gym, aside from some kids, including Pam, who'd stayed behind to stack and remove chairs. Metal legs cracked closed against metal frames and echoed in the gym. Cole found his eyes wandering over to Pam every few seconds.

"Was it because of her?" Eva asked.

Cole returned his attention to Eva. "What?"

"Did you just want to sit beside Pam? It's okay if you did. I'd just...if you just told me that, instead of making something up."

She knew he was making something up. She always knew.

"Eva, this isn't really...I don't want to talk about that right now. I mean, it's mostly about Mike. I'm trying to...I want to make that right, on my own, and I want to be your friend, and somebody please shoot me in the head, okay?"

"You don't want to talk about it right now, but you're talking about it right now, and you look like you just got kicked in the balls. Cole, help me out here."

"Can we talk about it later? Really?" Cole hopped off the stage. He extended his hand to help Eva off the stage, but she gave him a look like, *come on*, and jumped by herself.

"Since when do we do this? Honestly?"

Cole listened to the sound of metal against metal, counting each chair being placed on top of another chair. "Eva, I—"

"Fine. Can we talk tonight? What are you doing?"

Whatever he wanted to do tonight, and whether or not he wanted her around for it, Michael's face popped into his head. Michael's face with that familiar look: the furrowed eyebrow. The icy stare. The hardened features. "I'm kind of busy."

"Busy doing what? You can't go look for those files without me. That shit was done on me, too. Don't forget that."

"I haven't forgot, I'm just busy, alright?" Cole said. "Maybe tomorrow. How about tomorrow?"

Eva looked at him deeply. Sometimes, when Eva looked at him, it felt like she was looking *into* him. Then, resignedly, she said, "Okay, tomorrow. I'll see ya," and left.

"See ya." Cole said, but she was already gone.

Cole's shot hit the rim. In the empty gym, the sound echoed. He still couldn't shoot worth a damn. If only Choch had given Cole the ability to make basketball shots. Cole would have traded something like... strength...for that skill, but only if he'd be able to bring it back to Winnipeg with him after all of this was done (and if his coach was going to let him on the team at all, since he'd missed tryouts).

Cole picked up the ball by the three-point line. He hugged it between his arm and hip, ghosted a shot with his right hand, then took an actual shot. It rolled around the rim, before getting spat out. The old toilet bowl. Joe had told him who'd made the team back in Winnipeg. He was better than, well, all of the kids who made it. He'd be way better if he could hit a jumpshot. He chased the ball to the front corner of the gym, bounced it up to the hoop, and laid it in off the glass. He raised his arms in mock triumph, then took the ball with him to the free throw line.

He shot. It bounced off the rim, off the glass, off the rim, and onto the floor. The ball graciously bounced right back to him.

He'd asked Joe if Coach would take him onto the team if he got back before the season started, seeing as how he'd missed tryouts. Joe had texted back that he wasn't sure.

COLE: **What if you told him I was busy catching a serial killer?**

JOE: **Dude. Bullshit.**

COLE: **Wasn't it on the news? Nothing?**

Cole expected the story to have been in the newspaper. Nobody had interviewed him and he hadn't seen any news crews in the community, but surely the outside world would've gotten wind of *something*. Apparently, that wasn't the case.

JOE: **I'll talk 2 him, K? Make up real shit tho.**

Cole conceded, as he bounced the ball three times then twirled it in his shooting hand, that it did sound made up. But he'd lived it. All those deaths, all that craziness. Nothing on the six o'clock news? The radio? He hugged the ball between his left arm and hip, practised his form with his right hand again, then readied another shot.

"Oh, *that's* what that awful sound is. Bricks." Cole stopped mid-shot. The ball dropped to the floor a few feet in front of him. Pam was by the gym door.

"Oh, hey." Cole straightened out his sweats, like that would make him look more presentable. "I thought you left."

Pam picked up the rolling ball. "I was going to sweep your newly waxed floor, as a kindness."

"I did that already." Cole motioned to a pile of dirt and debris near the storage room. "I left a pile there if you wanted to…"

"No, that's okay, thanks. You should really finish a job once you've started it, hey?"

"If you only knew the half of it."

She bounced the ball a few times. "You really get zoned out, Harper."

"Yeah, sometimes I shoot around just so I can think." Cole tossed his arms out to the sides.

"Maybe you need to think more."

"Ha, funny." Cole received a chest pass from Pam. He aimed again, this time like he was shooting for a championship. The ball soared through the air, hit the front of the rim, skipped to the backboard, and off the side of the rim. "Yeah, maybe."

The ball rolled back to Cole quietly and slowly, like it was embarrassed for him. He picked it up and extended the ball to Pam, but she shook her head. "Not really my thing. I have a one-shot-per-day maximum."

"Right," Cole said, "Fortnite is your game."

"And I'd be just as nervous if you watched me play."

"What's the Fortnite equivalent of bricking a jumpshot?"

"Good question," Pam nodded thoughtfully. "Getting killed by The Storm when you're almost out of it? I'll get back to you on that one."

Cole missed another shot, rolled his eyes at himself, and chased after the ball as it journeyed to the corner of the gym. On the way, Pam called out, "So what were you thinking about?"

Cole considered how much to tell her, or whether to tell her anything at all, as he jogged back to the foul line. "Pardon?"

"Any specific thoughts? You said you shot around to think," Pam said, "*sometimes.*"

But what could it hurt? Since the assembly had ended and first period started, Cole had missed a bunch of shots, and he wasn't much further in his planning than going to the RCMP detachment tonight. And Choch wasn't around to help him brainstorm. Again. Cole was so lost for a good idea he actually wanted the spirit being around. He was ready to decipher whatever cryptic response Choch would give.

"Alright," Cole said, "I need to find something, but I have no idea where to look."

"Okay, that's vague. Care to elaborate?"

"Uhhh," Cole balked. "I'm not sure that I can."

"If you're worried that you're going to sound weird, just remember that weird is kind of our thing out here," Pam said.

Weird? Weird would be putting it lightly. Cole bounced the ball a few times, right over a dead spot. It sounded like empty thuds. Mihko waxed the floor, but they hadn't really fixed it. "Somebody saw who took this…thing…but I don't think they're the most reliable witness."

"Somebody like…"

"A kid. A kid saw it." Cole stopped bouncing the ball and took another shot. This time, it didn't even hit the rim. Off the backboard, onto the ground, and the ball rolled down to the other side of the gym. Cole left it. "She said she saw the boogeyman take it, okay? So, that's how much help she was."

"The boogeyman took *the thing*? Wow."

"I know it sounds dumb. I've been trying to think about what she really meant, and other than, you know, what Victor saw…"

"Oh, I heard about that. Bananas."

"Yeah, so I'm stuck."

Pam paced twice between the baseline and Cole. Then, she stopped. "You know, to a kid, a scary guy could be a boogeyman."

Cole nodded. "True." He started to think about scary guys, but nobody seemed scary to him. Scott, he supposed. But Scott was indisposed. *Ha! CB, that rhymed!*

Wait! Cole thought. *Come to the gym!* Choch didn't respond.

"Hey." Pam waved a hand in front of Cole's face.

"Sorry," Cole said.

"Maybe it doesn't matter, right now, who or what this boogeyman thing is," Pam said.

"It doesn't matter," Cole said thoughtfully, trying to let those words percolate.

"Maybe you should be thinking about the thing, you know? Back to basics. Okay, here's a question: what *is* the thing?"

"A folder with files in it," Cole said.

"Wow, boring. Didn't expect that," Pam said. "So, maybe it would be easier to think about the boring folder rather than who took the folder. Get me? Like, what are the files? Does it make sense that they'd be somewhere? Where is most likely? I search for files *all the time* on computers here. They're digital files, but the principle is the same, maybe?"

Where is most likely? Cole tossed that around in his head. Files on kids. Medical experiments that were done on his friends a decade ago, to be specific. A specificity that he didn't think he could, or should, tell Pam about. If it wasn't at the RCMP office, then where else could it be? The answer hit Cole hard, and when it did, he realized that it was obvious, and maybe that he'd been willfully ignoring it. Because of what it would remind him of. *The research facility.* Where his dad worked. Where his dad took part in the experiments. Where his dad died. Cole leaned forward, as though the breath had been sucked right out of him.

"Need Dr. Captain, Harper? Or did you just have an epiphany?"

"I think epiphanies are good. This sucks."

Pam walked towards the ball at the other side of the gym. She called out, "Thank you, Pam. You're super helpful, Pam." Cole watched her clumsily bounce the ball as she made her way back to him.

He straightened up. "Sorry. Thank you, Pam. You're super helpful, Pam."

"Not convincing." Pam tossed the ball from one hand to the other, then she bounced a pass to Cole that hit him in the stomach. "Harper, you look like you've seen a ghost."

Cole picked up the ball and stared at it, and he tried to just see orange and think *orange* and not think of anything else—not the facility, or the vitamins, or his dad. But it didn't work. He dropped the ball and neither of them said anything until it had finished bouncing, and rolled away.

"Care to tell me why you look like you might vomit on the newly waxed floor?" Pam asked.

"I just..." *breathe in five seconds, out seven seconds* "...think I have to go somewhere that I don't want to go. Sorry, it was helpful, just...I think I knew, in a way, and I just didn't want to know. If that makes sense."

"It makes no sense, but okay."

"Sorry."

"Oh my god, Harper, enough sorrys." She retrieved the ball and came back to him. "Okay, let's try this: when do you have to go 'somewhere that you don't want to go'?"

Cole shrugged. "Tonight, I guess." *After the RCMP detachment,* he thought. It seemed useless now, the files weren't going to be there. He knew that before. But Lauren might have information about Mikho or Scott. If the files were at the facility, then they weren't going anywhere. "Ooof!" Pam had thrown the ball again, and this time it hit him a bit lower than his stomach.

"Oh." Pam put her hand over her mouth. "*I* haven't said sorry yet, so sorry about that."

"Would you stop that?"

"Yes, I promise to not sack you again, but I will, however, continue to throw the ball at you if you keep zoning out on me."

Cole stopped short of beginning with sorry, and said, "Just got a lot on my mind."

"Well..." Pam picked the ball up again, and Cole winced, expecting another hard pass. "How about instead of thinking, you, I don't know, distract yourself."

"How?"

"Since I'm super helpful, I would be willing to take you out for dinner, and I promise to be totally forward and make you nervous only in the interest of keeping your mind off the boogeyman and the boring files and whatever ghost you just happened to see."

"Totally forward, like—"

"Wow, Harper. It's super easy to make you nervous. Not a date, okay? Just two people hanging out, if that floats your boat."

She tossed the ball at him, and this time he caught it. Cole looked at it again, rolling it around in his hands. Dinner with Pam. He looked up from the ball, to her, standing there, tapping her heel. Standing there in her white shoes, blackened with ink. Her ripped jeans which, Cole noticed for the first time, had letters and numbers written strategically all over the material. Code. Her baggy black shirt, which she still somehow looked cool in. Eva's voice popped into his head. *Was it because of her?* She sounded jealous of Pam. What would she think if he went for dinner with her? But then, Cole thought, what would Michael think? Maybe going out with Pam would help fix things with Michael. How could he be jealous of him and Eva, if he was seeing somebody else?

"Yeah," he said, "okay. Sure."

"Not so fast, tiger." She nodded towards the rim. "Hit the shot and it's a date."

"And if I miss?"

9

JAGGED VACANCE

"ARE YOU SERIOUSLY NOT GOING TO EAT ANYTHING? Since when do you not eat your food?" Brady was almost finished his second plate. He and Cole were at the kitchen table. All Cole had put into his mouth was water. Just a few sips.

"Sorry," Cole said.

"I slaved over a hot stove for, like, thirty minutes," Brady said, grinning.

Cole looked down at his plate of food. Kraft Dinner, mixed vegetables, fried bologna, and bannock. He calculated just how long he thought it would take Brady to put all of this together.

"More like fifteen minutes," Cole said. "Tops."

"You could've helped," Brady said.

While Brady had made dinner, Cole laid on the couch and stared at the ceiling as his *not*-date with Pam loomed closer with each passing second.

"I can hardly function," Cole said.

"You're always off staring at something," Brady said. "What is it tonight?"

"It's just…" Cole didn't even finish. He just shook his head.

"If you're not going to eat my food, then you're going to tell me why you're off moping in the living room," Brady said, "and *now*. You're so dramatic."

"I guess some advice would help, anyway."

"You don't say."

Cole shoved the plate away, not keeping up any pretense of eating. "I told Pam I'd go out with her tonight, okay? But now I don't know if I should've said yes."

"Pam?" Brady asked. "Really?"

"Yeah, Pam."

"She's awesome," Brady said. "So what's the problem?"

"Well, I didn't really say yes because I liked her. I mean, I *could* like her, maybe I like her, but it was more, just, trying to make Michael like me again." Cole's chin collapsed into his chest. "If that makes sense."

"If you'd told anybody else that, literally anybody, they would be totally lost," Brady said.

"But not you?"

Brady leaned forward. "You think Michael hates you because you're spending time with Eva, so you're going out with Pam to show him that he has nothing to worry about."

Cole raised his eyebrows. "Yeah, that's exactly right."

"So, I repeat," Brady started to sound tired, "what's the problem?"

"I keep thinking about not what Michael will think, but what Eva will think. I still…"

"You still have feelings for her."

"Yeah, and, you know, maybe she does, too? And what if I ruin that because I want to suck up to Michael?"

"You're supposing that Eva has feelings for you, too? She's with Michael, Cole. It should be irrelevant."

"But it's not!"

"So what advice do you need? How to keep secrets from one of your oldest friends?"

"We used to have feelings for each other. We were *engaged*, you know."

Brady rolled his eyes. "When you were *seven*, right? What do feelings really mean when you're seven? Let alone an engagement. Things change."

"It still means something to me. Anyway, I don't want to tell her anymore, but I want to be friends with Michael again, and I have no idea what I should do."

"I'm not playing this game, Cole." Brady leaned back and crossed his arms. He started to slowly shake his head.

"What?" Cole said.

"I want to tell you something, as a friend, as one of your best friends, but I don't want you to take it the wrong way," Brady said.

"Okaaay…"

"But at the same time, I don't think there is another way to take it. So, you'll just have to take it however you do."

"Okaaay…" Cole repeated and leaned forward.

"Does it ever register with you, in particular right now, that you're talking to me about love interests—"

"I don't love Pam. I told you, it's so Michael—"

"*Whatever.* You're talking to me about her and Eva and this huge problem you have, meanwhile, my boyfriend just got killed. Does that even cross your mind?"

Cole sighed. It hadn't, and he felt like an asshole. His whole body slumped. "No. I'm sorry. It should've. I'm an…I'm such an ass."

"And you're sitting there, on the couch, mulling over the same thing, I guess, and, you know, I'd really like to be doing the same thing sometimes, but I can't. Because you need *so much,* Cole."

"I just thought…" Cole leaned back. He felt his eyes start to well up. "…you're so much better at *this* than me, life, everything, and I trust what you say."

"That's fine, my friend, and I appreciate it. I really do. I don't want to guilt you, either. But Cole, once in a while, if one of those questions was, 'How are you doing, Brady?' I'd really appreciate that."

"You're right. Of course you're right." Cole slunk even lower in his chair. "I keep thinking about how Ashley died in front of me, and it's like the only thing I can see. Even at his wake, that's all that was in my head." Cole got up and started pacing around the kitchen. "And I'm talking about girls, and…" Cole stopped in the middle of the living room. He stared at the wall, away from Brady. He couldn't even look at him right now. He thought about everything Brady had done for him, taking him out on the land, taking him to a sweat, counselling him about what he'd been through, making him lunches and dinners—and what had he done for Brady? What meals had he made? "I do care how you're doing," Cole said through a shaking lower lip. "I'm sorry, man."

Cole felt Brady's hand on his shoulder. "Hey," he said, "hey." He turned Cole towards him. "Friends tell each other uncomfortable things sometimes, and they're honest with each other. They trust each other enough to be honest."

Cole had spent the first part of dinner with Pam picking at his fish and chips, a meal that he ordered without giving Rebecca any trouble. He still didn't have an appetite. With his eyes trained on the plate and the mutilated food, his mind was somewhere else entirely: Ashley and Brady. He imagined them sitting in this booth, eating together. Pam was almost done her supper because they weren't talking much.

"Do you really think I'm entitled?" Cole asked out of nowhere.

She quickly dabbed at her mouth, caught mid-bite. Aside from exchanging hellos and ordering food this was the first time Cole had really communicated.

"I think things are different in the city than they are here," Pam said.

"The longer I'm here, the less I feel at home. Is that weird or what?"

"You're not mad are you, Harper? Is that why you've been so quiet?"

"No, I'm not mad," Cole said. "I think you're right, that's all. I didn't at first, but now…"

"I usually am, so…" Pam put her napkin down and took another bite of food.

Cole stabbed at his fish. "I keep thinking about how Brady will never have Ashley around. I keep thinking how, I don't know, like, we're here, we can do this, and Brady can't."

"Not with Ashley," Pam said.

"Not with Ashley," Cole said, and Ashley's face displayed prominently in his mind again.

"Well, if it's any consolation, we're not actually doing anything, just eating," Pam said, "well, I'm eating anyway. So, don't feel guilty."

"Oh, I didn't mean…"

"Easy, tiger," Pam smiled, "I'm attempting to set you at ease by throwing you off-guard. You should know about that. Reverse psychology, right?"

"Right." Cole managed a chuckle.

"Brady'll be okay, you know. Eventually. Not right away, but one day. And he'll find somebody else, and they'll eat fish here. Some people will look at them weird, and some won't. It'll be good."

"And then I think of Maggie, too. And, you know, Alex. Keep thinking she's going to come out from behind the counter and mouth off or something."

Pam put her fork down. She leaned forward, tried to catch Cole's eyes, but he was being elusive, staring at his food again. She waved her hand over his plate, and he looked at her.

"Hey," she said softly.

"Hey," he said.

"Alex and I were friends, okay? Is this…do you feel guilty about that?"

"I'm feeling about one trillion things right now."

"I mean, that's pretty obvious."

"Why did you come tonight?" Cole asked. "I missed."

"Because I wanted to," she said matter-of-factly, "and the food's always good. I've actually been wondering why *you* came. You're not really here."

"Sorry. I wanted to come. This week's just been…a lot."

"The past, like, three weeks have been a lot for everybody, I think."

"Yeah."

Cole poked at a piece of fish. Pam ate the remains of her burger.

"Cool." Pam pointed at Cole's shirt with her fork. "Bon Iver, Bon Iver. Let's switch gears. What's your favourite song from that album?"

"'Holocene'," Cole said, trying to show some signs of life. "And best video, too. The beginning of it, with all the wilderness, reminds me of here."

"'Beth/Rest' for me," Pam said.

"Why?"

"Hmmm." Pam put up a finger, asking him to let her swallow food. When she had, she said, "Good question. I love the eighties and it kind of sounds like an eighties song. I don't know what most of the lyrics mean but I dig trying to figure it out. That being said, I do think it's about death, and it's really pretty. I like the thought of a pretty death."

"Because of Alex, or…"

"Just *because*. Now, your choice. Dissect 'Holocene', please."

"I just like the song," Cole said quietly.

"Harper, I'm doing all the work here, you know? Come on, your turn."

She was right. Cole was moping, again. Moping, and thinking, and being distant. Michael would not be jealous about what was happening here. The fact was, if he let himself, he might actually have a good time. Pam was easy to talk to, relaxing to be around, and she wasn't dating somebody else. If Eva wasn't around, would he be fully into Pam? Maybe he owed it to Eva, too, to just do this date, and not let it be about Mike or Eva. How about he let it be about Pam?

"*And at once I knew I was not magnificent,*" Cole said. "I like the idea of being small, knowing you're small, and that the world is big. That you're insignificant, and that's okay."

"But how can you feel insignificant when you're entitled? Riddle me that."

Cole stammered. "I…I mean…"

"Oh, Harper, what do I say?"

"Easy, tiger?"

"Very good," Pam nodded. "Now, you make a legitimate 'Holocene' case. Admittedly, it's my second favourite song on the album, so you're not far off."

Cole took a bite of a French fry. He looked behind the counter, where Alex used to work; at the pictures on the wall, trying his best not to count them as he went from collection of pictures to collection of pictures over each booth; and then at the people who were occupying the booths. Victor, the man with the story about the creature, was sitting by himself with a pot of coffee.

"Do you believe that guy?" Cole asked. "Victor?"

"Victor?" Pam gave a single shake of her head to one side, dabbed at her mouth with a napkin, catching some ketchup at the corner of her lip. "Crazy story, that. Scary as hell."

"So you think he's—"

"And yet…"

Cole leaned forward, trying to provoke Pam to finish her sentence. Finally, he said, "And yet what?"

"He's not one to run his mouth." She thought for a moment, chewing up and swallowing a French fry. "But maybe he just saw some kind of animal and came up with the first thing he could think of. Like your anonymous kid."

"The boogeyman."

"Yeah, like that."

"Do you think it could be, you know…?"

"Okay, well," Pam leaned back against her chair, took a deep breath, "if I were a betting girl, on the balance of probabilities, from what I've heard about it from Victor *and others*, sure."

Cole took a bite of fish.

"Or it could be an escaped monkey or something. A rabid monkey-man." Pam shrugged. "How about you? You believe in it?"

Let's see, Cole thought. *I have supernatural abilities, I talk to Coyote and also a half-burning ghost girl.* "I don't know."

Pam picked up the remaining fries on her plate and ate them. With a full mouth, she said, "I guess being away for ten years, in the big city no less, might've beaten that out of you, hey? Not to mention—"

"Making me entitled," Cole droned.

"Bingo," she laughed. "I guess I have to find some new material, hey?"

"I'm onto you."

"Whoa," she said, "you've gotta kiss me first. Holy!"

Cole turned white. His heart started to thump a thousand beats per second.

"Holy shit, I'm just screwing with you," Pam laughed. "But that's not to say a kiss is out of the question."

"Oh," Cole took a long breath in through his nose, "right. Totally." Expelled it for seven seconds.

"So," she said after allowing Cole to get his colour back, "how long are you staying out here?"

"I have no idea," Cole said. "I thought I was out here for one thing, and it turns out I either wasn't, or there was just…more things."

"Packed light?" she asked.

"Yeah."

Pam pointed at the shirt. "Brady's shirt?"

Cole felt flushed, like he'd lied. "That's still my favourite band," he blurted out.

"Harper," Pam pushed her plate away, "you have to stay at least long enough for me to help chill you out. Okay?"

She stood up.

"It's just—" Cole stood up, too. "I wish I knew what to do."

"About me or the boogeyman taking the folder?"

"How about both, among other things." *Like going to the research facility*, he thought. He wanted to ask Pam if they could sit down and stay longer, procrastinate longer, but he didn't want to ruin the few good moments they'd had.

"Welcome to being a teenager," Pam said, "the water's warm."

10

HELLO AGAIN

COLE ENTERED THE RCMP DETACHMENT, his presence announced by a little bell hanging over the door. The bell was a new addition, and it wasn't the only one. He'd been curious to see how Choch had fixed up the cell that Cole had escaped from the night of the memorial. Not only were the bars as good as new, no longer bent to the sides like they were pipe cleaners, but the cell boasted new bedding and over the bed there was a painting of a coyote emerging from the woods, and a potted plant hung from the ceiling.

Lauren's desk was covered in papers and reports, work that had undoubtedly increased since Wayne's gunshot wound. When she saw Cole, she put up a finger for him to wait a moment, and kept at it. Jerry had no papers on his desk. Jerry did not put up a finger for Cole to wait a moment. Jerry was dead to the world. He was leaning back in his chair, feet up on the desk, head tilted back, snoring. That's when Cole noticed the earbuds stuck into Lauren's ears, and heard the music playing in them, probably to drown out Jerry's snoring.

"Cole." Lauren took out her earbuds, picked up the piece of paper she'd been working on and slipped it into a folder. "Have a seat."

Cole, who'd been politely waiting at the front door, sat across from Lauren in an old office chair. He instantly started swivelling back and forth.

"How's everything going?" she asked.

"Some days are better than others," Cole conceded, silently debating where this day landed on the spectrum. Somewhere in the middle, he decided.

Lauren smiled. "It's hard to get over—" she started, before getting interrupted by a particularly loud snore. "Sorry." She picked up an eraser from the pencil holder at the corner of the desk, and tossed it across the room. It connected with Jerry's cheek, and he grunted and sat up straight.

"What's that?" he croaked, and looked around groggily.

"Just checking for a pulse," Lauren called across the room to him.

"God, Lauren, I'm on a break," Jerry said, and then he just rested his head on the desk and closed his eyes, not bothering to lean back.

"So that's what I'm dealing with," Lauren said, returning her attention to Cole.

"I don't even think I've seen him awake before," Cole said.

"He's my boss, Cole, okay? He's in charge of me, with Wayne in the clinic." Lauren slammed her palms against the desk in frustration. Jerry jumped and settled. At least his snoring was lighter now. "Whenever you think you've got it bad, just think of me, got it?"

"Got it."

"Where were we?"

"Ummm, oh, you were saying it's hard to get over..." Cole prompted.

"Right, it's hard to get over what happened, especially when you were in it." Lauren picked up a pencil and slowly spun it between her thumb and index finger. "I'm just glad the village idiot over there forgot to lock the cell, or else..." she sighed "...I don't know where we'd be now."

"I'm doing okay," he said.

Lauren tried to relax. She did her best Jerry impersonation and leaned back. "So how's school? Settling in?"

"School's, I don't know. New. Different than Winnipeg. There's less kids but it still feels like it's hard to breathe," Cole said.

"There are *fewer* kids," she said.

"I thought school ended hours ago," Cole said.

"Sorry, I get all grammar police when I write reports. Well, when I read Jerry's reports."

"There are less kids," Cole smiled, "how's that?"

"Better. You know, if it makes you feel any better, that's not just a Wounded Sky thing, how you feel about school," she said. "That's every high school for most kids."

"Yeah…"

"So what brings you here? Not that I don't appreciate the distraction, from this," Lauren pointed at her piles of work, "or that," she pointed at Jerry, who was drooling on a thin pillow of papers.

"The camp Scott was at," Cole started, "did you guys happen to clean it out? Any chance?"

Lauren shook her head. "When we finally got around to going back there, it was already picked clean. Figured hunters got there, went shopping."

"That's what I was afraid of," Cole said.

"Why?"

"Oh, nothing. Just something I'm looking for."

"Drop something, or—"

The tiny bell rang again. Cole and Lauren both turned their attention towards the door in time to see Reynold walk inside. "Evening, Constable. Mr. Harper."

"Everything alright, Mr. McCabe?" Lauren asked.

"Perfectly," Reynold said, "I came by to see my buddy Jer."

Sometime between when the bell rang and Reynold entered, Jerry had woken up, sat up, and busied himself with his paper pillow. Lauren looked surprised. Jerry working, even pretending to work, must have been a rare occurrence. Reynold crossed the room, stopped behind Jerry at his desk and gave the sleepy constable a hard squeeze around the shoulders and shook him.

"How's old Jerry Can, hey?" Reynold said.

Cole mouthed "Jerry Can?" to Lauren, who rolled her eyes.

"What can I do you for, Chief?" Jerry dropped the pencil he'd just picked up and turned around.

Reynold sat on the desk behind him. "I'll never get tired of hearing that, bud. *Chief.* Has a ring to it, doesn't it?"

"I'll never get tired of saying it," Jerry gave Reynold a wink and pointed at him with a finger gun.

Cole and Lauren exchanged looks. Lauren, at the "'Chief'" exchange, stuck her finger down her throat and feigned a dry heave. Cole chuckled, but it really wasn't all that funny. After all, it wasn't a joke. Reynold was Acting Chief.

"Speaking of which," Reynold crossed his arms, "at my party on Sunday…"

"Victory party."

"…absolutely. I'll need your presence, you and your," Reynold looked over at Lauren, who stopped pretending to puke just in time, "lovely assistant."

"Won't your cronies be there?" Lauren asked.

"Yes, I'll have staff there, but…" Reynold returned his attention to Jerry "…if any of our residents decide that they're…unhappy…with the results…"

"Ten-four," Jerry said.

"It's more for Lucy than me, of course. I want to have her in the safest possible environment after I win this thing."

"Who says you're going to win?" Cole asked.

Lauren kicked him under the desk, a silent scolding for his comment.

"Watch your mouth, kid," Jerry snapped, starting to get out of his chair.

Reynold put a hand across his chest, sat him back down. "Now, now, it's okay, Jerry. Cole, I have faith in the people, simple as that. I have faith that they'll make the right choice."

"Aren't you a bit worried after the assembly, though—OW," Cole stopped mid-sentence as Lauren kicked him again. Cole gave her an annoyed look, and she returned a concerned one.

Reynold walked halfway to Lauren's desk. "Remember, Cole, the kids aren't voting."

"Not yet," Cole grumbled.

"I beg your pardon?"

"Nothing."

Reynold stood in place and stared at Cole until Cole met eyes with him. Then, he turned his head to the side, "You'll make it happen, Jerry."

"I'll make it happen," Jerry said.

Reynold just nodded, and then strolled out of the RCMP detachment, at which point the room was silent until Jerry said, "You gotta watch your mouth with that crap, kid."

"Go back to sleep, *Jerry Can*," Lauren said.

Jerry grunted, and leaned back in his chair. He locked his hands behind his head and closed his eyes.

"You do have to be careful what you say, alright?" Lauren smiled almost apologetically. She hated to agree with Jerry, but in this case he was right. "The good will you've built up will only go so far with that guy."

"Yeah, I've kind of experienced that," Cole said.

"Right," Lauren said, "back to the matter at hand. We didn't clean out that camp, so I'm not sure how much help we can be. Sorry."

"Could you let me know if you hear anything?" Cole asked.

"Of course," she said. "If anything comes up, I'll let you know."

"Thanks." Cole stood up, sure that Reynold was a comfortable distance ahead of him. He started for the door. With his hand on the doorknob, Lauren called out, "Hey, what was it?"

"Huh?"

"What were you looking for?"

"Answers."

11

KIDDO

COLE PEERED OUT FROM THE EDGE OF BLACKWOOD FOREST towards the research facility. After a trip to the mall, Cole was appropriately dressed for a nighttime break-in. He'd found a black toque that said "Native Pride" on it, a black hoodie with a wolf design (not a coyote, most importantly), and thick, black long johns (which Cole had been assured weren't yoga pants).

He'd been in his hiding spot for several minutes trying to figure out the best way to get in. The entire building was surrounded by an electric fence and there were guards at each gate, as well as one at the front pacing from one end of the fence to the other. He'd settled on testing out whether he *could* jump over the fence or not, estimating that it was ten feet high. By now, he should've perfected the timing: when to run out into the open so the guard wouldn't see him, where to take off from so he had the best chance to clear the fence. But instead, he was staring at a park bench on the other side of the fence.

"Dad," seven-year-old Cole said, sitting across from his father, and beside his mother, on that same park bench.

"Yes, Cole?" His dad put down his sandwich, wiped a bit of peanut butter from his chin with one of the napkins Cole's mom had brought.

"Why do you have to go to work?" Cole asked.

Mimicking his dad, he put down his half-eaten apple and wiped at his mouth, too (only Cole wiped at his mouth with his sleeve).

His dad tossed the napkin into the brown paper bag with the rest of their lunchtime garbage—empty sandwich bags, apple cores, and used napkins. His dad pointed at the apple Cole had put down. Part of the core was visible. White parts at the edge of Cole's teeth marks were already browning. "Do you see that apple, son?"

"Yeah." Of course he saw it, it was right in front of him.

"Well, I have to work so that I can buy things like that apple," his dad said. "Out here, those things are expensive. If I want you to eat right, I have to be able to afford it. That's how it works."

Cole rested his cheek on his fist and he stared at that apple core, counting the seeds he could see. Two. Finally, he looked up. "So you work so you can buy us vegetables and fruit?"

Cole's mom laughed. His dad laughed, too. They looked at each other, and then his dad looked at him. "Yes, so I can buy us fruits and vegetables. The ones we can't grow in the garden."

Satisfied with his dad's response, Cole picked up the apple and took a big bite out of it.

Cole could taste the apple now, sitting in the darkness, staring at the park bench, old and broken and covered in peeling paint. He could taste it on his lips, as the juice curved over his bottom lip and ran down his chin. He could taste it on his tongue, its sweetness. He could feel the seed that he'd accidentally taken in his mouth, and he could remember picking it out from the back of his throat and throwing it on the ground. He had stared at it there, and asked his dad, "Couldn't we just bury that seed and grow an apple tree and then you don't have to work?"

His dad had smiled at him, at his inquisitiveness, and looked like he wanted to say something—Cole had an idea of what that something might've been now, the impossibility of what little Cole had wanted that apple seed to do. But his dad had just ruffled Cole's hair and said, "Sorry, kiddo."

Sorry, kiddo. That was the last time he saw his father. That night, his mother came into his room, interrupting his sneaky late-night comic book session.

"Cole," she sat down at the side of his bed.

"What is it mommy?" he asked.

She gathered him up into her arms. She squeezed him. "Your father, Cole. He died today."

Cole looked past the park bench, at the building. He pictured himself inside after jumping the fence and breaking the lock at the front door (he was good at breaking locks and door handles), and seeing his dad's body, maybe sitting in a chair, maybe sprawled out on the floor, having desperately tried to get out, get away, save himself, save others. The lady he died with. Her body would be there, too. At least, Cole thought, his dad wasn't alone, lying there, just a corpse covered in the clothes he had been wearing that day. Beige dress pants. White sneakers. Striped t-shirt. White lab coat. His hair might even still be there, messed but still looking good, like it had been messed intentionally. But Cole knew that his dad just got up and left in the morning, after feeding him breakfast. That's how his hair looked, asleep or awake. Or dead. *Sorry, kiddo.*

Cole knew it, of course. He knew what he was doing, staring at the bench, desperately replaying memories, imagining himself inside the building: Stalling. Just like he had been all night. He didn't want to see his dad like that. He wanted the last memory to be what it was. The best memory. He didn't want to have the bones. He didn't want that to be the last time he saw his dad. *Sorry, kiddo.* He kept hearing his dad say that. Then, those same two words played back at him, only in Choch's voice. *Sorry, kiddo. You have to do it. That's the deal. Well, it might be the deal. I misspoke. But, you know, it's promising, CB.* To shut him up, and only to shut him up, Cole waited for the guard to come back, then turn away, and when the guard was far enough, Cole sprinted towards the fence.

The task of leaping over the electric fence was as simple as dunking the basketball—jump high enough to get the ball over the rim, and then, once it was through the rim, land on the ground. As he ran, he calculated. Could he actually clear the fence? How much effort did he put into jumping to dunk? Not much. But getting over the fence was like trying to dunk on a twenty-foot rim, not a ten-foot rim. Wind rushed against his face. He was back in Blackwood Forest, running from the murderer, from Scott. Rushing towards Scott, trying to save Eva. *Faster, Cole. Build momentum.* Five feet away from the fence, Cole launched off the ground with his left foot and flew through the air. Up. Up higher. The holes in the fence blurred into trails. And then there were no trails, just the dark of night, just the outline of trees against the horizon. Just the northern lights hanging like fog over Wounded Sky. Just Cole, and all of this before him. For a moment, Cole felt like he could touch the ribbons of light. For a moment, he was bigger than his problems. For a moment, he left them behind, far below. The next moment, he came back to Earth.

Cole landed on the sidewalk in front of the entrance on two feet. He stopped himself by bracing his palms against the steps to the door. He stood up. Just an inch or two of metal between him and, if he was lucky, some answers. The folder. The files. His dad. Somewhere inside the building, behind those inches of metal.

Cole felt it all in his body—the beast rearing its ugly head—inside his chest, pounding to get out. It covered his body like a heat blanket, his skin breaking into a sweat. It whispered into his ear all the things he couldn't do, all the things he was too weak for. "I'm stronger than you," Cole whispered. It was spinning him around, making him feel unsteady, weak in the knees. It was covering his eyes with its midnight hands, coaxing him into unconsciousness. Cole shook his head, and he shook the beast off his body. He took a step a forward. He wrapped his hands around one door handle, then the other, and pulled as hard as he could. The handles scattered across the concrete.

A rush of air pushed against his cheeks, against his eyes. He blinked it away. He could see the checkered tile floor that led down the hallway and then forked off into two directions. He could see, in the natural light from the sky, from the moon, from the spirits dancing, the path laid out before him. He stepped forward, but stopped.

He felt a drop of water hit his head, although he knew it was a clear night. He heard growling. He looked up, and saw a figure on top of the building, a silhouette against the northern lights, its eyes burning red, saliva dripping from its mouth. Cole tried to look away, but he couldn't. The monster held him in place with its glower. With its awful stench and reaching arms. Reaching for him.

"Yooooou." It said, "Yooooou," like a howling wind. "Yooooou."

It descended towards him, its fingers digging into the side of the building. *Move. Move, Cole.* Cole backed away. Farther. Farther. It dropped from the building and stepped towards him. Cole looked to his left, to his right. He turned on his heel and ran. He could hear the thing chasing close behind.

"Yooooou. Yoooou. Yoooou."

Cole planted his left foot, strained to push off, but his knee collapsed. He landed halfway up the fence. He curled his fingers around the metal wires, and felt the electricity surge through his body. Steam rose from his skin. He could hear the thing behind him, and then he felt its scaly fingers scratching at his feet. He leaped forward, grabbed the fence—again and again.

"Yoooou. Yoooou."

When he was at the top, he let himself fall. He landed on his back, on the other side.

He pushed himself up.

His whole body felt on fire. His hands were like blackened wood after a bonfire. He ran, stumbled, got up, ran.

"Yoooou. Yoooou."

Its voice was farther away now. Cole didn't look back. He ran all the way to Elder Mariah's place. He could remember seeing it in the distance. But after seeing it, like a beacon in the nightmare black, he could remember nothing else.

12

BURNT

WHEN COLE CAME TO AFTER A HEAVY and unexpected rest, he knew exactly where he was. Brady's couch had become familiar to him. Over the last couple of weeks, he'd wedged an imprint of his body into the cushions, and he was stuck in that imprint now. The memory of last night came hard and fast: The shadowy figure chasing him across the grass from the research facility, and the surge of pain each time his skin connected with metal as he tried to escape.

His muscles ached and there was a burning sensation across his palms. He forced his eyes open to find the ceiling staring back at him, the tiles yellowed from water damage. He lifted his hands into view, and saw blackened lines on his palms, right over his scars, in a cross-hatch pattern. He winced at the memory of getting shocked, repeatedly, by the electric fence.

"Cole?"

At the sound of his auntie's voice, Cole's arms dropped to his sides. *No. Nope,* he thought. *Still dreaming.* He closed his eyes to get back there, to ensure this wasn't really happening.

But then he heard his auntie say his name again.

"Cole."

"Yes?" He didn't look in her direction. He just found one yellow patch on one ceiling tile, and held his gaze there.

"What happened last night?" she asked.

"I don't...I don't know what you mean." Cole's throat hurt from speaking, like he'd swallowed fire.

"Your kókom and I—"

"Grandma?" Cole's head shifted a fraction to the side.

"Tansi, Nósisim."

"Tell us what happened last night," Auntie Joan said. "Now."

This is happening, Cole conceded to himself. His auntie coming to Wounded Sky might be the worst thing that could happen. He grunted as he tried to get up into a sitting position, and ended up sprawled over the couch's armrest. Good enough. The morning got even worse when he saw not only his grandmother sitting politely at the kitchen table, but Lauren and Jerry as well, each with a cup of coffee.

"I want to know what's going on before I say anything," Cole said.

"Lauren and Jerry came to question you about something," Auntie Joan said to Cole, but then she turned to the two constables and added, "*without an adult present.*"

"It was just some questions, Joan," Jerry said.

"Don't tell me that I have to go over the law with you, Constable," Auntie Joan said.

"Actually, you probably do," Lauren said. "To one of us, anyway."

"Then what's *your* excuse?" Auntie Joan heated up.

"Sorry, Joan. We were just—"

"You're lucky I'm going to let you talk to him now," Auntie Joan said. "Clearly I came at the right time." She stared right into Cole's eyes. Her stare was a laser beam. "To protect you from them, but also from yourself."

"Protect me from them?" Cole looked back and forth between his auntie and the constables, which killed his head, but he was super confused. "Can somebody *please* just tell me? Grandma?"

"Something happened last night," his kókom said.

No shit, Cole thought. "I know that."

Nobody said anything for a moment. All the adults just stared at Cole, waiting for him to tell them something, but he had no idea what.

"What were you doing last night, kid?" Jerry asked. He had a note-pad out, a pen at the ready.

"Uhhh," Cole said, "just…" he straightened out on the couch.

"Just tell us everything you remember, alright?" Lauren said.

"I had dinner at the Fish before I came to see you guys," Cole said, "you can ask Pam. And then I went and got some clothes from the mall after I left the detachment…"

Jerry started scribbling notes when Cole mentioned getting clothes.

"…because I didn't bring enough clothes with me from Winnipeg. So I got some shirts and pants and a toque." Cole instinctively felt for the toque. He didn't want them to see his hair sticking up. Did electro-cuted hair even do that, or was that just in cartoons? The toque was gone, but his hair just felt matted and dry.

"Those the new clothes?" Lauren asked.

"Did you do anything else at the mall?" Jerry asked.

"What's this all about?" Cole's heart started to race, and his breath shortened.

"Could you not interrogate him?" his auntie said. "You said you were going to ask questions, that's it." She got up, walked across the living room, and sat down beside him.

"There was an accident last night," Lauren said, softer, to Cole.

"It was no accident," Jerry said.

"I'm sorry, what kind of accident?" Another death? Was it happen-ing again? His world started to spin. He felt like puking.

"Somebody set fire to the mall, and most of it's…" Lauren paused "…it's superficial, but—"

"It was *real*, Cole," Jerry said.

"Superficial means the damage was mostly on the surface, Jer, it doesn't mean it didn't happen." She said to Cole, "The back of the gro-cery store, along the exterior walls, got most of it. They're all charred and…anyway…"

"Somebody called in that they seen you there," Jerry said, seriously.

"Yeah, I told you. I got clothes. That's all. People saw me there."

"Those clothes new or not?" Jerry asked. "Answer the question."

Cole looked down at his body. His clothes were all dirtied, ragged. He could see his hoodie vibrating from his heartbeat. "Yeah. I...I h-have the receipt and everything," he forced out, but his lips were hardly working.

"Are you okay?" his auntie asked quietly so just he could hear her.

He nodded.

"Somebody called in that they'd seen you later on in the night at the mall, after it had closed. Saw you snooping around...all in black," Lauren said.

"Looks like those *new* clothes got kind of burnt from something?" Jerry said.

"They aren't necessarily burnt, Jer," Lauren said.

"I tried to climb a fence," Cole said quickly. "I got electrocuted."

"What fence?" Lauren asked. "At the facility?"

Cole nodded again, but it looked like he was freezing cold. He'd faint soon, he knew it.

"Why?" she asked.

How much to tell? Was trying to break in to the research facility better than arson? He wasn't sure. He couldn't even think straight, but he said, "I was looking for something."

"From the camp? What you came to see us about?" Lauren asked.

"Yeah," Cole said. "Since you guys didn't clean up the camp, that was the last place I could think of looking."

"The facility?" Lauren said. "Why there? What were you looking for?"

"Medical files?" Cole said.

"If they was medical files, you should've gone to the clinic, kid," Jerry said.

"If they *were*," Lauren said.

"They won't let anybody into the clinic!" Cole said.

"Since when?" Lauren asked.

"Like, yesterday," Cole said. "Shouldn't you guys know that?"

Lauren looked at Jerry, like he should've known.

"Can we get back to the fence?" Lauren asked. "Do you know how many volts are going through that fence?"

"Enough to make me look like this?" Cole pulled at his hoodie, on the sleeves, where it seemed like he'd gotten the worst of it.

"You'd be dead if you touched that fence," Lauren said. "Remember that kid, like, seven years ago, Jer? Tried to get over that fence…"

"Blammo," Jerry said.

"What? What the hell does 'blammo' mean? Is that somebody getting fried to death?" Lauren said.

"No, it was just…" but Jerry trailed off.

"The point is, Cole…" Lauren began.

"I broke the handles on the front door," Cole admitted.

"You did what?!" his auntie said, almost shouting.

"Cole…" his grandmother started.

"So you *did* climb the fence, you didn't just try," Lauren stated.

"Yes," Cole said.

"Cole, did you open the doors to that facility or not?" Lauren asked. "This is important."

"I don't…" Cole thought back to that moment. He'd broken off the door handles…and then he saw the shadow with red eyes. But he couldn't remember if he opened the doors or not. "…I can't remember. I don't think so."

"We have to check that out," Lauren said to Jerry.

"Now?" Jerry asked.

"Freaking yes, now, Jer. You can have your nap after that. Holy shit," Lauren said. "If those doors are open…is that registering with you? Do you remember what happened when that accident happened?"

Jerry shrugged. "Yeah, but…"

"*Yeah, but.* We have to make sure those doors are closed," Lauren said. "If they aren't…"

"Okay, fine," Jerry said.

"That was really stupid, Cole," Lauren said. "You're risking…I mean, you do your hero thing, and then this…I just don't get it."

"I'm sorry," Cole said.

"We'll be in touch," Lauren said to Cole's auntie and grandmother. "Come on," Lauren said to Jerry.

Moments later, they were out of the house and Cole was left alone with his grandmother and auntie. He looked at his grandmother, because he knew the look his auntie was giving him. He could hear his Auntie Joan breathing, or rather, trying to moderate her breathing because she was so worked up. Cole could relate to that. He was quietly trying to breathe evenly, too.

"So this is what you've been up to?" Auntie Joan asked following a long silence.

Cole wanted the silence back. "I didn't start that fire." He pleaded to his grandmother for help with collapsing eyebrows.

"I think Joan and I are more concerned about finding you on the ground outside the house this morning, Cole," his grandmother said.

"I what?"

"When we got here, you were laying across the steps outside."

"And if we found you like that the moment we got here," his Auntie Joan said, "what does that mean about everything else you've been doing here? You should've never snuck off like that."

"If I hadn't *snuck off* like that literally everybody in Wounded Sky would be dead."

"Oh, Cole, please," Auntie Joan said.

"I was trying to help last night!" The pounding in his head got worse.

"How?!" Auntie Joan got up and faced Cole with her arms crossed.

Cole stumbled with his response. He opened his mouth to say something, several times, but each time he stopped himself. Everything he'd planned to say was an explanation his auntie would never believe. "You don't even know what I've been through," Cole mumbled, giving up on any attempt to explain. All they knew at this point was what he'd told them last week, that he'd helped catch Scott, and that he needed to stay longer.

"Give me one good reason why I should let you stay," Auntie Joan had said.

"Because you can't make me come back," he said back.

"You're right, I don't know what you've been through, but I know you've been through enough." Auntie Joan pulled out her phone and started punching at the touch screen so hard Cole thought she might break the glass. "I'm not going to let you die out here like your parents," she said under her breath before putting the phone to her ear.

"What are you doing?" Cole asked, but she ignored him.

"Joan?" Cole's grandmother said. Whatever Auntie Joan was doing, she had been kept out of the loop.

"Yes, hi," his Auntie Joan said into the receiver. "The next flight out this evening, is there still room for—"

"No!" Eva. Brady. They'd die. Everybody would die. She couldn't take him. He wouldn't go. Cole started to think about how he'd avoid it. He'd run away, stay somewhere else, convince his grandmother to convince Auntie Joan to let him stay….

"I'm sorry, what?" Auntie Joan looked at Cole differently now, with worry and disbelief. Her face was melting with it. "That can't be right. We just…"

Cole tried to hear what the voice was saying on the other end, but the best he could make out was that it was a man.

"Fine." Auntie Joan ended the call, and tossed her phone onto the couch.

"You know I can't go, Auntie Joan. I can't leave here, it's—"

"Go to your room." Auntie Joan was looking down to the floor now, her hand on her face. "Now."

"I don't have a room here," Cole said weakly.

"Go to Brady's room!"

"Holy ~~shit~~ crap," Cole said, alone in Brady's room. He was sitting on the bed and staring out the window. He had many thoughts and not enough space in his pounding head to fit them. How bad was the mall? Who would've done something like that—and why? More to the point, who would've called the RCMP and said they'd seen Cole around the mall, when he clearly wasn't? By the time the mall was on fire, Cole was likely passed out on the steps. And how was he going to do anything with his auntie here? She'd watch him like a hawk. Worse, she'd find a way to get him out of the community, and that would mean disaster for Wounded Sky. "~~Shit~~ Crap."

"Boy, *that* escalated quickly," Choch said, "I mean, that really got out of hand fast."

"Could you not talk like Ron Burgundy please?" Cole asked.

"Well typically it's been *you* with the pop culture references, but I thought I'd throw my hat into the ring."

"I don't do that."

Choch snapped his fingers. "Right, sorry. Got you confused with somebody else."

"I'll have to meet this person you keep talking about that doesn't even exist, I bet," Cole said dryly.

"Oh, you have a lot in common," Choch said, "and by the way, speaking of which, I give up. You kids say the S-word way too often and it's impossible to catch all of them. So, if you could just not say the F-word that would be really helpful."

"I'm ignoring that," Cole said.

"So!" Choch clapped loudly. Cole might've worried about his over-protective auntie hearing the sound, but he guessed that Choch had probably muted the clapping. "Correct, I have muted the clapping for your relatives. Now, I came by because...oh...coffee?" Choch extended a cup, which had just appeared in his hand, to Cole. "Nobody makes coffee like a spirit being."

"I don't drink coffee," Cole said.

"Suit yourself." Choch sipped the coffee, then made an, "Ahhhhh," sound.

"Did you want...what did you want?" Cole asked.

"I thought I could help focus you," Choch said, "in light of the fact that, let me get this straight, you're looking for files, you're trying to make good with Michael, you're juggling girls, you're—"

"Okay, I get it!" Cole shouted. He felt comfortable shouting, knowing that—

"What's going on in there?" his auntie asked through the door.

Of course, Cole thought. "Nothing, sorry," he said to his auntie, and then waited to hear her footsteps recede. "Thanks for that," he said to Choch, "muting yourself but not me."

"One still has to have fun," Choch said. "It's not juggling girls, but..." Choch tried to hand him the cup again "...it's decaf by the way. I know how your nerves get."

Cole pushed it away. "So you just came to judge me or something?"

"*Au contraire, mon CB,*" Choch said, "I've always said that you need to find your own way. All I'm saying is that, perhaps you need to focus a little bit. It's fairly discombobulating. Granted, it's not all your fault. Certain storytellers might be a bit unfocussed, too."

"Should I even bother to ask if you have any suggestions? I mean, last night, all that other stuff, I was basically just...I didn't want to go to the research facility, okay, but I went, so..."

"Oh come on, you like having two girls on your mind. The drama, the hormones, the...well, any boy would like that." Choch stroked his thumb and forefinger against his naked chin "Except for Brady, I suppose. But you get my point."

"Don't even get me started about how I've totally ignored Brady's feelings about Ashley," Cole said.

"You know, if I were to offer advice, out of the goodness of my heart, I might ask you who might know something about those darn files, other than our precious little Jayney-kins," Choch said.

Cole thought about who else could know. *Who even knew about the—*

"Ummm, could you possibly ruminate aloud?"

"Fine," Cole said. "I was just thinking about who else knew about the files, anyway. Dr. Captain, Eva, Brady, Mike, Pam, Lauren..."

"Aaaaand..."

"Scott," Cole said.

"And you say I never—"

"I've already thought of him, though."

"And simply ignored the fact that he could know about the files? Boy, you really do stall, don't you?"

"It's just that," Cole said, "I figured he'd be guarded like Fort Knox or something."

Choch started to pace. "Gee whiz, how would CB ever get through a guard or two?" Then he stopped, turned towards Cole, and whispered, "That was rhetorical."

"My skills," Cole said.

"Yeah! I mean, you've got such great skills," Choch said exactly like Napoleon Dynamite. "That just might work."

"Spirit-being sarcasm is the worst sarcasm," Cole said.

"Why do you think I chose you, CB?" Choch started to flex his non-existent muscles.

"Okay, I get it," Cole said.

"The bonus is, readers love break-ins, heists, whatever. That's worthwhile detective work—exciting, engaging, all that. No other issues need to be addressed."

"You're being weird again," Cole said. "'No other issues need to be addressed?' There's always something you're saying that you're not really saying."

Choch took a fast sip of his coffee. "I don't know what you're talking about. Pfffft."

"You brought up all that stuff from last night, and you left out the fact that a fricking—"

Thank you for not swearing.

"—creature thing chased me last night. Don't you think that's important?"

"Frankly, I'd call that thing an 'easily avoided distraction.' You've got other things to do now. Break-in at the clinic? Hello?"

"What, are you worried I might get killed?"

"And also," Choch checked the time, "you're almost late for school. You do know what's first period today, don't you?"

"Why are you avoiding—"

"Gym! That's what! Do not be late, CB. I would hate to have to give you more man-makers, but I will."

And with that, Choch was gone.

"I'm going to have to go back there eventually, you know!" Cole shouted into thin air.

"Cole! Who are you talking to in there?" He heard his auntie stomp up to his bedroom door.

"Nobody," Cole said, and he realized that he needed to get used to his auntie's intrusions, just like he'd gotten used to Choch's.

13

#SHITCOLEDID

COLE LEFT BRADY'S ROOM CAUTIOUSLY, like he'd heard a sound in the night and was checking for intruders. He felt stuck in another reality. Seeing his auntie and grandmother sitting at the kitchen table was something he'd seen almost every day of his life since he was seven, up until about two weeks ago, but now it felt unnatural. On the other hand, they had settled right in, eating toast with peanut butter and drinking black coffee. They were talking about him. He could hear them, even though they were whispering.

"What could he have been doing?" his grandmother asked.

"It's not like him to be out drinking. He's never done anything like that," Auntie Joan said. "But maybe other kids have had an influence on him."

"No," his grandmother said. "We sheltered him, but we also raised him to make good choices."

"What good choice could have possibly brought him to sleep on the front steps?" his auntie asked.

"Maybe it wasn't his choice, he—"

Cole cleared his throat. Both of them turned towards him quickly and tried to act normal, like they'd just been having a normal breakfast conversation and not dissecting his life choices. But maybe that was normal breakfast conversation when he wasn't around. Who knew?

"Nósisim," his grandmother said.

"Can I come out now?" Cole asked.

"Thanks for asking," Auntie Joan said. "Yes, you can. I made you some toast." She pushed a plate of food with two pieces of toast slathered in peanut butter towards an empty place at the kitchen table.

Cole held his stomach. "No thanks, I'm already late for school. I'll eat a big lunch." He walked to the front door and stopped there. He stared outside, at the cracked concrete front steps, and pictured himself laying there, passed out. He might've thought he'd been drinking, too, if he'd found himself like that. Laying there, exposed to the elements, unconscious and unable to protect himself. Why didn't the dark creature just kill him then? Would it not come into the community? The research facility lay just beyond the perimeter.

"Cole," his auntie said.

"Huh?"

"I said that you better be home right after school, got it? Things are going to change."

Cole didn't look away from the spot. "I can't just be locked up in here, Auntie. I have a job to do."

"Which you've never explained, and until you do, you will be home after school."

"I told you that I can't explain it."

"Cole," she said sternly.

"Sure, yeah, home after school, got it," Cole said, but he figured that unless she literally came to the school herself, took his hand, and walked him home, she couldn't make him. He'd always listened to her in the city (mostly, anyway) but there, his compliance didn't affect anybody but himself. Now it could affect the entire community.

Cole headed to the research facility before going to school. He would be even later, and Choch would give him man-makers, but the spirit being had to know this threat was not a deterrent. He could do a hundred of them and *big deal*. Besides, Choch would know where Cole had gone, what had made him super late—because he was now headed in the "super late" category—and how could he be upset about that? He was doing his job. There'd be no break-in during the day, but seeing what sort of damage he'd left behind seemed important, if only because it would ensure his ass was covered. Since, because his life wasn't hard enough, somebody was trying to frame him for arson.

"Of course." Cole stopped on the path as soon as the facility came into view. The number of guards had tripled. He wouldn't be able to just run up and jump over the fence if he were to come back here. And at some point, he'd have to come back here. He could heal from a stab wound, sure, but how about multiple gunshot wounds? Not only were there more guards, but now they looked armed to the teeth. They weren't just carrying side arms, but rifles.

But what felt more distressing, because of the allegations he'd heard from Lauren and Jerry this morning, were the front doors. There were some people in what Cole thought looked like hazmat suits talking to Lauren and Jerry in front of the doors, which were perfectly fine, handles and all. He'd been "seen" setting a fire at the mall, and now, to the constables, he'd been lying about what he'd been doing. All he could really hope for there was that Lauren could put two and two together. More guards, guys in hazmat suits? Clearly something had gone down. Jerry would never make the connection. Cole wasn't sure if he could actually even add two and two.

"Maybe if Reynold asked him to," Cole said to himself. Cole took one last, long look at the facility, at the guards, the guns, the constables, the front doors, the handles. "Things keep coming up Cole." He sighed, and then turned towards school.

Cole thought being late could be looked at as a blessing. Everybody was in class and the hallways were clear. He didn't have a bunch of eyes on him, wondering if he tried to burn the mall down. Certainly, by now, news had spread across the community. In particular, his classmates must have heard about it, and been talking about it on the group text. What had Alex said before? #shitColedid. That's what it would be.

Gym class would be different. Cole felt like all the kids in his amalgamated class were just standing in there, waiting to jump out like a surprise party—the worst surprise party ever: "Surprise! You're an arsonist and we hate you!" He could just hear a chorus of voices shouting it. So, he took his time getting to the gym. He sauntered to his unlocked locker and stuck his backpack inside. He changed in the bathroom (not the boy's change room in the gym) and took his time getting into each new item of clothing, also selected from the slim pickings the clothing store had at the mall: a pair of black shorts and a white tank top. At least his new shoes matched his shorts. Cole shuffle-stepped all the way to the gym and by the time he got to the gym doors, he'd successfully killed ten minutes since he'd entered the school.

Cole opened the door a crack—just enough to peek inside. The good news was his fellow students were not, in fact, waiting to pounce on him for being an alleged arsonist. They were participating in gym class, and when Cole had cracked open the door he heard the distinctive sound of basketballs bouncing. Of course they were playing basketball when Cole wasn't there. The one time they'd played basketball in the gym for God knows how long, and Choch made sure they did because he was late.

"Guess you found a way to really punish me, if you weren't going to give me man-makers," Cole whispered to Choch, and he knew that the spirit being heard him even though he didn't say anything in response. The basketballs bouncing on the waxed floor was response enough.

He opened the door another inch and surveyed the class, kid by kid, until he found Brady. He was shooting free throws with Eva and Michael. Eva and Michael. Had Eva heard about Cole going to the Fish with Pam? What did she think about it? And if she knew, Michael did, too. What did he think? Would he treat Cole differently? *Oh but you do whine, don't you?* Choch pushed his way into Cole's head.

"I have a lot to think about," Cole whispered.

You whine like a little girl.

"You're teasing me like you're a student."

What did you say to Tristan again? When in Rome?

"Calling me a little girl because I'm whining is sexist, you know."

Gasp. I am not sexist, CB. Heck, I'm the world's first feminist. I created women! And men, but contextually, we're talking about women, so…

"Okay, well I'm going to go." Cole pulled out his phone and texted Brady. He hoped that Brady had his phone on him.

COLE: **Brady, I'm outside gym doors. Come here.**

Cole watched Brady intently. His friend took a shot and made it. Cole was the only person who couldn't make a shot, and the only student in his class on a basketball team. *There you go again, CB.*

"Get out of my head for the millionth time!"

Brady took a pass from Michael, but then bounced the ball over to Eva right away and fished his phone out of his pocket. Cole watched as Brady looked at his phone, shook his head, then wrote something back.

BRADY: **You come here. You're supposed to be in this class?**

COLE: **I kind of got held up BY MY GRANDMA AND AUNTIE!**

BRADY: **Yeah, your auntie kicked me out. Of my own house.**

COLE: **Sounds about right. So...**

BRADY: **Fine.**

Brady stuck his phone back into his pocket, motioned something to Eva and Michael, then jogged over to the doors. They talked through the partially opened door.

"How bad is it?" Cole asked.

Brady looked confused. "That's a loaded question. You could be referencing any number of things."

"The fire," Cole said.

"Okay, so, what sort of scale are we working with? What's really bad, and what's not so bad?"

"I—"

"Is really bad maybe something like finding you passed out on the front steps my house? And is not-so-bad the fact that you didn't tell Eva about you and Pam?"

"Did *you?*"

"What did I tell you about honesty, my friend? When Eva asks me what we did last night, and I have to tell her what I did, and what you did, do you think I'd lie to her?"

Cole kicked the ground and this created a squeak that echoed down the hall. "No."

"I mean, all you had to do was text her and tell her, right?"

"Okay!" Cole said. "So that's, sure, that's not as bad as the steps thing…"

"Which we have to talk about."

"Yes, but can we…"

"To answer your question, I don't think it's as bad as you think," Brady said. "And that's me knowing full well how you think."

"So no pitchforks?"

"No pitchforks, but some kids are saying that they saw you at the mall late, too."

"On the group text."

"It's, like, social media," Brady said apologetically, "what can I say?"

Cole turned away and the door started to close but Brady caught it. Cole slammed his palm against the wall. "One person says they saw me, and now others say they saw me. If it were somebody else, nobody would say a goddamn thing."

"Maybe, but honestly, it's not that bad. Just come in and act normal. For you. You did stop a murderer."

Cole faced Brady again. "Doesn't anybody think, you know, that I hate fire? Because of what happened? Why would I set fires?"

"Hey, you're preaching to the choir." Brady opened the door all the way, and held it that way. "Now, come on. It'll be okay, I promise."

Cole hesitated a moment longer, then he walked through the opened door and into the gym. "You better be right," Cole said while passing Brady.

For the most part, Brady had been right. Walking towards Eva and Michael, Cole noticed only a few negative looks. He felt better, as well, when he met eyes with Pam. He even laughed when he waved at her, and she, rather than waving back, made a cross out of her two index fingers before rolling her eyes like, *see? Told you people were fickle.* For Pam, maybe one student thinking badly about Cole was one too many. Shockingly, Michael was not one of the kids looking at Cole sideways.

In fact, Michael nodded at Cole, and Cole, in turn, nodded back. Had it worked?

"Hey, guys," Cole said when he and Brady reached Michael and Eva.

"What's up?" Michael said. Every nod and word from Michael right now raised Cole's spirits. Cole wasn't bothered, or he simply didn't take note, when Eva gave him a short and fast nod as though she were firing a shot at him.

"Hey, Mike," she said, "can you grab my phone please? It's in my locker."

"Sure, why?"

"I'm just expecting a text, that's all."

Michael looked at Brady and Cole and sighed, like, such is the life of a boyfriend, and said. "Be right back, I guess. Duty calls."

"See ya," Cole said.

"Text from who? Your dad?" Brady asked when Michael had jogged out of the gym.

"Oh no, he's still not texting back," Eva said.

"So…"

She looked at Cole. "I keep waiting for the text telling me that you're going out with Pam. It must've not sent, the connection here can be bad. Right?"

"I…" Cole stopped right there, but not by choice. He couldn't think of anything else to say.

"If that's why you were *kind of busy* last night, you could've just said that. Why didn't you just say that?" Eva asked.

"I didn't know how to," Cole said.

"And then what? You stayed out so late with her that you just fell asleep on the front steps?"

"Seriously?" Cole said to Brady. "*It'll be okay, I promise,*" Cole imitated Brady's promise from moments ago.

"I wasn't promising about this," Brady said. "I told you, honesty, my friend. Always choose honesty."

"I was going to!" Cole said.

"But it wasn't something you had to keep from me in the first place," Eva said. "I would've been like, 'Cool, Pam's nice,' or something."

"I wasn't out with her all night," Cole said, trying to get away from the part where he lied to Eva by omission.

"Do I get to hear where you were now?" Brady asked.

"I was looking for the files…"

"Oh!" Eva threw her arms in the air. "This keeps getting better! You *did* go look for them without me."

"Without us," Brady said.

"Why would you do that?" Eva asked. "We're a team, right?"

"I know," Cole said, "I just thought that if I went on my own, then we," Cole motioned to him and Eva, "wouldn't be alone, and Michael wouldn't hate me more, and if I didn't go with you, I wasn't going to ask Brady, and…"

"Cole, you sound ridiculous," Brady said.

Eva crossed her arms. That was never good. "So, did you find anything out?" She was talking now the way she'd nodded before. Short and fast.

"I—"

"Here," Michael came back and handed Eva her phone. She put it in her pocket without looking. "I thought you were waiting for a text?"

"Cole was just telling us how the search for the files went last night," Eva said.

"I thought you went out with Pam?" Michael said.

"I did, and then I looked for the files but I didn't find them," Cole said, "so it's not a big deal."

"It is when you promised you wouldn't go without us," Eva said.

"That *is* pretty weak, my friend," Brady said.

"I'm sorry, okay! I messed up, I know I did," Cole said. "But what I was doing, you wouldn't have made it." *Not over the fence, and not against that creature.*

"I made it through the whole Scott thing," Eva said.

Cole thrust his hands out, and turned them palm-up. The blackened crosshatch pattern from the electric fence was still prominent over his scars.

"Holy shit," Brady said.

"What's this?" Michael said.

Eva traced one of the black lines with her finger.

"I went to the research facility," Cole said. "Like I said, you wouldn't have made it."

"Wait, this is from the electric fence? You climbed it?" Brady asked.

"Kind of," Cole said, and hoped that they couldn't tell he'd left out information. They were usually very good at detecting when Cole was lying. But he *had* kind of climb the fence. Just after he'd jumped over it, and after that thing had chased him. Neither Eva nor Brady had brought up Cole's powers since they'd witnessed them—Brady seeing Cole crush a doorknob, and Eva seeing how Cole had healed from the knife wound—probably respecting the fact that he told them he couldn't say anything about his abilities, and he didn't want to give them something else to not bring up.

"How did *you* make it, never mind?" Eva asked.

Cole closed his eyes a moment and silently cursed himself. Not dying from a high voltage electric fence probably fell under *powers*, too.

"I guess that's why I ended up on the front steps of Brady's house," Cole said, praying they'd buy his answer and not keep grilling him. It was three on one, and the allure of Michael not hating him was wearing thin fast.

"But, remember that guy who touched that fence a while back, just touched it, and died?" Brady said to Eva and Michael, who both nodded.

"Not everybody dies when they're electrocuted, okay?!"

"*You* don't, anyway," Michael said.

Cole opened his mouth to respond, but—

"*Mr.* Cole Harper!" Choch shouted, followed by a whistle, from across the gym.

"What?!" Cole shouted at Choch.

Choch checked his watch, tapping on it for good measure. "Do you realize how late you are?"

Cole didn't even look at his phone or the clock. He just said, "Yes."

"Class is more than half over, young man! Man-makers. Now!" Choch shouted angrily.

"No!" Cole shouted back.

Choch walked to the centre of the court, stomping all the way. "What did you say?"

"I *said*, 'no,' do you need to get your ears checked!?"

All the kids in the gym gasped. Cole heard Pam snort, trying to stop herself from laughing.

"Do you want detention, too?" Choch asked.

"You're not even a teacher, *Mr. Chochinov*. I don't give a shit what you ask me to do *here*!"

"Man-makers, Harper!"

"Screw you!"

Well at least you didn't swear, I'll give you that. But, CB, first, I told you this would happen, and second, I'm trying to help you.

"I don't care!" Cole responded out loud to Choch's psychic explanation. "I'm not having the best morning, okay? Just back off!"

"You get to that line this instant, son." Choch pointed to the baseline, where the man-makers were to start. He blew his whistle again.

But Cole wheeled around, walked to the gym doors, and pushed them open so hard he was surprised they didn't break off their hinges.

Before leaving, he shouted, "And it's person-makers! Feminist my ass!"

"Hey!"

Cole stopped to let Pam catch up. He'd already ignored a text from Eva, another from Brady, and a couple of choice thoughts from Mr. Chochinov, but he wasn't annoyed at Pam. Things had ended up going well last night, after he'd actually started talking. He thought they had, anyway, until the walk home, when he'd gone quiet again. But it was hard for Cole to separate walking Pam home from walking Alex home, especially since Pam and Alex had been best friends. They'd stood on Pam's front step for a long time in complete, awkward silence. Cole was lost in thought, thinking about Alex kissing him on the cheek, and how she'd been killed probably minutes after the kiss. Cole was unreasonably worried that the same might happen to Pam. So, he didn't leave her and he also didn't say anything until she'd finally opened the front door and said, "Okay…so I'm going to go."

"See ya," he'd said.

"Hey," he said now, after Pam had caught up.

"Thought I'd double down on some post-dinner awkwardness," she said.

"Sorry about…" Cole's silence filled in the gap.

"Hey, what did we say about sorrys, Harper?"

"Enough sorrys," he said, repeating Pam's advice from the gym yesterday.

"Plus, you know, everybody needs a good awkward silence once in a while, right?"

"I just didn't know what to do," Cole said.

"Well, when in doubt, come on, tiger." Pam lunged forward, grabbed Cole on either side of his head, and kissed him on the cheek. She released him like some televangelist healer. "There, now we can just be normal."

Cole felt at his cheek, at Pam's intentionally sloppy kiss. He laughed. "Wow."

"See? Awkwardness averted," Pam clapped her hands together once. "And now that *that*'s out of the way, can we talk about how *that was epic*. I've never seen anybody talk to Mr. Chochinov, or any teacher, like that before."

"It was kind of stupid," Cole said. "It was just that, you know, people were looking at me weird because of the mall—"

"I called it."

"—you called it, and then my friends were bugging me. Cho... Mr. Chochinov was the victim of circumstance."

"If it means anything, I do *not* think you set the mall on fire," she said. "I mean, you're lit, but—"

"Oh-my-God."

"Ha, right? I hate that word, but sometimes it's too good not to use."

"If I'm lit, you just doused me with your saliva." Cole wiped at his cheek again, and hoped that she'd get the joke.

"Well played, Harper," Pam nodded, and Cole felt relieved. "Anyway, you left kind of upset and I wanted you to know that the group text is pro-Cole suddenly. See? Fickle AF."

"Hashtag shitColedid, right? I'm always trending, one way or the other."

"Buddy," Pam said, "you're going viral."

14

OUTSIDE IN

THE FISH WAS NEARLY EMPTY. Victor sat in the back corner, alone. A couple sat across the room from him, their distance intentional. Cole had found a spot near the front door. He was working up the courage to talk to Victor, watching him huddle over his coffee as though for warmth. Maybe he wasn't going to go back to the research facility yet, but Choch, avoiding the question about the creature, made Cole want to find out more. It had to be the same thing Victor had seen.

Cole had a glass of water in front of him and a cup of peppermint tea. He had ordered breakfast and was waiting for it, sure that Rebecca hadn't given it to him because she hated his guts. She was destined to be his server until the end of time, probably as punishment from Choch. He'd tried to flag her down once to ask when his meal might come, but when she ignored him, he gave up. He didn't want his food served with a side of spit.

Cole waited to make eye contact with Victor, and then be like, "Oh, hey, why don't I come sit with you? You can tell me stories about the shadow creature. It just so happens I saw it, too!" Where had Victor seen it? Near the research facility as well? What had it looked like to him? A boogeyman? Some black figure with red eyes? Were they all the same...thing? But Victor wasn't looking up from his coffee.

"Hey, space cadet, wanna move your elbows?" Rebecca had a plate of two eggs, toast, and bacon extended, wanting to put the food down, but Cole was leaning over the table.

"Sorry." Cole moved, clearing the way for Rebecca.

She tossed the plate down and walked away.

"You're seriously a terrible server," Cole said, now that she couldn't spit in his food (if she hadn't already).

Cold food. He wasn't about to ask her to heat it up. *Jayney,* Cole thought. A way better option.

She didn't show up.

Jayney! Cole thought.

Still no Jayne.

"Jayne," Cole said out loud.

The couple on the opposite side of the room from Victor looked up. Cole nodded at them awkwardly, and smiled awkwardly. Victor did for a moment as well, too quick for Cole to catch it.

"Hey, Coley." Jayne materialized with a big smile on her face. This was the Jayne Cole knew and loved. He could feel her swing her legs back and forth. Every second or so, one of Cole's legs would feel warm from her fiery foot.

"Hey, Jayney."

"What's up? You were thinkin' loud!"

"Oh," Cole pushed his plate over towards Jayne, "I thought you could maybe warm this up for me."

Jayne's flames grew brighter. "Could I!"

"Sorry, I hate using you like that," Cole said. "I hate when *he* uses you like that."

"But you wanted me to burn that gun?" Jayne cocked her head to one side.

"Yeah, but that was different. Scott was about to shoot me. You saved my life. And Eva's."

"Anyways, I was helping so…" Jayne's tongue stuck out as she waved her hand over the plate and the food began to steam "…I like doin' jobs."

"You helped a lot."

"I know. I did real good."

"Yeah, you did. Really good."

"Like that! Ta-da!"

Cole took the plate back. The food was much more appealing now. He took a forkful of eggs. "I think I just missed you. I didn't really need you to do this."

Jayne just sat there, kicking her legs, smiling.

"You're not hiding anymore?" Cole asked after another bite of food.

Jayne shook her head. "I don't need to hide at daytime."

"So where've you been?"

"With my friends, silly."

What about me? Cole thought, but he felt stupid for feeling jealous, *needy*, about where a ghost spent her time. Was it stupid to just want to spend time with her? But still, maybe she *could* help…

"Jayney…" Cole eased in, not sure of how to ask without scaring her. *She's a kid, don't forget.*

"Yeah?"

"Do you remember when you were watching the folder for me? And what you said took it?"

Jayne's bright flame dimmed. "Yeah. The boogeyman."

"Do you think…?" Cole put his fork down and took her non-burning hand. "Could you just tell me what it looked like?"

"I don't want to tell you about that." Jayne took her hand away from Cole, put it in her lap, and looked away from him. She started kicking her legs faster, like she was thinking about running away, right now, to anywhere.

Hiding.

"Jayney, I saw it, too," Cole whispered.

Jayne looked over at Cole quickly with a short burst of flames, like lighter fluid sprayed on a campfire. "You did?!"

"Last night," Cole said. "I just want to know what it is, and why it's here."

"But I don't know stuff like that, Coley," Jayne whined. "It's just scary, that's all."

"I know it is." Cole patted his hand on the table. Jayne looked at his hand, looked away, looked at it again, then slowly put her hand in his again. "Just…have you seen it again? Do you know where it is, where it comes from?"

"Why would I know where it comes from when I'm tryin' ta hide from it, stupid!?" Jayne's flames grew brighter and she took her hand away again.

"Okay, sorry." Cole leaned back. He crossed his arms and looked at the floor. He counted the tiles. One, two, three… "Where is it, when you hide from it?"

Jayne had her arms crossed, too. She just sat there for a while, tight-lipped. She glanced at him every few seconds. Finally, she said, "All over the place because he goes everywhere. Even talks to people, sometimes, when I'm peeking out at 'im in the day. He even talks to himself. He's so weird when he's not bein' scary."

"What? Talks to people? What are you talking about?"

"Yeah. With his *mouth*, okay?"

"This is so confusing." Cole knocked his head against his plate, which sent a clatter through the restaurant.

"Are you okay, Coley?"

"Yeah." Cole's face was muffled, half against the plate and half against the table. He realized that his forehead was in his eggs. "I'm fine."

"Are you mad at me?" Jayne's feet stopped kicking.

"No. Just frustrated at life."

"Oh." Jayne paused for a moment. Then she said, recapturing her joy, "Well I'm a good listener, you know."

Cole sighed deeply. "Well, if you can help me figure out why there's a scary boogeyman running around having conversations with people during the day, why patients in the clinic look sick again, why we aren't allowed *into* the clinic, and why the research facility is being guarded by soldiers or some shit—"

Jayne gasped. "Coley!"

"—or some *stuff*, sorry, and oh yeah, where the hell are the files?" It wasn't even worth mentioning the fire at the mall. That seemed a pittance compared to everything else.

"*Heck*...well, I like puzzles," Jayne said. "You know what I do? I just start at the outside parts and then I start putting together the inside parts."

"Yeah?" Cole asked. "So what are the outside parts in *my* life?"

"Just the easiest stuff," Jayne said. "The straight sides, and then all the other stuff you just find how it fits."

"Outside in," Cole summarized.

"Yeah, like that."

Cole could feel the yolk against his forehead. He stubbornly stayed face down. He wanted to lift his head, but he was simply too frustrated. If he could stay there forever, and just hide, like Jayne—only from everything—he would. Also, he was embarrassed by how his forehead would look once he came up for air. *Outside in.* What was easiest? What made the most sense? The whole diner seemed quiet. Cole could hear Jayne's fire crackling. He could feel her warmth. The door opened and somebody entered. Simultaneously, Cole heard a *poof* and smelled sulphur. Jayne left, and her warmth did, too. Cole didn't want to lift his head now, not until whoever came in had walked safely past.

But the footsteps stopped at Cole's booth.

"Sleeping?"

Reynold. Great.

"No, just..." Cole rambled off potential responses, settling on "...school."

Cole felt Reynold sit down across from him.

"School can be tough. Grade twelve. It really challenges you as you move on to, well...wherever it is you're going after this," Reynold said.

Cole patted around at the far side of the table for some napkins. Reynold handed him a bunch. Cole lifted his head slightly, hiding his forehead from view, and wiped off as much egg as he could. Finally, he lifted his head all the way.

"You've got, just…" Reynold pointed to the upper right area of Cole's face. Cole wiped at it broadly. "…there you go, son."

Cole put down the napkin. "Thanks."

"School must be even harder away from home, huh?"

"This *is* my home," Cole said. He picked up a piece of toast, one of the only pieces of food not impacted by his forehead. He took a bite, then put it down.

"Of course it is. I was just saying, it must weigh on you. You must have friends in the city, your aunt and kókom, of course."

"Actually they're here too, now, so I'll probably be staying for a while."

"Fantastic news." Reynold reached towards Cole's plate, stopping about an inch from his toast. "Do you mind?"

Cole shook his head.

Reynold picked up the toast, took a big bite, and then replaced it. Cole stared at the crescent-shaped mouth-mark Reynold left.

"I'm starving," Reynold said. "The election's been so busy, honestly sometimes I just forget to eat."

Cole pushed the plate towards Reynold. Half-eaten, half-smushed. "Well, be my guest." He didn't want to take one more bite now.

"You're too kind," Reynold said.

"I'm just not hungry," Cole said.

Reynold took another bite, then he clapped the crumbs from his fingers, and dabbed at his mouth with a napkin. "Lucy tells me she had a nice chat with you."

"Yeah, first day. I didn't know that she was your daughter at first."

Reynold pointed at Cole quickly and nodded his head approvingly. "That says a lot about you, son. That you'd show my daughter kindness without knowing who she was."

"It wasn't kindness, really, Mr. McCabe. I just talked to—"

"She can be a handful, I know that," Reynold said, "but she's my girl, and I love her fiercely."

"Of course you do, sir."

"Chip off the block, too, that one. Her mother..." Reynold shook his head to one side. "Anyway," he got up from the table and straightened his jacket. He stepped towards Cole, stopping uncomfortably close. "I just saw you while walking by and thought I should come in and check on you."

"Thanks," Cole said again. "I mean, I did see you last night. Not much has changed."

Reynold leaned over and put a hand on Cole's shoulder. "Still, if there's anything I can do for you, just let me know, okay?"

"I will."

Reynold started to walk out, but he stopped by the door, now behind Cole's back. Cole kept staring straight ahead.

"I can't imagine what you've gone through. Not only being away from home, but to have seen your friends..." Reynold sighed dramatically. "I just can't believe I never saw that in Scott. Ashley, Alex...such a tragedy. To think, it could've been my girl, you know? They were just innocent children, those two."

Cole nodded. Saw Ashley's face, Alex's. Memories flooded into his mind.

"And then for him to have tried to kill you as well..."

Cole thought of all the times Ashley checked in on him, just to see how he was doing down in the city. Coming to see his grade eight graduation. Alex, holding Cole's hand as they walked to her house. How her skin was cold, but he felt warm. Alex, tough little Alex, giving him a soft kiss against the cheek. But...

"At any rate, please. If there's anything, Cole. And do tell your auntie and your kókom hello for me, would you? They're perfectly welcome to vote on Sunday, too."

"What about Maggie?" Cole asked.

Reynold stopped. Cole looked down. He could feel Reynold staring at him.

"I'm sorry?"

"You said, 'Ashley, Alex...' but what about Maggie?" Cole asked.

Reynold cleared his throat. "Yes, of course Maggie. All of them. I just figured those were the two closest to you. Maggie's death is no less important. Naturally."

"*Naturally,*" Cole said.

"Do you have something to say to me, son?"

Cole remembered Lauren kicking his shin, like he shouldn't mess with Reynold. He paused just long enough after saying, "No," that Cole thought it was clear he had more to say.

Just not now.

"Good," Reynold said after his own pause, then the door opened and Reynold left.

Cole settled back into his seat. The plate in front of him looked like some weird art piece, not breakfast. Reynold's bite mark. Cole's fore-head mark. The scant collection of diner-goers was looking at Cole, maybe because they'd anticipated a bit more than what had happened between him and Reynold. The couple. Victor. He and Cole met eyes. Finally. Cole got up from his booth and walked across the room to Victor, who nodded an acknowledgement when Cole sat down.

"Hi," Cole said. "Victor, right?"

"That's right." Victor took a sip of coffee.

"I heard you saw something," Cole said, not wanting to give Victor any clues as to what Cole had seen.

Victor took one more quick sip of his coffee, then he pushed it to the side. "Out in Blackwood," he said. "I was goin' hunting. I didn't care that nobody else was goin' hunting. That's how we live out here, how we used to live anyways. That's when I seen it."

"Where did you see it?" Cole asked, maybe too quickly, too eagerly.

Victor wasn't fazed. "There was a clearing out there. I seen it in there…"

It must've been the same clearing where Scott had set up his camp, and where Jayne had seen the boogeyman. Where Cole and Eva and Brady had been just two nights ago.

"…I thought it was an animal at first, feeding on another animal. Seen that before. Then I seen it wasn't an animal it was feedin' on…"

Victor got lost in the memory. Cole tried to pull him back. "What was it eating?"

"Looked like a...a human."

"What? Nobody said..."

"Nobody gets far enough to listen," Victor said. "So, I came across it, and when it seen me, it got up, started after me. Growlin'. Runnin' real fast. It moved like a human, but I never seen its face. Just its eyes, y'know. Those eyes..."

"Yeah?"

"...*red*. Like they was on fire or somethin'. Heard it behind me all the way through the forest, all the way outta there, until I ran right inta here."

"What do *you* think it was?"

"I'm not goin' ta tell you what I think it was. I'm not sayin' that name, kid."

"Upayokwitigo."

"Hmph. Could be kid. Could be."

"I saw it, too."

Victor picked his coffee up, sipped it, and put it down, all without taking his eyes off Cole, assessing whether Cole was lying or not. But he must've seen something in Cole's eyes, because after a tense moment, Victor nodded knowingly.

"You made it out alive, anyways," he said. "You made it."

"Yeah," Cole said, "I made it. What do you think it wants?"

Victor shrugged. "Power? Fear? To feed off us? Literally. That's what it does, you know. It's got this hunger that it can't get rid of. Starts eatin' bigger things from that hunger. And the hungrier it gets, the worse it gets. I know it's bad, kid. I know it's bad because it's eatin'—"

"Humans," Cole said.

"That's right. Humans."

"How do we...how does somebody...stop it?"

Victor chuckled and leaned back against his seat. "You goin' ta stop it, there, kid? You thinkin' about stoppin' it?"

"Maybe," Cole said.

Victor got deadly serious. "It'll rip you to shreds. You'd be dessert, you."

"You sound pretty tough for a guy hiding in a diner."

"I'd kill it," Victor snapped. "If I had another chance I'd kill that monster."

"How?"

Victor raised his index finger, reached across the table, and pushed it right in the middle of Cole's chest. "Like that, kid. Just like that."

15

MWACH

COLE DEEMED IT SAFE TO RETURN TO SCHOOL after lunch following his outburst, and just kept away from the gym. It appeared as though his altercation with Choch had gone over well with the student body, which was a nice surprise. He noticed more smirks and fewer scowls, and he even heard the odd, "Person-makers!" shouted randomly. By the time Cole had reached his locker, the only thing he had left to worry about was the reception he'd get from Brady, Eva, and Michael. They were there, switching books at their lockers, from Biology to Cree. Cole got his out as well, before saying anything to his friends. The Cree textbook had been the only new one provided by Choch—a spiral-bound Wounded Sky Cree dictionary and phrase book.

All of them with their textbooks now, they stood in a kind of square, each at one corner, exchanging looks and not saying a word. Cole wanted it to end, but he wasn't sure what to say. Were they mad at him? Had he been that out of line? He started to replay their conversation, (argument?) in his mind. It boiled down to this: he'd not told Eva about hanging out with Pam and, seemingly worse, he had gone off to look for the files without them. Oh, and he survived electrocution. Cole couldn't think of doing anything other than apologizing. He felt like he was good at two things and two things only, sometimes: saying sorry and breaking locks (or door handles).

"Look," Cole started into his apology, but Eva suddenly lunged at him and gave him a huge hug.

"Oh, Cole, we love you! We're sorry for ganging up on you!" she said jokingly, like she was talking to a baby. Cole wasn't sure how he felt about that, but decided while still in Eva's arms that maybe he deserved to get talked to like a baby.

"Yeah, friend," Brady said, without baby talk, and made it a three-person hug.

"Just don't go off without us again, okay?" Eva said.

"And we know you can't tell us everything, but when it comes to the Pam thing…" Brady said.

"I know," Cole said.

"I mean, if we were around, maybe at least you wouldn't have passed out on the front steps, right?" Eva said.

"Maybe," Cole said.

They were all huddled, touching foreheads, but Cole looked up because he noticed one person missing from the hug, and he couldn't believe it but he wanted Michael in there more than Eva right now.

"Yeah, that's not happening," Michael said, but he didn't say it like he was mad or like he hated Cole, just that he wasn't a hugger.

Eventually, they let go of each other, and this coincided with the bell. Lunch was over, and classes were starting.

"How's your Cree?" Brady asked.

"Ha." That was all Cole could muster. He felt like he couldn't even say "Ha" in Cree, or if there was even a word for it. "I haven't spoken Cree, really, since I left Wounded Sky."

"It'll come back," Eva assured him.

"Say *yes* and don't even think about it," Brady said.

"Ehe?" Cole said.

"You sure about that?" Eva chuckled.

"Not now," Cole said.

"Relax," Brady said, "you're right."

"Ekosi," Michael said.

"Way to go," Cole said.

"See?" Eva said.

"Ehe, yes." Brady gave Cole a pat on the back. "It's like riding a bike, see?"

"That's, like, the easiest thing I've done since coming back," Cole said.

"Well, when you keep your gang on the sidelines…" Eva said.

"Trust me, you did *not* want to be around last night," Cole said.

"Hey," Eva said, "I've been in it pretty deep with you, Cole. Game recognize game."

Cole laughed. It felt normal, at least for right now, between them. "Fair enough."

"Part of me wishes I was there to see Scott get the hell beaten out of him," Brady said. "For Ashley. But…part of me thinks that violence for violence…it wouldn't have brought Ash back."

"Is it getting any easier?" Cole asked.

"Really curious, or do you think I'm still mad at you?"

"Can it be both? Either way, I care, man."

"I suppose the best way to put it is that I know I'll be okay, even if I'm not, get it?" Brady said.

"Yeah," Cole said.

"Now tell me you love me," Brady smiled.

"I love y—"

"Mwach. In Cree."

"Uhhh…"

"Come on, you got this," Eva said.

Cole pictured his mom, tucking him in at night just before she left, and him grabbing his flashlight and reading in secret. He pictured her face and tried to remember her words as he closed his eyes. "Kisaki-hitan," he whispered, then opened his eyes. He saw Eva and Brady looking at him, and somehow they seemed to know where he'd gone, where he had to go, to find the word. Eva reached forward and wiped a tear away from his cheek.

"Astum," Brady made a move towards class. "Come on."

Eva nudged him when they were halfway to class. "Can I ask you something that might sound weird, but I swear I don't mean it that way. To sound weird, or be weird."

"Now it's already weird," Cole said.

"Yeah, you're right."

"Yes, you can ask me something that might sound weird."

"Okay, so…" Eva tightened her ponytail, smoothing the hair back on top of her head "…you're good at math, and I suck at math, right?"

"I haven't seen your test scores," Cole said dryly, but he acknowledged that, yes, he was rather good at math.

"Well, I do suck," she said. "Trust me."

"Alright, I trust you," he said.

Eva was stalling, walking slower, giving herself more time to ask her weird question. Cole slowed to keep pace with her.

"What is it?" he asked. Talking to her, looking at Michael.

She smiled. "We have a quiz next week, yeah? I could use some tutoring help. Dad used to help me, but he can't even text, still."

"Tutoring, like, me and you alone? Like, me helping you, like, do you mean during school or…"

"School's not the most conducive place to just be quiet and learn together," Eva said. "I mean, you can't tutor me during class, so…"

Cole didn't answer. They switched places, and now Cole was stalling, hoping they'd get to class before he had to turn her down. He didn't want to say no, but he wanted to stick to his guns, to keep making Michael happy. He just got his friend back. But he made the mistake of looking at her just as she rubbed her lips together, as though spreading lip balm. She looked down, away from him, the olive skin on her cheeks carrying a suggestion of pink. She was embarrassed to have asked and not get a response. All of it made Cole's heart flutter.

Michael, he thought. *Michael, Michael, Michael…*

"Never mind," she said. "I shouldn't have asked. I'll just—"

"Sure, I'll help. What are friends for, right?" he'd said it all so quickly, like it was a race to get the words out.

"Ummm," she said, running her fingers over her ear to fix a few displaced strands of hair. "Okay, great. Can you come by tonight?"

"Yes," he said.

"In Cree, please."

"Ehe."

"Hey, Cole." Just outside of the classroom, Michael spun around to face Cole. And Eva. Tutoring. Tonight. Alone. Cole stepped to the side, away from Eva.

"Yeah?" Cole looked at Eva quickly, who shook her head. He gave her a questioning look, his head slightly tilted, trying to say through this gesture that she and Brady had literally just said to be honest and now he wasn't supposed to say anything about the tutoring? What did that mean?

"We'll be in in a second," Michael said to Brady and Eva, who raised their eyebrows at each other, but went inside the classroom, leaving Cole and Michael together.

"Excuse me, ladies." Lucy walked between them on her way into class. She stopped just before entering the class, looked at them both, and said, "huh, I thought you two hated each other," then went inside the room.

"What's up?" Cole asked. *Please do not tell me you heard Eva asking me over,* Cole thought.

"Still play hockey?" Michael asked.

Thank God. "That's debatable," he said.

"How horrible would you be, scale of one to ten?"

"Minus five million-billion?" Cole said. "One is bad, right?"

"Seriously."

Cole pictured himself trying to skate while getting choked out by Tristan. "I'd say a solid two, maybe three."

"We can work with that," Michael said.

"Maybe three and a half. Work with me how, and for what?"

"The game's back on this weekend, not sure if you heard or not."

Cole showed Michael his phone. "Not on the group text."

"Right," Michael said, "well, we need another player, since…"

"Yeah, I know."

"I think it'd be really nice if you played."

"Michael, I don't know." Cole wanted to keep building up good will with Michael, but at what cost? Making an ass of himself in front of the whole community? How would it actually feel to suck at a game that was super intense, to be an ankle-bender around really good hockey players?

"You'll be fine," Michael said. "And, you know, you could honour Ashley, right?"

"Okay, that's not fair."

"*I'd* appreciate it, okay?"

"Oh, way to double down," Cole said. He wanted to say, "Mwach," so badly. He ruffled his own hair and closed his eyes tight, like Michael would go away when he opened his eyes again. No luck. "Alright fine. Ehe. Whatever."

"Thanks." Michael extended his fist to Cole.

Cole looked at it. He hesitated, and then touched his fist to Michael's.

"So, how *are* you doing, anyway?" Cole asked as he and Brady left school on their way to Brady's place. "Now that we're alone, and you don't have to, like, put on a front or something."

"I don't have to put on a front for Eva, or Mike."

"I just wanted to ask, and not just because you told me I wasn't asking you about it," Cole said. "Can I ask you?"

Brady managed a smile. "Yeah, you can ask me. I'm, you know, okay. There are times where I don't think about him for a moment or two. I like those times, but…"

"But what?"

"I guess, when I remember him again, just sitting in class, or whenever, I feel guilty that I wasn't thinking about him."

Cole put his hand around Brady's shoulder and gave him a man-hug. How could he tell Brady not to feel guilty, or give him advice about it, when he literally felt guilty all the time? So they walked in the quiet, the ominous calm that Cole at once loved and hated, and Cole kept his arm around Brady's shoulder, giving it a squeeze every few steps.

But Cole stopped in his tracks when Brady's house came into view, and Brady slipped away from Cole's one-armed embrace. He walked a few steps before noticing Cole had held up. He stopped, too, and looked back at Cole.

"What are you doing?" Brady asked.

"What the hell…?" Cole said under his breath.

Out in front of Brady's house, Cole's auntie and grandmother were standing with their suitcases and Cole's backpack and shopping bag from the store, too.

"That." Cole pointed at his relatives.

Brady looked away from Cole, towards his house. "Oh, crap. What's that about?"

"I don't know, but I doubt it's good."

"What's going on?" Cole asked when he and Brady had come to the same front steps Cole had been found on. He thought that his grandmother and auntie were standing right on top of that spot intentionally to make a point. But what point?

"We're going home," Auntie Joan said.

"No, I can't go back to Winnipeg, you don't understand. I—"

"Not Winnipeg," Auntie Joan said. "If we're staying here, then we're going home. Your home *here.*"

"Mwach," was all Cole could say. "Mwach."

Somehow, this was worse.

16

MY NORMAL

HOME.

Cole hadn't been home since he ran there the morning after the school fire. He remembered it now. He'd been found in Blackwood Forest sometime in the night, his palms burned, his shoes gone, his clothes charred and torn. He'd been brought to his auntie's place, but as soon as he could, he'd gone home. He'd burst in through the front door and rushed through the house, through each room, screaming "Mommy! Mommy! Mommy!" hoping she would be there, that the fire had been a nightmare. Then he ran outside, ran and ran, ran until he couldn't run anymore.

He never set foot in the house again.

"I'm not going there." Cole's grandmother, Auntie Joan, and Brady, had been waiting patiently for him to say something. "I can't go there. You *know* I can't go there."

"I think it's important that you do," Auntie Joan said. "Isn't that what your psychiatrist had talked about once? What did she call it... exposure therapy?"

"She never mentioned going back into that house," Cole said. "And also I wish I'd never briefed you about my sessions!"

"Cole, we're just trying to help you get through this," his auntie said.

"Well, I don't think you should use my *private* sessions as ammunition!"

"Joan thinks you should be home, with *us*," his grandmother said. "Nobody is using anything as ammunition."

"Do you want me to…?" Brady motioned to the house, sounding like he really wanted to be sent inside.

"If you don't mind, Brady—" Auntie Joan started.

"No, I'd like for you to stay." Cole put his hand against Brady's chest, keeping him right where he was. "Brady knows about my anxiety."

"Seems kind of like a family thing, that's all." Brady sounded very uncomfortable, but Cole needed him here.

"You are family," Cole said to him.

Brady relented. "Alright, cuz." He forced a smile, but stayed put.

"Grandma," Cole looked for another ally, "you can't think this is a good idea. Please. Tell her."

"It's always been up to you," his grandmother said, "but I do think Joan has a point."

"Well, I'm not going," Cole reiterated. "It's bad enough that you guys wasted…I mean, holy shit, Auntie Joan, we hardly have enough money day to day and you just threw down $2,000 to get here? Does grandma have another envelope or two under her mattress?"

"I have savings, and I can replenish those savings," Auntie Joan said.

"We are trying to support you," his grandmother said.

"Brady and Eva have been supporting me," Cole said. "I've been buying groceries and everything. Plus, *plus*, Brady's kókom's in the clinic, you know that, and I don't want Brady to stay alone!"

"Friend," Brady said, "don't hate me, but I agree with them."

"But…"

"Don't flip things on their head. I've loved having you here, *mostly*," he smirked, "but…I don't know…don't you think it's kind of weird you've never even gone within a hundred yards of your old house?"

"No, it's not weird because I literally set up an invisible boundary that I promised myself I wouldn't cross," Cole said matter-of-factly. "I know that I won't be able to handle it, and then what good will I be?"

"If I can give you some advice you haven't asked for, I think you should go," Brady said.

"You *can* handle it," his grandmother said.

"And we'll be there with you," Auntie Joan said.

"What, am I on A&E or something? Is this an…an intervention?"

Brady put his hand on Cole's shoulder. "Cole, whether you want to believe it or not, you're as strong as they come. And I don't mean…the stuff I've seen. I mean, even just coming home and facing what you've faced, almost daily. You can do *this*, too." Brady paused, then added, "Also, you're not allowed on my couch anymore."

Cole looked at Brady's shoes, then at his own. He looked back up and smiled at his friend. A soft, quiet smile. Then, he patted Brady's shoulder in return. "I hate you."

Brady laughed. "Kisakihitan."

Cole picked up his backpack, and handed it to his auntie. "Fine, you win. You can sit there and watch me collapse into nothing from the worst panic attack ever."

"We won't watch you," his grandmother said. "We'll hold you up."

His auntie nodded.

"If I do this, you can't just tell me what to do all the time," Cole said. "I have things I need to do. That's why I'm here."

"Sorry, Cole, but you're a kid, and we're responsible for you. You will do what we say."

"Auntie, you don't understand."

"I understand, and I am not changing my mind. If I can't bring you back to Winnipeg, then things are going to change here for you," she said.

"Grandma…" Cole pleaded.

"I already lost your parents," his grandmother said. "I can't lose you, too."

"You're not going to lose me," Cole said.

"You're right, we won't," Auntie Joan said. "I mean, look at you. You're having a panic attack right now, aren't you?"

"You're giving me one! Just wait until I get home for fricks-sake!"

*(CB did **not** actually say frick.)*

Auntie Joan reached into her purse and pulled out a full bottle of medication. She handed it to him. "Here."

Cole hesitated for a moment, but took them. He gave the bottle a shake, rolled it across his fingers, then put it in his pocket.

"I'll be there later." Cole started to quickly walk away.

"Where do you think you're going?" Auntie Joan said.

Cole stopped. Did he want to be defiant now? It would only make them watch him more, and make it harder for him to go out when he had to do something more important than tutor a friend. He swallowed hard. He could feel his pride sliding down his throat. "Can I go to Eva's? I'm supposed to tutor her."

Auntie Joan paused, and it felt like a power play, letting him know that she could keep him here, or allow him to leave. "Be home by nine."

"Nine?" Cole calculated whether he could tutor Eva, break into the clinic to talk to Scott, and get back in time. It would be close, but he relented. "Okay, fine."

"Not a minute later," she warned.

"Yeah," he said, and he continued to walk, feeling the bottle against his leg with each step.

"Hey." When Eva opened the door she checked her phone for the time. "You're early."

Cole felt stupid, standing on the doorstep indecisively.

Eva leaned her hand against the door frame. "You can come in, you know."

Cole nodded and stepped inside.

"Where's your textbook?" she asked.

Cole pressed his palm against his forehead and grunted.

"No big deal, we can use mine." Eva turned and walked towards the dining room table—expecting Cole to follow her, he decided. He tried not to notice how pretty she looked in her sweats, plaid shirt, loose ponytail, white tank top, and bare feet. He joined Eva at the dining room table, leaving an empty chair between them.

"Weird," Eva said. That didn't last long. She slid over to the chair beside Cole.

"I just didn't want to seem like—"

"He speaks!"

"I don't want Michael to be pissed at me. We were, like, friends today. Actually friends."

"I noticed," Eva said. "Big step."

"Maybe it can be normal again," Cole said.

"And all it took was a date with Pam," Eva said.

"I'm still sorry about that," Cole said, "but it wasn't a date, really. We were hanging out."

"Over dinner, alone?"

Cole stammered. Eva noticed.

"Sorry, I'm being stupid, it's not my business," she said. "I really won't tell Michael you came tonight, if that'll make you feel more comfortable."

"I kind of suck at lying," Cole said.

"He won't know, so he won't ask," Eva said. "You won't even have to lie, you'll just have to keep your mouth shut."

Cole sighed.

"Glad you agree so emphatically." Eva chuckled and pulled out her math textbook.

She started to flip through the pages. Meanwhile, Cole tried to breathe normally. Knowing he was going home after this, knowing he was jeopardizing his just-fixed friendship with Michael, and not wanting to leave even though he was aware of the risks, was making him sweat and shake. Eva started to write down some questions onto a pad of paper, flicking her hair behind her ear every time a lock fell against her cheek, looking frustratingly pretty, and Cole's heart started to pound harder and harder. He mindlessly patted the bottle of meds in his pocket.

"Could you stop that?" Eva asked without looking at Cole.

He stopped patting his leg. He hadn't noticed the soft rattle the pill bottle had been making. "Sorry."

Eva put down her pencil. "What is that, anyway?"

"What's what?"

"The thing in your pocket making sounds."

Cole decided to show her. Still, he took forever, out of nervousness, out of embarrassment, because he didn't want to seem weak, because he *was* weak. He placed them on the table, then he turned the bottle so that the label was facing her.

She picked it up, read it. "Alpra…"

"It's anti-anxiety medication."

"I'd get anxiety just trying to read the name of it." Eva read it over a few times. She was reading to herself, but her lips were moving. "Would you be offended if I told you that I'm not surprised?"

"Zero percent offended."

"And the whole…" Eva shook the bottle like it was a maraca.

"Nervous tick, I guess…involving nerve meds…" Cole said. "Go figure."

"*Apropos.*" Eva handed Cole back the pills. He put them back in his pocket. He decided he was going to do his best not to tap on them again, but he was so much better at that when he didn't have them.

"I think I could've used something like that when I was younger," she said.

"Sometimes they're like…they make things too easy, and then you don't deal with it. I mean, *really* deal with it," he said.

"Just, you know. When things got a bit hard."

"Yeah, I know," Cole said. He pulled the textbook towards him and scanned the page, but he didn't actually read through any problems. "I don't think you would've needed them, though."

"How would you know that?" she asked.

"Brady told me tonight how strong I was, and how I didn't know it…"

"That's because you are."

"But even if I am, I know you're stronger. You and Brady are both stronger."

"I don't think having to take pills makes you weak, Cole."

"Do you think part of that is because you stayed? That nobody made you leave? I mean, you didn't run away from what happened. You faced it."

"I think you're used to feeling like you screwed up somehow," Eva answered, "and so you think you *are* some big screw-up. But it's just different, Cole." Eva tapped on the pill bottle—which was now back in Cole's pocket.

"Don't worry, that's a pill bottle, I'm not just happy to see you." He actually said that. For real. When he realized that he said it he tried to fix it. "I mean, I *am* happy to see you, it's just that…"

"You kind of want a pill now, don't you?" Eva stifled a laugh.

"Yep."

"How long have you been taking them?"

"Since I was, I don't know, thirteen?"

"*Cole*, thirteen?"

"That's just when I started taking them. I've kind of felt the same way since that night."

"And how's that? How do you feel?"

Cole squirmed. Talking about anxiety usually gave him anxiety. He moved his hand towards his pocket, but Eva intercepted it. She held his hand in place to keep him from touching the bottle.

"How do you feel?" she asked again.

"I thought we were going to do math," Cole said quietly.

"Math can wait."

Cole took a deep breath, and it shook on its way out. It was how he remembered feeling when he was younger. "I guess it's just this…unsettled feeling. Sometimes, I don't think I can eat. I used to lose weight, now I just eat anyway. It's like I've always got a gun to my head. Always like I'm getting chased, even when I can't…when nothing's there."

"Always?"

"I got good at ignoring it, when it's not bad. I just try to do things anyway," Cole said. "It's, like, *my* normal. I don't know how to feel anyway else."

Eva still had her hand on his. She squeezed it now, rubbing her thumb against the outside of his. Her subtle touch was calming in a way he wasn't used to. He couldn't tell her that.

"And when I have to, I take a pill. When it's too much," he said.

"I hate that you feel like that," Eva said. "I didn't know it was that bad."

"It's okay." Cole, looked away. "It's like you said, thinking I'm a screw-up all the time. I do it to myself."

"I didn't mean it that way." Eva reached over, placed a hand on his cheek, and made him look at her again. "I just want you to go easy on yourself. You never want to think about the good you've done, always the bad."

"I've gotten used to feeling like that, too," he said quietly, almost breathing it out. "Of doing that."

They stared at each other. Cole wanted to know what she was thinking. He spent too much time with his own thoughts. He knew them too well. He was breathing heavy. The house felt hot. She slipped her hand from his cheek.

"What are you thinking now?" she asked.

"You make me feel calm," he said. "I should feel so nervous right now, but I don't. Right this moment, I don't."

"Huh," Eva said, "you can't swallow me, you know that, right? I don't come in pill form."

Maybe she was trying to find her way out of the moment, but it didn't really seem like she wanted to. That's what he wanted to believe. There was only her and him, and there were no problems, there was no deal. There was just now.

"That sucks," Cole said.

"This is the weirdest flirting," Eva said. "We should just shut up."

"And do what, if we shut up?" Cole asked.

"Shut up." Eva leaned forward, eyes closed, her lips lined up with his. She drew closer. He could feel her breath against his lips, inches away…*crack!* Eva's body jerked as the front window shattered. Cole put his arms around her, and felt around her back.

"Eva!" He looked down at his shirt, to see if there was any blood. "Eva!"

Thump. A large rock landed against the floor and skipped to a stop just under the television.

"What the hell!" Eva ran over to the window from the dining room table.

She's alive. Cole kept thinking that over and over. *She's alive.*

"Cole!"

Ashley. Cole was trapped with him now, in the trailer, watching Ashley's blood spray on the walls, the furniture. Watching Ashley's body fall to the ground. Looking at the hole in the glass made by Scott's bullet. Kneeling beside Ashley, holding his hand, watching him die.

"Cole!"

Eva's voice sounded distant and hollow, as if calling his name from the far end of a tunnel. Cole pushed himself back into the present. He looked around the room. *Deep breaths.* Everything was spinning. *In. Out. Five seconds. Seven seconds.*

"Cole, come here!"

He could see the rock underneath the television. *A rock, not a bullet.* He followed the broken glass speckled across the floor up to Eva's naked feet. He looked up to find her staring at him, her head tilted to one side.

"Wanna come here?" she asked. "Please?"

"Yeah, sorry." Cole got up from the chair, trying not to look like his knees felt as weak as they did, and joined Eva at the broken window. They both looked out across the field around her house, to the few other houses in view, but they saw nothing.

"Who would've done that?" Eva asked, still looking back and forth. Without waiting for a response, she went out onto the front step.

Cole followed her. But whoever had thrown the stone was long gone. "People don't do stuff like that and wait around."

Eva hugged her arms against her stomach. It was cold out. "I guess you're right."

"Do you get that ever?" Cole asked. He was shaking, too, only not from the cold. "Kids wanting to mess with the sheriff?"

"He's not—"

"I know, it just sounded better, for…you know."

"No, people respect him, for the most part, unless your last name is McCabe," Eva said. "Plus, everybody knows he's at the clinic."

Cole stopped looking for the perpetrator, and he looked at Eva instead. She was still scanning the area, her brow furrowed, her eyes fixed. He watched her jaw muscles clench and relax. He watched her breath escape, like she was exhaling smoke. Her lower lip shook from the chill. "Do you think Michael would've…"

"Mike?" Eva shook her head. "No, no I don't think so."

"You don't sound too sure, and I'm not either. What if he came by and saw us, what if…" Cole felt like fainting.

Eva took a deep breath and then let it out, like a weight. "But throwing a rock through my window?"

"We just—"

"I know." Eva took one last look and went back inside. She grabbed a broom and started sweeping up the glass.

Cole grabbed the dust pan and crouched at the pile Eva had made. She scooped it into the pan. Cole took it to the garbage and dumped it in. He handed her back the dust pan.

"Thanks," Eva said.

Cole nodded, trying to smile.

"That probably shouldn't have happened, back there," Eva finally said. "That shouldn't have happened."

"Right, yeah, I was thinking that, too," Cole said. "Big mistake, right?"

"Right." She gave him a quick hug. "Friends?"

"Friends." *But maybe not with Michael anymore,* Cole thought.

"Why do we have to confirm our friendship on a daily basis, right?" Eva shook her head, smiling, then went to replace the broom. She leaned against the fridge and started fidgeting with the sweetgrass ring. She played with the sweetgrass ring like he played with his pill bottle.

"We were just seven," she said.

Cole walked a step closer to her and leaned against the kitchen counter. She noticed she was playing with the ring, but didn't take her fingertips off it. She was staring at a square of the kitchen's vinyl flooring.

"I remember making that," he said, hesitantly. He wasn't trying to recapture the moment, but the memory was so clear right now, ready to bust out of him.

"Yeah?"

"I was sitting by Silk River, across the field. I found these, like, little blades. I had to chew them down a bit, too…"

"For my finger."

"…for your finger, yeah. Anyway, I was sitting right by the river, and the current was, you know, it was fast, but not…so I was staring at the bank, just before the river, and the water was rushing past, and it looked for a second like *I* was moving, not the water."

She tucked the ring back underneath her shirt, pushed herself off from the fridge, and walked over to him. She leaned against the counter across from him.

"And I remember thinking that I never wanted to leave. Because, we were getting married, so…"

"Of course."

"…and then, when I was in the city, it was different. It was like, yeah, I'm gone now, but I always wanted to come back, I think. Just, on my own terms."

"And you're not back on your own terms."

"No." Cole started crying—from everything he'd been through over the last two weeks. From every moment, every struggle, every loss, every feeling of being home at exactly the worst time. Eva walked across the kitchen. She took his cheeks in her hands, and made him look at her. She kissed him on the cheek, tasting one of his tears. Then she just hugged him. Not a man-hug, not a more-than-friends, but something different, and Cole didn't want to analyze it. He put his arms around her and hugged her back.

"It'll be alright," she whispered.

"Guys?"

Eva and Cole let go of each other, and found Brady standing in the doorway. He looked at the hole in Eva's living room window. "What's up with that? I'll ask about that, not about the...you know..." he clasped his hands, referencing Eva and Cole hugging.

"Don't ask," Eva said, "about either thing."

Cole busily wiped tears away from his cheeks. "What're you doing here?"

"I tried to see my kókom again just now, and they still won't let me in," he said.

"And I still haven't gotten a text from my dad," Eva said.

"Cole, do you want to do something for *me* for once?" Brady said. He wasn't kidding. No smile. No laugh. Deadly serious.

"Of course." Cole knew where this was going. He knew where he planned to go, and knew that he'd now have company. And that's how it should be.

"We need to get into that clinic."

17

FIRESTARTER

COLE, EVA, AND BRADY POSITIONED THEMSELVES in a tree-covered area a short distance from the clinic's front doors. They'd been watching Mark at the door for half an hour, and he hadn't moved.

"He's like some mutant that doesn't have to pee or move or anything," Brady said. "I think he was in that exact same position half an hour ago."

"So what's the plan?" Cole asked.

"Knock him out and get in there," Eva said.

"He has a gun," Cole said. "Maybe we should try something else first."

Brady stood up, stepped outside their cover. "Why don't we just try to get in first, the normal way?"

"But you just—" Cole started.

"Yes, I'm aware of that, my friend, but now there are three of us," Brady said.

Eva and Cole exchanged a look, and then followed Brady. The three of them walked towards the clinic, and within moments they were standing in front of Mark. Brady and Eva stepped right up to him, but Cole slunk back. He knew he wasn't Mark's favourite person. After all, it was Cole's presence that got Mark fired the first night Cole returned to Wounded Sky.

"—Oh-hi-Mark," Brady said.

"Brady, back again," Mark sighed, but he wasn't looking at Brady. He was looking at Cole, who was trying to disappear while standing in plain sight.

"Do you have to piss or something, city?" Mark asked.

"Huh?" Cole instinctively looked down at his pants.

"You're a weird little shit, you know that, right?" Mark said.

"Mark, can we just go inside for a second?" Eva asked.

Mark looked behind, into the clinic, as though he were considering it. "No way. I literally just told Brady he couldn't come inside. What are you guys, stupid?"

"Stubborn." Brady said as he took another step forward, closer to Mark. "Come on. I just want to see my kókom, that's it. I haven't seen her since…"

"What are you, trying to charm me now? You know I'm not a homo, right?" Mark said.

"You'd be lucky if he gave you the time of day," Eva said.

Mark snorted out a laugh. "Yeah, okay."

"Asshole," Cole muttered.

"What was that?" Mark said.

"Why can't you just let us in for a few minutes?" Cole asked. "What's the big deal? They can't be afraid of the flu spreading if all the patients are recovering."

"Look," Mark said, "I'm paid to keep people the hell out of the clinic. If there are times Brady can visit his kókom, or Eva can visit her dad, they'll post it. Until they do that, sorry."

"Why can't he even text me?" Eva asked.

"Maybe his phone's dead. What do I care?" Mark said.

"I haven't seen her since Monday!" Brady shouted. "They won't let anybody in anymore!"

"God, if you need somebody to look after you just go back to your folks," Mark said.

"Screw you," Brady said.

"What do you and Cole do at your place, anyway?" Mark asked, looking back and forth between them with a disgusted look on his face.

"You're such a jerk," Eva said, "in case you didn't know."

"Have a great night," Mark said, "Bye." He waved with his middle finger.

A minute later the trio was back in their spot.

"I don't know why I thought that would go any different," Brady was trying to calm himself for once, and not Cole.

"I mean, this doesn't change anything," Cole said. "We were always going to have to break in, right? Not ask nicely to be let in?"

"True," Eva said.

"Okay, there's no point waiting for what we know is going to happen," Brady said, and just like that, both he and Eva were looking at Cole. "Time to do your thing, my friend."

Cole looked the building over. He could see Mark at the front door and another guard by the door at the side of the building. The clinic was smaller than the research facility. Even though the guards weren't patrolling, Cole couldn't get in through a window or jump onto the roof without being seen. There wasn't much Cole could think of doing short of just beating the shit out of Mark and going in through the front door. But, again, Mark had a gun. Cole stared at Mark, thinking.

"You've got some awesome, *Ocean's Eleven* kind of idea, right?" Brady asked.

Cole didn't answer. He was still watching Mark, who was alert but smoking a cigarette. Cole could see the ember light up orange when Mark sucked in every few seconds. Then, Cole noticed a garbage can by the front entrance. That was it. *Jayne!*

"Cole Harper," Brady said.

"This happens a lot," Eva whispered to Brady.

"No kidding," Brady said.

Jayne, I need you! Please! Cole kept repeating this over and over again, while Eva and Brady complained about Cole's whole Space-Man act. *Jayne, it won't hurt you while I'm with you. I promise! Just for a moment.*

"Cole!" Brady whisper-shouted.

Mark didn't look in their direction. He was far too busy trying to blow smoke rings, but failing miserably.

"Yeah, sorry," Cole said to Brady and Eva. "I have an idea, but—"

"You better not get me hurt, Coley." Jayne appeared right beside Cole, lighting up the bush they were in.

"*But...*" Eva prompted.

"But nothing," Cole said.

"Why does it feel, like, ten degrees warmer all of a sudden?" Brady asked.

"Maybe you're having hot flashes," Eva laughed.

"Ha-ha," Brady said dryly.

"So do you actually have a plan, Cole?" Eva asked.

Cole stared at Jayne, but to his friends it looked like his eyes were trained on the clinic, on Mark. "I don't think I need one," Cole said.

"Are we going to wait for Mark to fall asleep or...?"

"No, Mark's been throwing his butts into the garbage can." *Follow me, Jayney, please.* "Have you seen that?"

"No," Eva said.

"It's *on fire*," Cole said.

Brady shuffled forward and took a good look. "What? No it's not."

"Yeah, Coley, it's not on fire," Jayne said.

Cole rubbed one hand across his cheek, anxious and frustrated. "Yes it is, look. There's a little fire in there and it's going to get really big."

"What're you talking about?" Eva asked. "It's totally *not* on fire."

"I swear it is, or it's *catching fire*," Cole said directly to his invisible companion.

"Are you feeling okay, friend?" Brady asked.

Jayne shook her head, wide-eyed and confused.

Would you just go and set the can on fire, already!?

"Oooooooohhhhh," Jayne nodded. She appeared in front of the garbage can.

"Just watch. There's a bit of smoke now. Wait."

"I'm just going to make him let us in." Eva started to get up, but Cole grabbed her arm and held her there. "Hey!"

"Look!" Cole said.

Jayne raised her burning hand in the air, pointed a finger, and then dipped it dramatically into the garbage can. The can went up in flames, an eruption of fire and sparks and smoke.

"See?" Cole said, proudly. He was proud of Jayne.

"Holy crap," Brady said, "that exploded."

"You didn't…?" Eva started what sounded like a question.

"Shhhh," Cole said.

Jayne gave Cole a thumbs up, and then she disappeared. Her cloud of black smoke joined the smoke from the can and billowed into the air. Mark swore when he saw the fire. His body jerked in the direction of the burning garbage can, then stopped, as though he were chained to the spot he'd been occupying since the trio had arrived.

"Come on," Cole whispered.

Mark ran over to the can, which was burning quite spectacularly.

"Let's go," Cole said. "Now!"

They ran out of the bush while Mark tried his best to smother the fire, emptying a bottle of water on it with little effect. Eva, Brady, and Cole closed in on the clinic and only slowed down when they were near the entrance, where they sneaked through the front doors while Mark resorted to scooping up dirt and tossing it onto the flames.

The lobby was empty.

"Listen," Cole started on his way to the unoccupied nurse's station, "you guys go check on your people, I'm going to track down Scott."

"Meet back here in what? Fifteen?" Eva suggested.

They all agreed. Eva and Brady ran off to see Wayne and Elder Mariah respectively, and Cole hopped over the desk at the nursing station to try and find the room assignment for Scott. He started to finger through papers. Nothing on the desk. That'd be too easy. The top drawer had a nursing schedule that was over a week old. Were the nurses also told not to work? Did Dr. Captain know that? If they weren't working, who was looking after the patients? Second drawer... some snacks, pencils, an extra stethoscope...useless. The computers were on, but password protected.

"I guess we're doing it the old fashion way," Cole said to himself, opting to jog through the halls until he tracked Scott down—and, hopefully, information about the folder.

As Wayne had said, people in their hospital beds looked almost as sick as when they had the flu, but not the *same* sick. Still, Cole wondered if something was wrong with his blood. Did the cure in his blood only half-work, or just work for a period of time, and then people got sick again? Was that because they'd administered his blood the way they had? If any of this were true, it made sense why they were guarding the clinic and not letting people in anymore.

"Was that why you didn't let me leave?" Cole asked Choch out loud, but why had they let people visit patients in the clinic in the first place? That didn't make sense. They'd been kicked out just when Eva had asked about the vitamins. It couldn't have been a coincidence.

He needed answers.

He jogged down a hallway, whipping his head from left to right while he ran, checking each room. No Scott, just sick-looking Wounded Sky residents. Wayne was right. They didn't *look* flu-sick, just sunken. Pale. Tired. Depressed. He made a mental note of the symptoms, and to discuss them with Dr. Captain later.

At the end of the third hallway, Cole found a locked door.

"Hello?" he called, and he pressed his ear against the door to hear a response.

But none came.

He knocked, lightly at first, and then, when nobody answered, he knocked louder.

"Alright."

It seemed to always come to this. He wrapped one hand around the doorknob and pressed his other hand against the door, then gave one hard, fast push. The door swung open and crashed against the wall. Cole looked down the hallway to see if the sound had alerted anybody, but it remained deadly quiet. Comfortable now that the coast was clear, Cole turned his attention to the room.

There, handcuffed to the clinic bed and attached to a heart monitor and an IV drip, was Scott.

18

GETAWAY

THE LIGHTS WERE OUT IN THE ROOM, and Cole kept them out. He walked over to the bed and stood over Scott. The beating Cole gave Scott at the camp was still tattooed all over his face in discoloured blotches, his blackened eyelids swollen shut. Cole felt a hint of regret that he'd hurt somebody that badly, despite what Scott had done.

"Scott," Cole whispered.

He didn't stir.

"Hey!" Cole said. There was no point whispering. Nobody came when the door slammed against the wall, and they weren't going to come because he'd raised his voice.

Cole poked him in the arm. "Hey, Scott."

This time, Scott grunted in response, moving his head from one edge of the pillow to the other.

"Scott!"

Scott tried to lift his arms. The handcuffs stiffened and his arms recoiled. His eyes blinked open. "What the fu—"

"Scott." Cole inched closer to the side of Scott's bed. He checked the clock on the wall. He had a few minutes before he had to meet Brady and Eva in the lobby, and he needed to be there. If Mark had gone back to his post, and there was no reason to think that he hadn't, they'd need Cole's help to get out.

"You...you're alive." Scott sounded like he had the worst sore throat ever.

"They didn't tell you?"

"I haven't talked to nobody." Scott tried to inch upward, to sit up a bit, but gave up. "Thought I killed you."

"I thought I killed you, too…before you stabbed me in the heart," Cole said. "And after you killed my friends."

"What do you want me to do? Say I'm sorry?"

"No," Cole said, "I want information."

Scott turned his head away from Cole. "I'm not gonna tell you shit."

"Who hired you to kill my friends? What else are they doing? What have they done?"

Scott didn't respond.

"Answer me."

"I told you, city boy. You're barkin' up the wrong tree."

"Was it *them*? Who are *they*?" Cole reached over to Scott's arm, and squeezed it. "What do they want?"

Scott let out a yelp.

"Tell me who *they* are," Cole demanded.

"If I tell you anythin', they're gonna kill me. They'll *really* kill me, bro."

"Who!?" Cole put his left hand on Scott's forehead, and turned Scott towards him. He placed two fingers against one side of Scott's windpipe, and his thumb on the other side. "Do you want to die then, or now?"

"What the hell are you doin'?" Scott croaked.

"I'm going to *Roadhouse* you, asshole," Cole said.

"*Roadhouse* me? What the hell does that mean?"

"What the hell does…you seriously haven't seen *Roadhouse*?"

"What's that? A movie or somethin'?"

"Patrick Swayze?" Cole waited for a response, but Scott's eyes were glazed over. Cole sighed. Now he felt like an idiot. "I'm going to rip out your windpipe if you don't tell me what I want to know."

"You wouldn't do that."

Scott was right. Cole wouldn't do that. But he needed to make Scott believe that he would. Cole took his hands off Scott and wrapped them around the hand rail. He ripped it off the bed and bent it into a U shape. It clanged against the floor. Cole put his hand back on Scott's windpipe. He was committed to the *Roadhouse* thing now, even though Scott didn't know what he was talking about.

"Shit, how did you—" Scott breathed.

"Now." Cole pressed down.

Scott started to choke under the force.

"All's I…know, if you're lookin'…for answers *here*, you're in the wrong place, kid. Far's I know."

A bit more pressure. "What's the right place?" Cole hissed.

"They got big…plans for the facility. I heard them…" he coughed, "…heard them talkin' about it."

"Of course the facility," Cole mumbled to himself. "What were they saying?" he asked.

"Screw…you. I'm done. *Roadhouse* me or whatever."

Cole's fingers began to shake thinking about going back to the research facility. His whole body started to shake. Cole took his hand away from Scott's throat. He gave him as tough a look as he could, despite feeling as weak as he suddenly did. "You've told me enough."

Scott tried to reach his throat, but the handcuffs prevented him. He swallowed, and it looked painful. "You go there and you're as dead as I am."

(Say it, CB! Please say it!)

Cole rolled his eyes. "Then I'll see you in Hell," he mumbled reluctantly.

(YAAASSSS! You could work on your delivery, but it was still worth it.)

"Excuse me!"

Cole had been walking down the hallway towards the lobby, but he turned in stride to find one of the doctors he'd seen at Elder Mariah's room just after his blood had cured her. "Yeah?" He tried to remember her name.

"Hold up!" she demanded, coming quickly out of a room.

Cole stopped in his tracks. He was almost at the lobby. He listened for Brady and Eva, but didn't hear anything. He figured he had some time.

"Yes?" Cole waited until the doctor caught up to him.

"What do you think you're doing here?" The blonde-haired woman had a clipboard in one arm, and she pulled down a surgical mask to reveal the bottom half of her face.

Cole put on his best acting effort. He looked around as though he were lost. "I don't know. I was trying to check on my Elder."

"Elder? Your grandparent, or..."

"No, my Elder. A community Elder. Mariah Apatagan?"

Dr. Ament! That was her name.

"She's in the other wing," Dr. Ament pointed broadly in the direction of the other side of the building, and then, as though she'd forgotten that he wasn't supposed to be here, she added, "are you... was there not somebody at the front door?"

"Oh," Cole turned towards the lobby, then back to Dr. Ament, trying to think quickly. "He was preoccupied, so..."

"Well, Mr. Harper, you're not, like I said, you're not allowed in here." Dr. Ament hugged the clipboard to her chest. Cole wondered what was on that clipboard. He brushed past her, into the room she'd come from. She chased after him, grabbed his shoulder, and turned him around just as he saw yet another sick patient.

"Well, *Dr. Ament*," Cole said, "I want to know what's going on here. People want to see their friends and family."

Dr. Ament looked for some indication of how he knew her name because it wasn't anywhere on her clothes. "That's just not possible, we're keeping community members out until—"

"But everybody's recovered, right? Why would you need to keep family away?"

"We need to understand *how* it happened, their condition, how it improved so quickly and drastically, and until we do…look, we're looking out for Wounded Sky's best interests."

"The patients look terrible. When Elder Mariah got better, she looked better than all these people right away. What's happening with them, if they got better *so quickly and drastically?* Huh?"

Dr. Ament looked like she was scrambling to think of something. "Just, ummm, unforeseen complications in the recovery."

"You don't get better from something, then get sick again right after!"

Dr. Ament took a deep breath. "You know, it might help matters if you would allow us to confirm some evidence we have access to, and take a blood sample."

Cole took a step back. "*You* have the files," he gasped.

"The files? What files?"

"You know exactly what I'm talking about! The experiments when we were kids, how mine worked and the others didn't. Ring a bell?"

"It certainly does not." The clipboard dropped from her chest to her hip, and she raised her own two-way radio. Pressed the button. "I'm calling security."

Cole slapped it away and it skidded down the hallway.

"What do you think you're doing?" Dr. Ament went for the radio, but Cole held her back.

"I think one of your patients needs your attention," he said.

"What?"

Cole ushered Dr. Ament into the room she'd come from. He closed the door and snapped off the door handle, trapping her in there for the time being.

"Let me out of here!" her muffled shout escaped the room, but it wasn't loud enough to alert Mark or anybody else.

"Sorry-not-sorry," Cole called back, "but while you're in there, try being a doctor!"

Cole got to the end of the hallway and turned the corner to find Brady and Eva in the lobby, out of Mark's sight. They had a guest with them, too. In a wheelchair, looking weak, pale, and cold, sat Elder Mariah. When Cole saw her, he didn't question Brady and Eva about why they decided to take her away. She was dying. Again. He rushed over to her, knelt at her side, and put his hand on her hand.

"Elder," he said through tears. "What did they do to you?"

"She won't say." Brady stepped around to the front of the wheelchair and looked at his kókom with a pained expression, as though he were sick, too. "I asked her a bunch of times."

"Elder..." Cole looked her straight in the eyes. She didn't look away, but she didn't say anything. Instead, she put her hand on his. Her skin was like ice. She turned his hand palm up, then raised her index finger and started to trace his scar. All the while, she didn't take her eyes off him.

"Yeah," Cole said, "scars. The northern lights. I remember." He thought back to the time they'd spent by the fire, and the story she'd told him about how the northern lights were created. That the sky had been cut, and out of the wound came the heavens. The northern lights were the scars that came from that wound.

"We need to get her out of here," Brady said.

Elder Mariah shook her head.

"That's all she does when..." Brady put his hands on his hips and stood up "...when I talk about getting her out of here, she just shakes her head, like she wants to stay."

"Not safe," she said weakly.

"Why?!" Brady asked.

Cole grabbed Elder Mariah's hand and squeezed it. "We're getting you out, Elder. We have to. I'll keep you safe."

"Not worried...for...me," she whispered.

"Is your dad this sick?" Cole asked Eva. "Should we get him out too?"

"He said he's fine," Eva said. "He told me not to worry. I mean, he looked fine, so..."

"But is he?"

"Let's just worry about Elder right now, okay? How do we get her away from here?" Eva asked.

"Mark will flip when he sees us," Brady said.

"Leave Mark to me," Cole said. "There's no other way to go. There's a guard at the side exit, too."

They left the lobby, with Cole walking at the front, Brady pushing his kókom behind him, and Eva at their side. Cole first noticed the extinguished garbage can fire, the wood and metal receptacle charred and smouldering. Then he saw Mark. Mark gave Cole a good stare-down, and then he looked the group over, paying special attention to Elder Mariah.

"You're screwed now," Mark said.

Cole saw Mark's hand tightening around the handle of his gun. "We don't want trouble, Mark. We just want to leave."

"You asked for trouble when you broke in." Mark unclipped the strap on his holster. Before he could draw, Cole stepped forward and took a swing at him. Cole's knuckles connected with Mark's chin, and he spun around and collapsed to the ground. His gun came to rest near the garbage can. Cole picked it up and shoved it in the back of his jeans.

"That," Eva said, "was awesome."

"Seconded," Brady said.

"Let's get somewhere safe," Cole said, all business.

Soon, they were out front of Brady and Elder Mariah's place, standing around the fire pit in the front yard, a modest fire burning, not high enough to attract attention. Cole was standing a few feet farther away from the fire than anybody else.

Brady added a piece of wood, then stoked the fire. It snapped, and a few embers jumped into the air. Elder Mariah reached for him and brushed his arm. "Nósisim."

Eva backed away and stood beside Cole, giving Brady and his kókom space.

"Nókom?" Brady said.

"You need to…take me to the land," she said. "Do you know where I mean?"

Brady nodded. "Yeah, your cabin. Why?"

"Because they don't…know about it. They won't find it."

"Nókom, what are you afraid of?"

"I'm more afraid of losing you…than I am of them," she said. "You'll need to come with me…to the land. You'll be safe there…you can help me get my strength back."

"Safe from what?"

"I can't…"

Brady sighed. "How long is this…how long do I have to go for?"

"Don't know," Elder Mariah said, and then she hesitated. She tried to talk, but she couldn't, or wouldn't. "You…"

"What?" Brady took his grandmother's hand. She was shaking. "You're scaring me."

"You need to call…your parents. Have them come, too."

"What?" Brady stood up. He paced back and forth. He crouched down in front of his grandmother, covered his face, and then he rubbed it like he was trying to peel off his skin. Finally, he looked up. "Do you know what you're asking me to do? I haven't talked to them for—"

"I know. But for all they've done, and said…they're still family. Right now, they're in danger."

"Your cabin is…it's really small, Nókom. They're not going to stay in a small cabin like that, not with me. They won't do it. I won't, and they won't."

"I'll figure this out, Brady," Cole said. "It won't be long, I promise."

Brady looked at Cole. "What, now your mission is saving me from my homophobic, intolerant, jerk-face parents?"

"I…" Cole started "…just call it a bonus."

Brady shook his head. "I can't believe this."

"If Elder thinks you need to do this," Eva said, "don't you need to? I couldn't deal with anything happening to you."

"Me neither," Cole said.

"*You* know who you are, B. Screw 'em," Eva said.

"Why do I have to still love those assholes?" Brady asked himself, looking up at the sky, as though trying to temper his anger with the ribbons of light overhead. He threw his arms up in the air. "Alright, fine. Whatever."

Eva walked over to Brady first. No words were exchanged. She just took him in her arms, and gave him a bear hug. Then, she turned to Elder Mariah, leaned over, and kissed the Elder on the forehead.

After Eva, Cole took his turn. He gave Brady a hug, too. They kept hugging while they talked.

"Does this mean I can stay here?" Cole joked, kind of.

Brady laughed into Cole's shoulder. "No."

"Okay." Cole squeezed Brady, but didn't let go. He asked, "Can I at least raid your closet?"

Brady laughed again. "Oh my Gosh, Cole. Yes, you can borrow my clothes."

"Thanks, man."

"Figure yourself out, okay?"

"I will, I promise. I'm sorry, Brady."

"Stop feeling sorry for yourself. If you came here to fix things, then that means stuff was going bad before you got here, and that means it's not your fault." Brady put both hands on Cole's shoulders. "You can do this. Got it?"

"Got it."

Cole leaned over to Elder Mariah. He put his hand on hers. Put his forehead against her forehead. "Elder Mariah," he whispered. "I won't let anything happen to you or Brady."

"I know."

He gave her a gentle hug, then backed away. Brady waved at them, smiled weakly, then walked behind Elder Mariah's wheelchair. He pushed her towards their house to pack whatever they were going to bring. Once they were inside, Eva nudged Cole on the forearm.

He turned to her. "Hey."

"Hey," she said. "What a night."

"Yeah, what a night," he said.

They stood together, looked at each other, trying to cast comforting looks, but they were unconvincing.

"So," she said, "you're heading home now?"

"I guess." He checked the time. 8:57 p.m. "Can't really do anything to avoid it now."

"I could walk you home," she said. "You know, keep you safe. I'm kind of good at that, right?"

"Yeah, you are."

"What would you do without me?"

Die. That's what he would have done. Literally. She held his hand, playfully. She swung it back and forth, as though they were already walking together. She tilted her head towards his house, where his auntie and grandmother were waiting for him.

"Come on," she said.

"You know what..." Cole looked around, at the night, and he thought about what was lurking in the shadows in Wounded Sky. He checked the time again. 8:58 p.m. He only had two minutes, but it didn't matter.

He could be late, for Eva. "I think I should walk you home instead."

19

ALL OVER AGAIN

COLE STOOD ON THE FRONT STEPS of his parents' house, frozen in place, wishing he'd stayed at Eva's when he'd dropped her off. If there were more rocks through the window, then there were more rocks through the window. He would've ducked. He would've been hit. Getting hit with rocks was better than this. His knees were buckling, his pulse was racing, and his muscles were shaking from exertion. He put his hand on the door to steady himself. He tried to breathe in slowly, but he couldn't. His lungs were full already, and there was no room for air. He was blacking out. The darkness was coming.

"Help."

"Cole."

He could feel a hand take his. Tears were running down his cheeks. Auntie Joan was standing in the doorway. Cole's grandmother was standing behind his aunt. She looked sad for him, worried for him.

"Let's get you up." She was strong. She led him inside, towards the kitchen. He was a little boy again. Wearing a yellow shirt and blue over-alls. Two years old. He was running down the hallway. A monster was chasing him. He was too scared to look behind. He looked ahead, only ahead. He turned the corner into the kitchen. His mother was there, sitting on the chair, arms out. She saved him.

His first memory.

Auntie Joan brought him to the kitchen table. Dust exploded from the chair as he sat down. She went to the fridge. It groaned and wheezed, clinging to life, as she opened it. She took out a bottle of water. He could feel his grandmother behind him, her hands on his shoulders. Groceries were spread out on the kitchen counter. Bread. Peanut butter. Cereal. Auntie Joan came back with the water and handed it to Cole. He could hardly hang onto it. Water spilled out because his hand was trembling.

"Where are they?" Auntie Joan said as she felt at his pockets. She found what she was looking for. She curled her fingers inside his pocket, and pried out the pill bottle. She took out two pills. Cole counted them as he kept trying to take deep breaths, but they were shallow. *One, two.* She placed the pills into his free hand and told him to swallow them. He hadn't taken a pill in days. Something felt wrong about it.

"Take them," she said.

She put her hand under his, and moved his hand towards his mouth. He tried to stop her. "I don't..." he started to say, but said nothing else. He was weak.

"You're having a panic attack." She took the pills from his palm, and placed them into his mouth herself, then guided the water bottle to his lips. He could feel some of the water spill against his pants. He could feel the pills dissolve on his tongue as cold water seeped into his mouth.

He swallowed.

"There," she said.

His grandmother squeezed his shoulders. "It's okay, Nósisim."

"Give it a minute." Auntie Joan closed the pill bottle, shoved it back into his pocket.

"Twenty-six minutes," he said.

"What?" she asked.

"It takes twenty-six minutes," he repeated.

"Give it twenty-six minutes," his grandmother said behind him.

The act of taking the medication helped to calm him—at least enough so that he could breathe, and as he breathed a bit deeper this, too, set him more at ease. He could only feel so much calm, however, with his auntie and grandmother staring at him. He knew they were trying to help, but still, the last thing he ever wanted during a panic attack were people breathing down his neck, loved ones or not. He needed to be alone, in the dark, and with music. "I want to lie down."

Auntie Joan looked at her mother and then nodded quickly.

"Sure," she said. "Of course."

Cole pushed himself to his feet. His auntie grabbed his forearm to help him, but he was already almost standing.

"Do you need—" she said as Cole started to walk out of the kitchen using the wall, the door frame, whatever he could get his hands on for balance.

"No, I'm good." He wasn't. Not really. Not yet. But he needed his Auntie Joan—God love her—to leave him be. His knees were tenuously supporting his weight. He kept telling himself that he was almost there. *Twenty more steps, Cole. Come on. Nineteen, let's go.* And eventually, he got to his bedroom.

If it wasn't for the early work of the pills his auntie had stuck in his mouth, being there might've made his panic worse. Everything in the house would have. Clear memories, like they happened yesterday, came to him. The kitchen smelled of the food his mother and father used to make him. Oatmeal for breakfast. A bowl of rice and ground beef, mixed together with ketchup, and vegetables on the side for supper. Down the hallway, with each step, his dad, carrying him from the bathroom to the bedroom, wrapped up in a towel, making him fly through the air with spaceship sounds. In his bedroom, it was the night his mother told him that his father died. The clearest of all memories, and the one from this house that had stayed with him more than any others. Hiding under the comforter, reading comics. Her careful steps, unsure of what the future would be like after she told him. The smell of her as he buried his face into her shoulder.

Lilacs. Laundry.

Fifteen minutes had passed by the time Cole made his way across the bedroom, and to his bed. He pulled the comforter from his bed, and shook the dust off. He put the comforter back onto his bed the same way his mother used to after she'd returned from the mall with clean laundry. He lifted it up in the air, where it floated for a moment, like a feather. He let it fall, slowly, until it wrapped itself around the bed. He lay down on top of the comforter, propped his head up onto the pillow, stuck earbuds in his ears, and played his go-to music when he needed to get through an attack. *For Emma, Forever Ago.*

That's where he was. Forever ago. Stuck there now, counting down the minutes until his brain would allow him to just be there, just exist there, without the fear, the pain, the panic. Seven minutes to go. The length of two songs. *Breathe. Just breathe.* He closed his eyes. He listened to the music and moved his lips as though he were singing. Finally, twenty-eight minutes after his auntie had given him the pills, he slipped into sleep.

Cole heard distant shouting. He had been having this nightmare over the last decade. Soon the shouting would turn to screams of terror and desperation. Screams from children. He'd be running—running from the banks of Silk River towards the screams—and how odd that amid those screams of horror, the horizon would look so beautiful. A sunset. The evening sky painted liberally with oranges and yellows and reds. He'd be running, and then he would stop in front of the school and see it burning.

"No," Cole whispered, his eyes closed.

He buried his face into his pillow and pushed the sides of the pillow into his ears. There was muffled shouting. Not terror, maybe, but Cole heard desperation. And he wasn't sitting by the banks of Silk River. Gradually, he realized that he was awake in bed—that he wasn't dreaming. Like so many times in the last two weeks, the nightmare was real.

The pills. They made him feel disoriented—level, somewhere close to calm, but detached. It was a wonder that he'd woken up at all. He checked the time quickly. 2:07 a.m. He sat up in bed, and looked out the window, to see why people were shouting. Something was happening. He'd failed. Again. He slept through it. There'd be more blood on his hands. He couldn't see anybody out the window, but the waking nightmare continued. The nighttime horizon was beautiful again. Like a sunset, painted in oranges and yellows and reds.

"No!"

Not again. Not now. Cole charged out of bed, out of his bedroom, out of the house, and ran faster when he got outside. *No, no, no,* he kept thinking as he pushed his legs to go faster than they'd ever gone before. The gravel pathways that weaved their way through the community were like rivers of brown water flowing beneath Cole's feet. The trees that lined the pathways blurred like scenery outside a car window on the highway. The sting of Wounded Sky's autumn breeze whipped against Cole's face.

No.

He ran towards the horizon, tears streaming from his eyes. His arms working furiously. His legs pushing, pushing…towards the pretty colours, and the horror. The shouting was behind him now. Still coming, but not as fast as he was. Not nearly.

The Fish. Cole slid to a stop in front of the diner. The heat enveloped his body and started to burn his skin. The whole building was up in flames.

"No!" Cole shouted.

He listened for screams, for somebody trapped inside. All he heard was the fire. Crackling. Roaring. Somebody could still be inside. Passed out from smoke inhalation. Dying. Burning. He pictured his friends, his teachers, his mother, in the gym, at the school, ten years ago. Dying. Burning. There was a time when they stopped screaming, too.

Cole didn't wait a second longer. He ran into the building, through the flames, through the smoke. He ran through the diner, behind the counter, into the kitchen, squinting through tears, from pain and smoke, looking for bodies. Within moments, he was certain that there weren't any. Within moments, his clothes and skin were burning. He found his way back to the front doors, or where the front doors used to be, and ran outside. He collapsed on the sidewalk leading up to the diner. He was coughing. Crying. He clawed at the ground and pulled himself farther away. When he'd inched far enough onto the main path, which forked off to the Fish and the X, he pulled himself up to his feet and stood there watching the diner burn. There was nothing else he could do. Smoke rose from his own body, and into the night sky.

"Harper!"

Tristan was at the front of a gathering crowd of Wounded Sky community members just now arriving. Cole looked across the sea of faces, all lit in warm colours by the relentless flames. Some were staring at the burning building in disbelief. More were staring at Cole. Cole knew the look on their faces. It was the clinic all over again. Everybody thinking—knowing—that he had done it. That he had murdered people. That he had brought the sickness to the community. That he had set the Fish on fire. He started to back away as Tristan kept walking towards him.

"I didn't…" Cole raised his arms, extending them towards Tristan. His skin was red, burned, still steaming. "I was trying to…"

"Trying to what? Get back at everybody for turning on you?"

"I'm not getting back at anybody, Tristan. I saw the fire out my window, I…"

"And you got here that fast?" He was standing in front of Cole, and shoved his finger into Cole's chest.

"I ran…" Cole said weakly.

"You ran, from your house to here, that fast?" Tristan looked around. "We all ran, Harper. You were already here. Already…" Tristan grabbed at Cole's shirt, burned and ragged "…like this. How?"

"He did it!" somebody shouted from the crowd.

"I…stop…stop moving." Tristan was spinning. The crowd was spinning. The fire. Everything.

"I'm not moving. I'm standing right here. Be a man."

"Stop…" Cole backed away again. He stumbled and fell backwards, bracing himself with his arms. He felt one of his forearms snap. But that pain didn't matter. The real pain was around him, the sea of faces closing in on him, looking at him. Shouting at him. Again.

Cole got to his feet. Tristan shoved him with both hands, and Cole staggered back again. This time, he turned around and used the momentum to propel himself away. From Tristan. From the crowd. From the fire. He was running again. Running away. Running home.

20

DISCOVERY

COLE RAN INTO HIS HOUSE AND LOCKED THE DOOR. He rushed past his auntie and grandmother into his bedroom. He slammed the door, shoved a desk in front of it, and went to bed. But Cole couldn't fall back asleep. He was sitting up, back against the wall, listening. Listening for the mob. Listening to his auntie and grandmother whispering in the hallway. Listening to them pace in front of his bedroom door. Listening to the doorknob jingle every few minutes. Listening to the repeated attempts to talk to him. Attempts that he ignored.

Cole heard footsteps approaching from across the yard, and reaching the front door.

Knock, knock.

He heard voices. Lauren's. Jerry's.

"Constables?" he heard his auntie say.

"Can we come in?" he heard Lauren ask.

They were standing behind the screen door. It creaked open. Lauren and Jerry walked inside and stood in the hallway.

"What's going on?" his grandmother asked.

"The Fish burned down," Jerry said.

Cole got up from his bed, walked to his bedroom door, and moved the desk out of the way. He stood there at the door and waited.

"What?" his auntie said.

"That's what all the commotion's about," Jerry said.

"We need to talk to Cole," Lauren said.

His auntie and grandmother didn't say anything for a few seconds. They were probably thinking about how Cole had ran out of the house, and then, soon after, ran back inside.

"Why?" his auntie finally asked.

"Because he's a suspect," Jerry said.

"He was there before anybody else," Lauren said.

"Says who?" his grandmother asked.

"Says everybody," Jerry said, "alright?"

Footsteps were coming towards his bedroom door. Cole backed away, as though he'd been shoved by Tristan again. But now, there was nowhere to run. The door opened.

"Cole, the constables—" his auntie started.

"I know," Cole said.

"Of course you do, you little pyro," Jerry said.

"*Jerry*," Lauren said.

"We got you dead-to-rights this time, boy," Jerry said.

"I only went there because I saw it was burning, too. I wanted to help," Cole said.

"You and your helping. Look where it's gotten us," Jerry said.

"It got us down one murderer, that's where," Lauren said.

"You can't prove anything," Cole said.

Jerry laughed. "Look at you, are you kidding me? Your clothes are all burnt, your skin's all red…"

"I went inside to see if anybody was trapped inside," Cole pleaded.

"…to see if you'd killed anybody trying to send a message, more like," Jerry said.

"Oh, what message would that be?" Cole's auntie piped in. "Why would my nephew burn down the Fish after he'd found a killer? Saved people?"

"And after the community had just honoured him," his grandmother said.

Jerry ignored Cole's grandmother and auntie. "His arm's hurt just like people said. I mean, come on. Nobody's blind here, kid."

"Tristan did this," Cole lifted his arm, which now only looked swollen a bit.

Jerry shook his head. "Doesn't matter what you say now, anyway. Doesn't matter if the whole damn community saw you standing there all burned up from what you did." He took a plastic evidence bag out from behind his back. Cole recognized the toque he'd purchased at the mall. Black. Native Pride. "Because we got this, too. Not burned. Right outside the diner."

"Where'd you get that?" Panic fought to get out despite the medication. Cole could feel it thumping from inside, banging on his ribs for release.

"I lost that the other night." Cole tried to touch the bag, but Jerry took it away.

"Oh, you mean the night of the *other* fire at the mall?" Jerry took out the plastic bag again, and shook it in the air like a bell.

"This really doesn't look good for you, Cole," Lauren said.

"No, I heard him leave, he wasn't gone that long," his auntie said to the constables.

"Maybe not, but Cole's our number one suspect right now," Lauren said. "Our only suspect."

"We need to look around," Jerry said.

"For what?" Auntie Joan asked.

Jerry looked at Lauren for some help. Lauren just shrugged, like: *you go ahead.* Jerry gave it a shot. "We're looking for stuff Cole might've used. An acc...accel..."

"Oh my God, Jerry, it's like you're reading *Green Eggs and Ham,*" Lauren tried to say under her breath, but it came out clearly. She took over. "We want to see if there's anything here that could've been used as an accelerant for the fire—"

"And matches," Jerry added proudly.

"Yeah Jerry, and matches. Look, Joan," Lauren said, "if Cole really didn't do this...I mean, we could get a warrant."

"No, go ahead and look around," Auntie Joan said. "We've got nothing to hide."

Lauren nodded at her. "We'll try not to be too long."

Cole hovered around his room while Jerry and Lauren started to look around. It probably wasn't a good idea. Watching the constables look through his stuff made him look guilty. That is, if he could've possibly looked guiltier than he did now, first person at the fire, and the whole community there to see it. Who would've found his toque and placed it there? Probably the same person that called and said they'd seen him at the mall.

After Cole's bedroom, Lauren and Jerry went from room to room the same way, with Jerry tossing things all over the place and Lauren (compensating for her acting-boss) being as tidy as possible. Jerry didn't even look like he was trying to find anything. He was just pulling things out of drawers, books out of book shelves, cutlery out of drawers. At one point, he mentioned to Lauren that they were finally doing some real police work. Lauren shot back that it was amazing what you could do when you were actually awake.

By the time they got to the last room, Cole's father's office, they had been searching for over an hour. His dad's office had lots of stuff in it. Cole's dad, Donald, had been really smart, and really disorganized. Books upon books were crammed onto shelves that lined the walls. Stacks of papers, files, and notebooks were piled on top of his desk so the surface wasn't visible anywhere. Lauren and Jerry looked through any place Cole could've hidden an accelerant. Circled the room in some kind of weird dance. Crossed the room, walked around the perimeter, almost bumped into each other a few times. Cole started to count floorboards, from one end of the room to the other. Back to front, left to right.

One floorboard seemed to depress deeper than the other boards each time Lauren, and especially Jerry, stepped on it. It let out a *creak*, the same one Cole tried to avoid when he'd sneak into his dad's room. Each time they stepped over it, he hoped they wouldn't notice and pull it up. He was sure there was something underneath it. His mind began to race.

After Jerry and Lauren's search was over, Auntie Joan, Cole, and his grandmother, followed the constables to the front door.

"Not even a single match, huh?" his auntie confirmed as they stepped outside.

"It's very possible he hid stuff elsewhere," Jerry said. "Not like we don't have enough to go on right now, anyway."

"Anybody see him start a fire?" his auntie asked.

"We'll be talking to everybody who was there tonight, who saw him at the Fish," Lauren said. "See what they all have to say."

"Don't go anywhere, kid," Jerry said.

"I couldn't even if I wanted to."

"Are you okay?" his auntie asked him after the constables had left.

They were all standing in the hallway, and it had been quiet for several minutes.

"We know you didn't do this," his grandmother assured.

"Everybody else will think I did," Cole said.

"Not everybody," his auntie said.

"I can think of two people who wouldn't." Cole pictured Eva and Brady. Brady wouldn't even know about the fire, though. By now, he'd be at the cabin, deep within Blackwood Forest. "Maybe three." Cole added Pam to the group, hopefully.

"Five," his grandmother said.

"Against how many?" Cole took a deep breath, and thought about something he could control. Something he could do, now. "You know what? I'm exhausted. I need to just sleep."

"This is why we came home, nephew," his auntie said. "You know that, right?"

"Right." Cole went back to his bedroom, where he lay down and pretended to sleep. He waited until he heard his grandmother and his auntie go to bed, too. Waited until they were actually asleep. Then, he went back to his dad's office.

He stood in the middle of the room, looking at the floorboard, waiting for his dad to catch him and kick him out. He'd done the same thing the day after his dad had died. He'd gone into the office, sat at his dad's desk, and waited, *prayed*, for his dad to come find him, yell at him, and kick him out.

He sat at his dad's desk for hours that day.

Cole got onto his knees and felt around the floorboard. He pushed at it and ran his fingers along the edges. It definitely felt different than any other area of the floor, but it was still nailed down. If his dad had been hiding anything underneath, whenever he took it out, he pulled out the nails, and then when he put it back, he nailed the floorboard back again.

Cole couldn't find a hammer. He tried to get a grip on the edges of it in order to pry it open, but wasn't able to. He got a knife from the kitchen as quietly as he could. No use. The knife was too fat to wedge between the cracks. That left Cole with one option. Punch the floorboard and break it open. He got the comforter from his room, and placed it over top of the floorboard to muffle the sound. Then, he raised his fist in the air, and struck down as hard as he could. He stifled a scream as he felt his arm re-fracture.

The sound wasn't catastrophic, but it was still loud. He waited a minute to see if he'd woken anybody up. He listened for movement. When he was sure it was safe, he slipped the comforter away from the floorboard, and then pulled the broken halves from the floor. Inside, there was a black carrying case. Cole pulled it out, using his good arm, and opened it up. An old laptop.

Unsurprisingly, the laptop was dead. Luckily, the power cord was in the case. He found a power outlet by the desk, and plugged it in. He waited as the machine whirred to life. His excitement faded quickly. The laptop was password protected. Cole tried three different passwords—his mom's name, his name, his birthdate—and they were all wrong. The computer locked him out after his three failed password attempts. He slammed the laptop shut.

"What do I do now?" he asked.

The answer came quickly.

21

PAM

THE LIGHTS WERE OFF IN THE SCHOOL'S COMPUTER LAB, both in the main room and a little side office, and all the monitors were off as well. There was no familiar, steely glow given off by computer screens in the dark. Still, he walked through the lab and into the office to be sure. You never knew with gamers. Maybe she'd fallen asleep there, and he could wake her up.

But Pam wasn't there. Just the suggestion of Pam. An empty can of Coke resting beside the keyboard. A small bag of baby carrots beside the can. She had an awesome chair, and Cole didn't know how she had swung it. It was like she was either going to hack into a website or command the U.S.S. Enterprise.

(Choch here. I know it's been awhile, folks. I'm interrupting, on one hand, just because I miss you. But really, I wanted to add, and I don't usually give Mr. Robertson much credit, that you should appreciate what he just sacrificed for art. You see, he's a Star Wars *fan, but the chair reference required a* Star Trek *connection. I have to tell you, it was tough. Whatever you give the book on Goodreads, just know that.)*

Cole took off his backpack and sat down. Rather, he *sunk* into the chair, and into a deep and satisfying oblivion. He told himself that he was staying in the chair because he was waiting on the off-chance that Pam showed up, but really it was so damn comfortable. And he was so damn tired.

"Harper."

Cole opened his eyes. The lights were on. He sat up and checked the time. 8:38 a.m. He'd fallen asleep.

"Hey." Cole rubbed sleep from his eyes, got up from the chair. "Sorry."

"All good." Pam sat down, rolled up to the desk, and flicked her computer on. Cole watched as it fired up. She opened up a black screen with green letters and digits, like she was in *The Matrix*, and started typing. Cole wasn't sure what to make of that. He'd managed to sneak his way through Wounded Sky, and to the school, without encountering one person. He'd left his grandmother and auntie sleeping. Pam was the first person he'd seen. Did she hate him?

"Are you about to hack into the mainframe? Can you change my Land-Based Education grade to an A? No, B. I don't want it to seem too obvious."

"Oh, you're funny now, are you?" Pam kept typing. Faster than ever. "Just hang on a sec, okay?"

Was that annoyance? Was she annoyed at him because she thought he was some arsonist? Because she thought he'd gone and burned down the diner, the spot they had their first date? He said, "Okay," with his tail between his legs. He sat on the desk behind her and waited, with the laptop bag hugged between his hand and his hip. He waited for an uncomfortably long time. Cole wasn't sure if she was doing actual things, or if she was intentionally making him squirm. Either way, with one last, pronounced keystroke she finally finished, and swivelled her chair around to face him.

"Sorry about that," she said breathlessly, like she'd been running a marathon.

"What was that?" Cole pointed at the computer screen.

"Oh, that?" Pam turned the monitor off, then faced Cole once again. She waved her hand once over her head and made a *whooosh* sound.

"Over my head."

"Slightly," Pam said, "sorry."

"Don't be." Cole sighed enormously.

"Rough day at the office, or what?"

"You tell me."

"Well, if I were you, and thank God I'm not…"

"Rough day at the office," Cole agreed.

"If it makes any difference, I'm sure not all the kids think you're the worst person alive?"

"That bad?"

"Know how I said to join the group chat?" Pam didn't wait for a response. "Don't."

"Yeah, that sounds pretty damn bad."

"In their defence, and not saying that I believe it, you *were* at the diner before everybody else, and by all accounts, your clothes were all burned up," she said.

Cole looked at his shoes. "When I saw the fire from my window, all I could think of was the school fire. I felt like I was back there. So I ran there like I could, I don't know, run back in time. Ran into the Fish in case…"

"Nobody got hurt," Pam assured, "except…" she grabbed his arm, turned his forearm around, inspected it carefully "…people said your arm was, like, in an S shape. Tristan pushed you or something?"

Cole took his arm back, covered his forearm with his other hand. "Probably just the shadows or something. I think it's just sprained."

"Oh, right." Cole wasn't sure if Pam sounded convinced or not. He thought not, but she didn't keep at him about it. "So, wanna know what I'd do? Because it'll just get worse. I mean, there're kids on here saying they saw you set the fire, all that."

"I wish that surprised me."

"I'd just ignore all this bullshit and concentrate on the people who're also ignoring all this bullshit," Pam said. "Those are your real friends anyway."

Cole slid off the desk, walked over to Pam, crouched down beside her. "Thanks."

They looked at each other for a moment.

"That's screwed up, though, about the Fish. How am I ever going to accurately relive the first time we hung out outside of school?"

"I think they should fix it just the way it was," Cole said. "I bet they can fix it like that."

"Maybe by that time you might actually ask *me* to hang out."

Cole rested his forehead against the armrest of her chair, then lifted his head back up. "I'm sorry. Things have been so crazy. It's not that…"

"You don't have to, you know. I can take it."

"No, it's not that I don't want to. Really, I've had, like, no time to even breathe."

"Well, there's a million things to do here, so…" Cole still had the laptop bag clutched against his body and, more and more, Pam was noticing it. Her eyes were darting back and forth between him and the bag. Cole wasn't subtle. He may as well have been carrying a baby. "But this isn't a social call, is it?"

"Not exactly, sorry," he said. "But I was glad I had to come see *you* for this."

"Not just any geek?"

"You're my favourite geek, and also not a geek."

"I like being a geek," she said. "It's all good. Plus, lucky for us, I'm kind of the only one. Whaddya got?"

Cole sat on the floor and flipped the bag onto his lap. He pulled out the laptop and handed it to Pam. "I found this in my dad's office last night."

"What are you, trying to get some pictures off it or something?" she asked.

"I mean, it'd be awesome if there were old pictures of me and him," he said, "but I think there's stuff on here that's…different than that."

"Files-related?" She placed the laptop onto her table, shoving her keyboard to the side, and flipped it open.

"Maybe," Cole said. "Maybe answers of any kind, I guess."

"Ahhh," the login screen popped up, "you got booted out."

"I tried, like, three passwords and that was it."

"You want me to break into it."

"Could you?"

Pam locked her fingers together, and extended her arms out, with her palms facing away. Her knuckles cracked in unison. "I thought this was going to be a challenge."

Cole pumped his fist. "Thank you."

"Is this super urgent, or…"

"I'd put it at the super urgent level, yeah. But, just, however long it takes."

"I'm totally cool with skipping ELA, so…urgent it is."

Cole leaned forward and kissed her on the cheek. He was surprised by the kiss as much as she was. He wished he hadn't done it, because he felt stupid, and at the same time he wished that he'd tried two inches to the left, on the lips. But now didn't seem like the time.

"You've got to buy me dinner first, Harper." Pam turned towards the laptop, stared at the screen like she was meditating. "Or at least carrots and Coke."

"Sorry."

He saw Pam smile a half-smile, and then she flipped him the bird. "Get the hell out of here. I've got work to do."

When Cole saw his locker, he fell back against the opposite wall. Rumours travelled fast in Wounded Sky. His locker had been beaten to a pulp, probably by a baseball bat or two. On what Cole could see of the metal, there were words spray painted all over. *Burn in hell, Harper. Eat shit & die. Fake.* He gave himself a minute or two to digest what he was seeing, and to calm himself. The pills were out of his system now.

He approached his locker and pulled it open.

Textbooks and notebooks had been ripped up, defaced with more colourful language. His gym clothes had been torn apart, and his new basketball shoes had been slashed with a knife. Cole picked up the shoes and stared at them. He stared at them for what they'd meant when he first received them, and what they meant now. He dropped them to the floor. Then he dropped to the floor himself. He took his bottle out and slipped a pill into his mouth. He chewed it up and let the morsels dissolve under his tongue, staying there for several minutes, unmoving, even as students began to file into the halls. They opened lockers near him and whispered to others when they saw him, angry words, colourful language, like they were reading the words on his locker, on his textbooks, on his notebooks.

Cole just stayed there, counting one floor tile over and over again.

One. One. One. One. One.

"I mean, what's really sad about this, to me, is the whole counting thing. There's something that tugs at my heartstrings, like when I watch *Armageddon*. You know, the part where the kid sees his dad on TV and asks his mom who he is, and his mom says—"

"Not now, Choch." Cole didn't look up.

"I thought you would've seen the movie, CB. You like watching old movies, don't you? Oh, and the other time I *always* cry is when Bruce Willis calls Ben Affleck 'son.' I can't *even*..."

"No, I've seen it. I'm just not in the mood right now. You've seen my locker, haven't you?"

"Yes," Choch said, and then he recited all the words on the locker to Cole out loud. When he finished, he said to himself, "Not really altogether imaginative now, are they? Just vulgar."

"Could you not join in on the chorus?" But Cole couldn't hear any whispers anymore, or footsteps, or lockers opening and shutting. He looked up to see that every student in the halls was frozen in time. "Oh."

"Just thought we needed some alone time," Choch said.

Cole might've been surprised if he hadn't seen this trick before. "It'd be way worse if it weren't so familiar," Cole said, referencing the graffiti on his locker.

"At least they were using full sentences, and not text-speak. That would have been even more upsetting," Choch said.

"You mean like GTFO?"

Choch gasped loud. "Saying that to *me*, your friendly neighbourhood spirit being?"

"Can you really blame me? Plus you were being an asshole with the whole man-makers thing."

"I was keeping up appearances, CB. No offence intended. What would a class full of teenagers think if I let you get away with coming to class late? Next thing you know, *everybody* would be coming late, or not at all. You know kids. I mean, look at your poor locker."

Cole pushed his back against the locker next to his, staring at the painted bricks on the wall. *One, two, three...*

"Well at least you're actually counting past one now," Choch said. "And like I've always told you, I'm actually very helpful if you listen."

"What, exactly, did you want?" Cole didn't want to listen in the least.

"I was concerned about you, that's all. I came to cheer you up."

"Awesome job. I feel *so* much better."

"Would you care to brainstorm? Run some thoughts by your old buddy? I'm all ears." Choch turned his ears into coyote ears, and said, "Huh? Any takers?" and then he twinkled them.

Cole shook his head. "I'm doing things one at a time. I'm going to get Pam to try and get into the laptop..."

"For your mission, or for yourself?"

"Both, I hope," Cole said. "Then I have to go back to the research facility and try to actually get inside this time. Hopefully, you know, there's no shadow thing waiting for me." Cole paused. Choch allowed for this by not interrupting. Then, Cole shrugged. "But maybe I have to kill it anyway, so it might as well be there."

"I wouldn't try to tussle with that thing." Choch was deadly serious, Cole noticed. "If you don't mind my advice, I'd find the long way around and avoid that thing altogether."

"If it kills me, it kills me."

"What is this I hear? Are you giving up so soon?"

"I'm getting tired. Tired of not knowing, tired of *this*," Cole motioned to his locker, "just tired."

Choch gave Cole a nudge on the hip with his foot. Cole looked the gesture off. "Come on, let's go play HORSE. Better yet, COYOTE. That way, we can spend more time together. And I promise I won't cheat."

"I DON'T HAVE BASKETBALL SHOES!"

Choch knelt down right beside Cole, put his hand on Cole's shoulder. "CB," he said quietly, "you really need to find your calm place. If you get all worked up like that, well, we know how your anxiety is."

"I took a pill. I can shout as loud as I damn-well want. And no, I don't want to play COYOTE with you, or HORSE, or whatever game you think of."

"Look, all I'm saying, relax. Do some mindfulness. That's all the rage right now. Cross your legs, close your eyes, concentrate on your breathing…"

"I do that already."

"Have you considered Buddhism?"

"Considered it how?" Cole turned to the right, away from Choch, as though the spirit being would get the message.

"As a state of mind," Choch said. "Knowing that everything is in a state of change, nothing is static. That means *everything* is connected. People, animals, nature…even laptops."

Cole looked at Choch quickly, who winked back at Cole.

"Well, that might be a stretch. Specifically, manmade things are—"

"Were you actually just trying to help me?"

Choch looked at Cole coyly. "Look at the time. I have to go and inflate some basketballs. Somebody came in and deflated them all, if you can believe it."

"My fan club."

Choch headed back to the gym. On the way, without looking back, he said, "But do try the whole mindfulness thing. I've found it very helpful, when I feel like breathing and, well, just enjoying the human experience. It does get stressful managing all my little jobs."

"Sorry I'm such a screw up!" Cole called out.

Choch stopped, turned around. "Look, don't be so hard on yourself, to echo your friends. Just, I suppose, keep things moving. Yes, the boss is breathing down my neck, but all you can do is try, right?"

"Right."

"If I can say one thing about you, my boy, you do put your heart into it."

"Thanks."

"See? I'm not all bad." Choch moved to leave, but he stopped and poised his fingers in a snapping position. "If you decide to, you know, do the thing with the thing at the thing…"

"The monster, at the research facility," Cole clarified.

"Yeah, the thing at the thing, like I said," Choch said. "If you *do* decide on that, I only ask that you attend to that, err, *situation*, heavily armed. See you later."

Choch snapped his fingers, and the students moved instantly. A kid dumped a bottle of water on Cole's head.

"Cool off, pyro!"

Cole didn't even resist. He just sat on the floor, stared at the wall, and counted painted bricks. He counted bricks up and to the right, until he stopped at the clock.

How long would it take Pam to finish?

22

SAY IT AIN'T SO

COLE STAYED THERE, ON THE FLOOR beside his locker, and endured the abuse he was getting. Kids repeated the words that had been written all over his locker. Kids kicked his feet on purpose, or stepped on them. Glared at him. Threw stuff at him. Pencils, pens, erasers, spitballs, paper balls. He endured all of this until Eva showed up. She just stood in front of Cole's locker, staring at it, staring inside it, her arms crossed, eyes darting back and forth, looking at the damage, reading all the words, and then doing it all over again.

"Hey." Cole got up and stood beside her. He mirrored her, arms crossed, staring at the locker.

"Cole…"

"Things kind of went downhill last night, after I dropped you off."

"You keep running into trouble," she said. "Maybe you should try running the other way next time."

"You know I can't do that."

"What happened?"

Cole walked over to his locker and shut it as best as he could. The metal was warped, though, and it stayed ajar. Cole just shook his head at Eva's question. "I don't know what I'm supposed to do, you know, so when anything happens, *anything*, I have to do something. If I don't…"

She shook her head, too, mirroring him. "How'd you get there so fast?"

"Reading the group text?"

"Just trying to understand."

"You don't think…"

"No, no of course not. It's just, God, Cole, you must be the unluckiest person ever."

Cole nodded and moved back beside Eva. They both kept staring at the locker. He read the graffiti over and over during the silence. *Fake.* Kept reading that word. *Fake. What did that even mean? Fake. Fake hero?* Somebody shouldered him. He turned around, but it was impossible to tell who. Everybody was looking at him. There were so many kids walking by.

"So where's Mike?" Cole asked.

"I don't know, not answering my texts. Maybe he's sick."

"Maybe he doesn't want to admit that he broke your window."

"There's less evidence for that than there is against you, Cole," Eva said, and it made Cole feel small, like he should've kept his stupid mouth shut. "Deflect much?" she added.

"Sorry," he said.

"No," she said, "I'm sorry, I…I feel so guilty about what we did."

"What we almost did."

"I wanted to, that's enough."

"I wanted to, too."

"Like Mike needs that. Like he needs that right now."

"I know."

Eva looked around, like she was expecting Michael to show up just then. Somebody threw a paper airplane at Cole's head. "Listen," she said, "I'm going to get to class, okay?"

She wasn't inviting him to join her. He didn't blame her. He didn't blame anybody for staying away from him.

"Sure," he said. "I'm going to, I guess, just clean up this mess a bit."

But she was already gone, already off to class. ELA. Cole approached his locker, opened it, crouched down, and started to pull items out. His shoes. His gym clothes. He started in on the ripped up textbooks when he felt a hand on his shoulder. He turned quickly, aggressively, and shouted, "What?"

Lucy flinched, but recovered quickly. She kept her hand on his shoulder long enough to pat him twice, and smiled with her eyebrows raised.

"Sorry," Cole said. "It's been a rough morning."

"How bad is it that I totally want to make a joke about you being hot under the collar or something?"

Cole shrugged. Lucy took a step closer.

"Are you a closet bad-ass, Cole?"

"I didn't—"

"Hey, you're getting shit on by people who think their shit doesn't stink, and you decide you've had enough. No judgment here."

"It's not like that." Cole wasn't sure if her proximity or attitude made him feel off-balance. The bell rang for class. Cole started on his way there, hoping that she'd leave him, but she followed him.

"I'll burn this place down with you, whaddya say?"

Her eyes were fiery and fearless. Cole at once felt scared and envious of that. If he were that way, all of this crap now wouldn't hurt him as much. "Hard pass," he said, "since I didn't set anything on fire."

"Yeah but, what about now? You may as well have a target on your shirt."

"And what's different for you? You don't hate me?"

"Nah," she said, "I've been in your shoes. I'm *in* your shoes." She kicked him on the side of the foot in stride.

"Because your dad is…"

"Because my dad *is*, yeah."

"That sucks."

"It is what it is," she said. "You get used to it. Trust me."

"When?" Cole asked, maybe a bit too desperately. "When do you get used to it?"

"Just wait until my dad does something dumb again. They'll forget all about you. Patience, Cole. Dad's good for it, believe me."

They got to class. Cole gave Lucy a genuine smile, and then he turned to head into the room, wondering if he'd get hit with a paper ball or a spitball first. Lucy grabbed his arm.

"Hey," she said, "there's that debate tonight. My dad and Anna Crate. At the community hall."

"I hadn't heard about that."

"Wanna come with me? You can do something *actually* lit."

"Very funny," Cole said. "No thanks. Big crowds and me don't mix. Especially now."

Lucy's shoulders slumped dramatically. "What's a girl have to do to piss off her dad?"

"Sorry," Cole said, "not interested in getting knocked out again."

"God, do you play hard to get. Suit yourself." Lucy pretended to brush some dust off her shoulder, then she pushed past Cole into class.

Cole waited outside of class for a moment, opened the door a crack, and looked inside at the students in the room. All of them, except for Eva, and maybe Lucy, were ready to make the next hour a living Hell. Just because he was used to it, it didn't make it any easier. So, instead of going in, he closed the door quietly and turned away. He moved down the hallway, to the back door of the school, and left. He walked across the field and found a spot just outside of Blackwood Forest, at the edge of the school grounds.

He sat there and tried not to think about anything that had happened, any word that his classmates had said or written, and not about the things he still had to do, or the things he had done. He just sat there and waited. He closed his eyes, and breathed. *In five seconds, out seven seconds.* Sometime after that, maybe minutes, maybe an hour, maybe more, Cole felt his phone buzz in his pocket. As it turned out, it was close to noon.

PAM: **Where you at?**

COLE: **Hiding.**

PAM: **So are we playing a game or do you want your laptop? If I'm "it" I'm cool with that.**

COLE: **Back of the field.**

PAM: **You suck at this game.**

A few seconds later, the back door to the school opened, and out walked Pam, the laptop bag hanging from her shoulder. She handed him the laptop bag once she'd crossed the field, then she sat down beside him. "I thought you were going to give me something hard to do."

"Wow, thanks. I thought it would take all day."

"Cole," she said glibly. "All I had to do was use a Hirens Boot CD."

"Right, a Hirens Boot CD. *Obviously.*"

"I'm just being a shit. I know you don't know what that is. But it *was* easy."

"This seriously made the day not so shitty."

"But still pretty shitty."

Cole shrugged. He opened the bag and pulled out his dad's laptop. Fired it up, and found that it was no longer password protected. "Awesome."

"I should leave you to it," she said, and got up.

"You don't…"

"Yeah, I do. This was your dad's, Cole. You need your privacy. It's cool."

Cole stood up. "Hey, thanks." He gave her a hug, and patted her on the back.

"Let me know how it turns out," she said, and then she headed back towards the school.

"'Kay," Cole said with Pam already too far to hear. He sat back down, clicked on his dad's first name, Donald, and got to the home screen. Whatever the desktop wallpaper used to be couldn't have been important. Cole laughed when he saw that Pam had taken the liberty to change the wallpaper to a shot of her, in her computer room, flashing devil horns at the camera, her tongue sticking out. He stared at it for a solid ten seconds before starting on his search for information. He checked the browser history first, but there was nothing of interest there. His dad was interested in NHL and NFL, movies, MySpace, and medical sites like the Mayo Clinic.

"Okay, Dad." Cole searched through the folders on the desktop. There were lots of "medical and research type documents" in those folders (as Cole put it), but nothing he could understand, and nothing, from what he could tell, that was anything like the files he'd found at the camp. Still, showing Dr. Captain all the documents wouldn't hurt. He'd throw them on a jump stick and give them to her when he had the chance.

Next, Cole checked his dad's email. Most of the messages were to and from co-workers at the research facility. He also found short emails between his mom and dad. Cole read them over and over again. They weren't about anything, really, but that didn't matter. He could hear his dad's voice, his mother's, and that was enough.

DONALD: Hey, can you bring me an extra sandwich for lunch? I didn't eat anything this morning.

BEV: Yes. Cole will probably eat another, too. You need to remember to eat, Don. Especially when you aren't sleeping!

DONALD: It won't always be like this. It's just busy right now. We're close.

BEV: You've been close forever.

To Cole, all of these emails were like poetry, like songs with the most beautiful lyrics. It was a while before he moved on from them, and he only did because he saw other emails exchanged between his dad and another woman. Vikki Folster.

DONALD: I think we should do it tomorrow. Why do you keep waiting, Vik?

VIKKI: He'll know. He'll find out. I know he will. I can't do it tomorrow. I don't know if I should do it at all.

DONALD: You said that last week, too. If we're going to do this, we have to do it. It will never feel like the right decision, but it is.

VIKKI: Have you talked to Bev? Does she know?

DONALD: No, she doesn't know, and she doesn't have to. It's safer that way. It's just between us. When people have to know, they can know.

VIKKI: I'm too scared. What about my girl?

DONALD: I have a place where you can both stay. I can see you there until we can get you somewhere more permanent.

VIKKI: He'll kill me, I know he will.

DONALD: I'm worried about what he'll do if you don't leave.

VIKKI: He doesn't know about you. If he doesn't know, then I'm safe, and so are you, and so is my girl. We should just leave it, and forget about this.

DONALD: You know we can't do that.

VIKKI: Fine. Okay. Tomorrow.

The last message had been sent the day before his dad died. Cole closed the laptop shut slowly, as though if he shut it with any force it would explode.

Everything looked different. Every-goddamn-thing about his father. Cole was only seven at the time, but how the hell could he not have known, not have noticed anything? How could his mother not have known? Did she know? Somebody had to have known. The timing was too perfect. Too horribly perfect. The woman his dad had died with was Vikki, and their death wasn't, couldn't have been an accident. Whomever Vikki was talking about, the person that was going to find out about them, killed them.

Nothing else made sense.

23

HERE LIES...

COLE WALKED TOWARDS THE SCHOOL IN A FOG as the bell rang for lunch. Kids poured onto the field, making camp on the grass to eat their food. Tossing the ball around with lacrosse sticks they borrowed from the gym. Kicking the soccer ball. Listening to music. Yelling profanities and accusations. None of this registered with Cole. He just kept going, step after step, hardly aware of what was happening around him. Nothing felt real. Maybe he was dreaming. He wanted to be dreaming. Maybe it was a nightmare. It had to be a nightmare.

"Cole." Eva was walking beside him. "Where were you this morning?"

Step. Step.

"Are you mad at me? Don't be mad at me."

Step. Step.

"Cole! What's gotten into you?" She grabbed his wrist and tried to hold him up, to turn him towards her.

"No." He shook his head and pulled his wrist away from her hand. She kept walking with him.

Step. Step.

"Seriously. You're scaring me."

Cole didn't answer. He looked ahead, and walked ahead.

"Is there something you're not telling me? What can I do?"

Eva's voice was a hundred miles away. The emails between Cole's dad and Vikki—they were screaming at him.

"Cole!" She was crying. Her voice was shaking, trembling in the autumn wind.

He stopped. He looked at her. Tears glistening, falling down her cheeks. Tears streaming out of her brown eyes.

"Please," she said.

"Leave me alone. I need to be alone."

He could feel her stand there while he walked away, watching him.

He felt like he was walking in the middle of winter, naked. Numb. The cold seeped into his body, into his soul. It was like his body was protecting him from the trauma. Not letting him feel anything. Not anger. Not sadness. Not confusion.

And he walked.

He found himself at the entrance to the cemetery before he realized where he was. He opened the metal gate, oblivious to the shrill squeal as the metal joints ached into movement. He meandered between headstones, framed by granite and marble, wooden crosses, and crumbled stone. He walked away from the well-manicured area that housed his classmates, teachers, and mother, to where the grass grew a bit longer. Where the flowers weren't as fresh, drying at the base of graves. He found his father's headstone and sat down on the long grass in front of it, knowing that there was nothing underneath him. He hugged his knees against his chest and rocked back and forth. He read his father's name, and the inscription, over and over again. *Here Lies Donald Harper. Husband. Father.*

"Lies is right," Cole said to the gravestone, as though not only was his father's body there, but that he was alive and listening. And maybe he *was* sitting beside Cole, having come down from the northern lights just for this moment.

Cole looked around. He saw a stone a few feet away. He reached over and picked it up.

He hit the stone against the inscription, against the word *father* as hard as he could. Again and again, harder and harder. Chunks of marble flew all over the place and disappeared into the grass. Within moments, *father* was almost illegible.

"You shit!" Cole shouted at the headstone.

The words started to blur, as tears welled up in his eyes. Cole threw the stone with all his strength. It disappeared into the sky. He collapsed forward, forehead against the marble, arms resting on top of the headstone.

"Why'd you do it? Answer me! I know you can hear me!"

"Coley?"

Cole was breathing hard. Sobbing harder. He could feel Jayne's heat, but he didn't turn around to see her. He was trying to breathe deep, in and out, but couldn't. His breath quivered despite the warmth.

"Coley, you okay?"

He felt fire against his back, then the heat was taken away.

"Sorry!" She'd used her burning hand to touch him. He wanted to ask her to put that same hand back, to feel the fire. To burn his thoughts away.

To burn everything away.

"It's okay," he said.

"What're you doing anyways?" she asked.

Cole fell backwards, to the spot where he'd been sitting before, knees to chest. He wiped his tears away with his jeans. "Nothing, Jayney. I'm just seeing…" he stopped at calling his dad, *Dad*. Didn't want to call him something so intimate, personal, affectionate.

"He's not here though, you know that," Jayne whispered, like she didn't want Cole to feel stupid, but everybody knew his dad wasn't actually buried there.

"Yeah," he said, "I know that. I know. I just didn't know where else to go."

"Why're you so sad?" she asked. "I can feel it all over."

Cole looked at her. Her flames were low. She looked almost normal.

"You don't have to be sad, too," he said.

"Yeah I do, you're my friend," she said.

Cole smiled at her, and her flames flared up a bit. He stood up and looked at his dad's headstone for another minute. He looked at the damage he had inflicted on the word *father*. "He's just not what I thought he was."

"What, like he was a secret agent or something?"

"No, not like that." He thought of how to explain it to a seven-year-old girl, ghost or human. "He did things I didn't think he'd do, that's all. And it made me mad."

"You were hitting that with a rock." Jayne pointed at the headstone.

"Did I scare you?" he asked.

Jayne nodded. "Yeah, but I was more sad, that's all."

"Me, too." Cole reached out, and took Jayne's non-burning hand. Gave it a comforting squeeze. "You don't have to be sad anymore."

"Okay." She grew a little brighter still.

"Come on." He wasn't sure where to go, so he just kept dragging Jayne along with him. She thought all the zig-zagging was fun. She kept getting brighter and hotter. Finally, when Cole saw the headstone he was looking for, he stopped abruptly. Jayne let out a groan, sad that their trip all around and through the cemetery was over. Cole stared at the name on the headstone.

Vikki Folster.

"Ever see her up there, dancing?" Cole asked.

Jayne leaned forward, squinted her eyes at the name, sounded it out. "Vi...Vikki...Fos...no...Fol...Folster. I don't know. Maybe. I never saw that name before so I don't know who she is. What does she look like, do you know that? Because then I'd know."

"I have no idea what she looks like."

"We don't really have names up there, you know. We just kind of dance and we just know our colours and stuff. Why do you wanna know about her?"

"I just do. I just need to know, Jayney."

"Well she's not down there, you know that? I can tell. She's not anywhere here at all." Jayne looked around the cemetery, presumably for spirits that she could see, and he could not.

"Yeah," Cole said. "But I know exactly where she is."

24

DONALD

COLE WALKED INSIDE AND PAST THE KITCHEN, where he dismissed questions from his auntie and his grandmother. He walked down the hallway—ignoring the pictures of his father and his mother affixed to the walls—and into his bedroom. He shut the door and sat on the edge of his bed. He stayed like that, hands interlocked and resting on his lap. No music. Just staring at a piece of flooring that had been chipped off at some point. He couldn't remember how it had happened.

Cole didn't know what time it was when he heard a hesitant knock on the bedroom door.

"Cole." The knocking doubled, the sound of knuckle against wood increased.

Cole didn't respond. Finally, his grandmother opened the door, and stood in the doorway.

"What's going on, grandson?" she asked.

Cole shrugged.

"Do you have spares this afternoon?" she asked.

He leaned back onto his hands, looked away from the floor, to the window, imagining what lay beyond the blackout blinds.

"What's wrong? Did something else happen?" she asked.

Oh, just my life crashed down right on my head, he thought. *No big deal.* He tried his best not to redirect his anger towards her. But how do you do that when you're mad at the entire world? What could he say to her? What if she didn't know about his dad? Of course she didn't know about his dad. His grandmother had never said a bad word about him. If she knew what he'd done, she might not have said anything bad, but she wouldn't have said anything good, either. His auntie didn't know. She didn't hold back on anything, and she wouldn't have held back on his dad. She'd always spoken well of him. Cole decided he could not tell his grandmother what he'd found on his dad's laptop. On *Donald's* laptop. That's what he was going to call him from now on. Did he deserve any better? Did he deserve to die because of what he did?

"Cole, you're making your old kókom nervous If it's just the fire, they'll figure out it wasn't you. We know it wasn't."

He heard his grandmother, kind of. He lifted his legs off the floor and sat like he was seven. *Crisscross apple sauce.* His grandmother walked across the room, sat on the edge of his bed, a safe distance away, careful not to intrude.

"Why are you sitting here in the dark?"

Cole let out a deep breath. All his breath. He breathed in. "I just am."

"You know I won't make you tell me anything."

"Will you make Auntie Joan not make me tell her anything, too?"

His grandmother chuckled. "Yes, I'll tell my daughter to let you be. I just worry about you."

"I know." Cole finally turned to her and rested his head on her shoulder. She gave him a pat on the cheek, and a kiss on the top of his head. "You don't have to. I'm fine."

"If it's one thing that I know, it's that you're not fine."

"I will be then. I will be fine."

"Of course you will be." She gave him another kiss, got up from the bed, and crossed the bedroom.

"Grandma?"

She stopped just at the door.

"Yes?"

"What if you thought you knew somebody, and then, I don't know, you found out something about them, and they were…different? Like you never knew them, ever."

She put her hand on the doorknob. "You need to figure out what version you can trust."

"How do you do that? How do you know what to trust?" Cole thought about the emails. He could recite them, word for word. They were there in black and white. They said what they said. Could he trust that? Why couldn't he? But then he thought about Donald making him breakfast in the morning. Donald holding his hand and taking him away from the exploding Coke bottle they'd just put Mentos in. Donald sitting with him at the picnic table outside the research facility, sharing sandwiches with him, telling him that he worked so hard to buy them good food. Veggies and fruit. Ruffling his hair. Tucking him in at night with a kiss.

Sorry, kiddo.

His grandmother started to back out of the room, closing the door on her way out. "Trust comes from truth. You need to find that truth, grandson."

She closed the door and left Cole sitting in the dark. The blinds let in little slits of light that fell across his body, cutting him into pieces.

25

VIKKI

A TRAY OF COLD FOOD HAD BEEN LEFT INSIDE COLE'S bedroom door over an hour ago, and had remained untouched. After his grandmother left, Cole moved from sitting at the edge of his bed to lying flat on his back. He'd stuck earbuds into his ears and had been listening to *Sleep Well Beast* by The National on repeat. He'd taken more medication, which had helped calm his mind.

After he'd read the emails a fire started to rage inside. Now, underneath his skin he felt charred bones, ashes, and embers. This sensation was new. He hadn't yet encountered it over the years that he'd been living with anxiety, but it was just as unpleasant. The meds had only done so much to soften the feeling.

His legs were spread out, pointing at the edge of either side of the bed, one arm was resting at his side, and he had one hand spread across his chest to monitor his heartbeat, and as though he could push down the burning feeling. He stared at the ceiling. Back in Winnipeg, his therapist had told him to visualize in order to address his anxiety. He now pictured the ceiling as snow, cold and white and falling over him and through him and inside of him.

It did little good.

His favourite song on the album cut out. "The System Only Dreams in Total Darkness." In its place, the *Knight Rider* theme blasted into his ears. Cole ignored it. He didn't even look at his phone, just waited for the ring—one he never downloaded onto his phone—to cut out, and for his song to cut back in. But it didn't. The theme song kept repeating—for how long, Cole didn't know, but its stubbornness won out. He lifted the phone and found a selfie of Choch, from the shoulders up, staring back at him. The spirit being was wearing a purple blazer, orange dress shirt, purple tie, and a vicious little smirk. Cole pressed his thumb against the decline button, but the phone kept ringing and the *Knight Rider* theme song kept playing. Cole answered the phone.

"Yes." Cole let the phone fall against the mattress along with his arm, and returned to staring at the ceiling.

"I'm just checking before I actually do this, because I understand you've had a hard day, but may I please make a pop culture reference?"

"No, you may not."

Cole heard Choch groan through the receiver. "Okay," the spirit being said through gritted teeth. "But don't say you're not my special little guy."

"What did you want, Choch?"

"I have a proposition," Choch said.

"I think we've talked about how I'm not doing any more deals with you. That includes propositions."

"You sound *soooo* much like Ferris trying to sound sick on the phone in *Ferris Bueller's Day Off*," Choch blurted out lightning-fast.

"And then you made the reference anyway." Cole tried to hang up, but his phone—or Choch—would not allow it. Cole took the earbuds out of his ears so that he could no longer hear Choch.

"If you throw the phone out the window next," Choch's voice blared through the phone's speakers, "I will just appear in your room, CB. I'm sure you'd rather speak on the phone than have me talk to you in person, then, afterwards, visit with your auntie and grandmother, then—"

Cole stuck the earbuds back in his ears. "Okay, okay. I'm here."

"Better. Now, with all that out of the way, I have to ask what you've been doing all day."

For such an easy answer, it took Cole a while to respond. He'd been in bed all day, doing nothing. He hadn't eaten, hadn't talked to anybody, hadn't so much as put a toe on the floor.

"But there's a whole lot of something in that nothing, isn't there?" Choch asked.

"Yeah, I guess," Cole said.

"So what were you thinking about, while doing nothing?"

"Just images flashing in my head," Cole said. "Of Donald. All the memories I have of him, and how they all feel different now, like they were lies."

"Fake news!"

"And then of *her*…Vikki…but she has no face, because I've never met her, I don't know her. This girl, too. Vikki's daughter. They look like mannequins, you know?"

"That's super creepy, CB, just saying. This is *not* that kind of story."

"It's not a story, this is my life." It was something Cole felt he'd told Choch repeatedly.

"But I digress. It sounds to me like you could kill two birds with one stone."

"How?" It was partly a question, and partly Cole playing along, in all his frustration, to get Choch off the phone.

"We have this deal you may have heard of, correct?" Choch continued without waiting for an answer, "and you're also very curious about the identity of this woman and her child. What if finding these things out may or may not assist you to some degree in working towards fulfilling some of the requirements our deal entails?"

"That was, like, the most non-committal sentence ever spoken in the history of the world. You know that, right?"

"You have two lovely ladies sitting in the kitchen, worrying about you over cups of black coffee, whom you could simply ask."

"Yeah, but…"

"Is this where I draw it out of you by saying, 'Yeah, but what?' or something to that effect?"

"I don't want them to know about Donald. Some part of me doesn't want to ruin memories of him for other people."

"How sweet of you," Choch said. "While I don't necessarily think any memories will be ruined, I wonder if you can't simply just ask them about Vikki without mentioning your father. *Donald*, sorry. I'd forgotten that you aren't referring to him as *daddy* any longer. I mean, after all, not asking people right outside your door might be something one would call a plot hole, if this were a story and not your life."

Cole sat up and felt a little dizzy from doing so quickly. "Fine, okay, I'll go ask them. Happy?"

"Delighted. You're the man, CB. Ta-ta."

Cole ended the call, and it really ended. He took out his earbuds, left his phone on the bed, stepped over the plate of food, and exited his bedroom.

Auntie Joan and his grandmother were in the kitchen, hunched over cups of black coffee, just as Choch had said. When Cole entered, and sat down at the table in front of them, they stopped talking. Choch was right about that, too. He'd been the subject of their conversation.

"Did you eat?" his auntie asked.

"How are you, nósisim?" his grandmother asked.

"Who is Vikki Folster?" Cole asked.

Auntie Joan and his grandmother looked at each other, confusion written all over their faces.

"Vikki?" Auntie Joan asked. "Why would you ask that? Where did that come from?"

"It doesn't matter where it came from, I just want to know," Cole said.

"She worked with your father," his grandmother said.

Cole tried to assess his auntie and his grandmother, to suss out any weirdness, any evasiveness, any sense at all that they were once again protecting him from something.

"For, what, two years?" Auntie Joan said to his grandmother, who nodded.

"And that's it? They just worked together," Cole said.

"They and a bunch of other people, from the community and from outside the community," his grandmother said. "What's this all about, nósisim?"

204

MONSTERS

Cole may not have been as astute as Eva and Brady were at telling whether somebody was lying or not, but they seemed to be truthful. Donald and Vikki had worked together, so what? Whatever they were up to, they kept it a secret.

"Who was she with?" Cole asked.

"With? Like, who was she dating back then?" Auntie Joan said.

"Yeah."

Auntie Joan and his grandmother exchanged looks again, like they could telepathically communicate, but it seemed like neither of them were sure. And it wasn't important to them, either. Why would it be? They had no idea that the person Vikki was with very likely murdered her and Donald.

"I think it was…" Auntie Joan kept looking at his grandmother for help.

"Was it?" his grandmother said.

"Reynold McCabe, wasn't it?"

Cole's heart exploded. Thundered. He rubbed instant cold sweat from his forehead with trembling fingers.

"I think so."

"You…you're s-sure? You sw-swear." Cole's face felt like it couldn't move.

"Positive, right?" Auntie Joan asked his grandmother.

"Yes, I remember seeing them around back then. They had that girl together. What was her name again?"

"Lucy," Cole breathed.

"That's it," Auntie Joan said.

"Cole," his grandmother said, "are you feeling okay?"

Cole braced himself. He placed his hands on the table and pushed himself up from his chair. He stumbled backwards. Auntie Joan leapt forward and took his forearm, but he pulled away.

"I have to…" Cole started "I have to…I have to…"

He willed his legs to move forward, one at a time, until he collapsed out of the kitchen, against the hallway wall. Pushed himself forward toward the front door, slid his shoulder against the wall on the way for support. Pictures of Donald crashed against the floor.

"Cole! It's getting late and you are *not* going out!" Auntie Joan followed after him.

"I h-have to go!" Cole fumbled to open the door. His fingers couldn't grip the doorknob. He used both hands, and tried to turn the knob.

"Nósisim, lay down. Rest."

"No!" He pulled the door open. The doorknob went flying and punctured a hole in the wall. He fell forward through the screen door, then outside.

"Come back here, Cole Harper!"

Cole didn't respond. He kept falling forward, and used the motion as momentum to carry him farther and farther away from the house.

"That fu...that shit..."

Cole was hyperventilating. He could hardly see through his tears. The world was distorted. He could hear his auntie and grandmother calling after him, but their voices were like his vision, getting softer as the space between them grew.

And he didn't need vision.

He didn't need medication.

He didn't need their voices.

He only needed one thing: to get to Reynold's house.

26

FALLOUT

REYNOLD MCCABE LIVED AT THE FAR EDGE OF TOWN. Cole had to force his way through the dispersing crowd leaving the debate at the community hall. He first saw them from a distance. He almost turned back, but he pushed himself onward—head down, heart racing, sweat pouring, and his body forever threatening to shut down in a sea of black spots that were as crowded in his vision as the debate-goers.

"Cole Harper! On your way to burn the hall now?!"

Keep going. Don't look up. Don't stop.

"Keep running right the hell out of Wounded Sky, city!"

Head down. Breathe.

Somebody shouldered him and he fell hard against the ground.

He clawed forward, planting his scarred palms into the dirt and gravel, and got up. *Ignore them. Go. Get there.*

"Cole!"

Footsteps followed behind him. They closed in. He didn't look back. *One leg in front, then the other. No giving up.*

"Harper! Stop!"

Pam? She grabbed his hand. Through his numbness he could feel her fingers curl over his skin. He could feel her pull backwards, keeping him from his destination. He yanked his hand out of hers and kept moving forward.

She grabbed his hand again.

"Come on!"

Cole pulled back. Could she feel it? Could she feel the sweaty palms? Through his skin, with her soft fingertips, could she feel his heart race? He could feel it throughout his body, he could see the thousand tiny blood vessels in his eyes pulse through his vision, through the crowd, through the black spots. He stopped, let her turn him around. She looked scared, confused. Her eyebrows caved in, her mouth opened slightly.

"Wh-what is it, P-Pam?"

Pam put her hand against Cole's forehead and pulled it back like she'd touched an oven element.

"Holy shit, are you okay? This is like when I saw you in the hallway times ten," she said.

"But I'm running. I can run. I don't need your help," he said.

"You don't need my—okay, sure. You're not yourself, that's fine."

"I need t-to go, okay? I just need to g-go."

"You needed my help this morning, remember? You needed more than my help." She touched her cheek, where he'd kissed her. He remembered. He could feel her cheek against his lips. He could feel it through the numbness. He needed her. But at what cost? To be like Donald? He could feel Eva's breath against his lips. So close. So achingly close.

"I'm not my father!"

He shouted at her, but it wasn't at her. It was at Donald, wherever he was. He looked up, to the sky, to the northern lights. He imagined a ribbon up there was him. Blue. Cold. Numb.

"Cole..."

Pam took his hand again and squeezed it.

He looked down. Saw her hand clutching his. Their fingers mixed together. Her thumb rubbing the outside of his hand, trying to comfort him. Her perfect, olive skin. She didn't care what his hand felt like. She didn't care that he was cold, that he was sweating, that he was who he was. But— "I'll hurt you."

"What?"

"I'll hurt you, like he hurt her..."

"What are you talking about? Hurt me? What are you talking about, Harper?"

She moved forward, arms outstretched. Moved to hold him, to squeeze him, squeeze the panic out of him. Out of who he was.

"No." He backed away. "You can't."

How to stop her. How to keep her away from him. He thought of Reynold. He thought of Vikki. He thought of Donald. How to save her? From him.

"I don't understand," she said.

She came forward again. This time slower, tentatively, her body echoing the confusion on her face.

"I love Eva," he cried. "Okay?"

She stopped.

"I'll hurt you," he said. "Don't let me hurt you."

She backed away now. She shook her head. A tear fell from her eye, like she'd shook it out. They stared at each other. He could feel tears fall from his own eyes. *Faint now, faint and leave here. Wake up somewhere else. Not here. Not now.*

"You hurt me already," she whispered.

"Pam…"

But she was already gone. Running away from him, from the mess that was Cole.

Compared to most housing in the area, Reynold McCabe's house was a mansion; a rare two-story structure that appeared even bigger with its attached garage. Whenever Reynold desired he could drive around in his big truck, even though everything was within walking distance. And it wasn't quite within the boundaries of Wounded Sky First Nation proper, either, as though that house and that truck and that man were too good for the community. Cole stopped on the path in front of the house and fell to his knees, exhausted.

On his hands and knees, trying desperately to catch his breath, to gather strength, Cole looked up. Reynold's house was surrounded by security, a guard at the front door, at the side door, and probably at the back door, too. A roaming guard paced back and forth from one end of the house to the other. All the guards were dressed in black, and all of them had handguns on their belts. He had come this far for nothing.

"Shit." Even if he weren't in the state he was in right now, he didn't think he could get inside, close enough to confront Reynold, or to tear through the place to see what he could find, anything that would connect Reynold to Donald and Vikki's murder. He'd be asking for a gunshot wound, an end to everything. And while that may have been a relief for Cole, dying so foolishly would be making a decision for everybody else in Wounded Sky.

"I'm not like you," Cole said to an absent Donald. He wasn't selfish like Donald, to do what he'd done, to impact his son's life, his family's, in exchange for Vikki. How was she worth giving up so much? His life? No, he wasn't like Donald in any way.

Cole stood up, and managed to stay up. Shaking knees. Trembling body. Racing heart. He took out his pills and put two in his mouth. Tonight wasn't the night. But the guards would be there tomorrow, too, and the next day. Cole had to find another way in. He scanned the area, as though the answer was there, as though it would walk right past him. And then he looked at the house, at the one light that was on: a room on the second floor. A silhouette crossed the window, behind the curtains. It wasn't Reynold. It wasn't round enough.

And the idea came to him, came right through his mind, like a silhouette moving behind a curtain.

"Lucy."

Buzz.

Students were leaving classes. Cole had stood at the end of a row of lockers, close to the classroom, for a full hour. He'd stood there, and stared at the floor, and the ceiling, and the wall, counting tiles and speckles and bricks, waiting for this moment. In anticipation of enduring more abuse, Cole had slipped a pill into his mouth twenty-six minutes ago. The meds were now built up in his system. If he stopped taking them, he was asking for the panic attack to end all panic attacks.

When he saw Lucy walking past, he called to her. She stopped, and jokingly acted as though she wasn't sure whether he'd meant her or not, though he'd said her name.

Cole did his best to play it cool, not act awkward. "Yes you," he said.

"You know what?" she walked up to him, "I've got an even better idea of what a day in the life of Cole Harper might feel like now."

"No, you really don't." Cole said. "How could you, aside from…" Cole tried not to explode "…your dad being your dad." *Your dad being a murdering sack of shit.*

"Not aside from, *because* of my dad being my dad," Lucy said. "Shit went next level after last night, boy."

"Last night…" Cole pictured himself running against the tide of community members leaving the debate "…right. How'd that go?"

"Cole, aren't you on the group text? It's the Twitter of Wounded Sky."

"No, and I've been advised to stay off it."

"Actually that's a damn good call, most of the crap on there's about you anyway. No, spoiler alert: dad got killed. Big time. No contest."

"That doesn't always translate into a loss, though."

"Here it does. Here it does when you're running against a Crate. Not only are they fricking popular but, you know, they've got the sympathy vote, too."

"I guess."

"Moral of the story," Lucy leaned into two passing students, "our fellow classmates are *talking shit today.*" She shouted those last three words to their faces. "Anyway, what did you want? You called me over, remember?"

"It doesn't matter anymore." Cole had moved on. Already thinking of another way into Reynold's house.

"You're so depressing, look at you." Lucy grabbed both of his shoulders and tried to straighten them out. "Just tell me anyway, I'm curious now."

"I thought I could come over and help plan the victory party for Sunday, that's all."

Lucy scrunched her brow and tapped at her lips, all while staring at Cole. "You want to help plan a party for the guy who knocked you the hell out?"

"Maybe I just wanted to hang out with you." How good a liar could he be? The pills helped here. They kept him calm enough.

"Having the town pariah over to hang out, hey?" Lucy didn't give it more than a second's thought. "Yeah, I'm down. We can plot our revenge."

"I was thinking more like watch a movie?"

Lucy rolled her eyes. "There's never been a more likable pariah, that I can tell you. Sure, no plotting, just a movie and chips and Coke, like good little angels. Do we need a chaperone, or…"

Cole forced a mostly believable chuckle. "Does tonight work?"

When Cole got back to his parents' house, his auntie and his grandmother were out, and he was glad for it. He ate an uninspired lunch just to get something into his stomach—soda crackers with peanut butter spread clumsily on them, and an apple—then went directly to his bedroom and closed the door. There was nothing to do but wait until the evening. At 7:00 p.m. he'd go to Lucy's place, then figure out a way to search through Reynold's house and find something that would give him answers.

Lying in bed was cathartic. He enjoyed being there, staring at the blank ceiling and trying to match his thoughts to it. He stuck his earbuds in and turned on some music. *OK Computer*. "*Let down and hanging around.*" Never down lower, maybe, but still here. He had to be here. Hanging around. His eyelids were heavy. Each time he blinked they were heavier. "*One day I am going to grow wings.*" He closed his eyes.

He wasn't sure when he woke up. He heard his phone chime. A message. He rolled over onto his side and checked his messages.

EVA: **You avoided me all day.**

Cole propped himself up on his elbow and two-thumb typed a response.

COLE: I avoided everybody.

EVA: Mike's pissed you skipped practice.

COLE: That would've gone well.

EVA: Still...

COLE: Did he say anything about throwing rocks?

EVA: Says he didn't.

COLE: Can you tell when he's lying or only me?

EVA: I just want to get it, Cole. I don't get it. I don't get anything.

Cole typed and deleted several responses. He wondered what she was thinking on the other end of the line, wherever she was, whatever she was doing. She would have seen the three dots on her screen for a long time. She would have thought he was writing some long, drawn-out message.

COLE: I said I just need to be alone. Would you want to be around people, if you were me?

Then he got a taste of his own medicine. Fair enough.

Three dots from Hell.

EVA: I just thought you should know about Anna Crate, if you haven't heard.

COLE: What.

EVA: She dropped out.

COLE: What? Why?

EVA: Later, Cole.

27

NO SURPRISES

COLE ARRIVED AT REYNOLD MCCABE'S HOUSE after pausing several yards away to gather some courage and swallow a pill. He'd felt the meds wearing off when he'd left the house, after he got into an argument with his auntie about where he was going. Cole had just left. She'd shouted after him. He cursed himself that he'd not taken his pill at the house rather than now. It wouldn't do any good for his nerves. It wouldn't help him confront the security guard at Reynold's front door. The guard had a sneer on his face and when he saw Cole, his hand fell instinctively to his gun.

"Where do you think you're going?" the guard asked, and put a hand on Cole's chest.

"Inside?" Cole tried to hide the fact that his entire body was shaking.

"Nobody goes inside."

Cole tried to bravely push his way towards the door. But the guard stepped directly in front of him. The other guards took notice, made their way over, and Cole took a step back.

"I have a date with Lucy."

"Nice try."

"I do! Seriously, go and ask."

The guard looked at one of his colleagues who'd joined them. That one, a superior, gave the guard standing in front of Cole a nod towards the house.

"Hang on." The guard walked over to the front door, opened it, and went inside. The other two guards stood flanking Cole with their hands on their guns, too.

"What do you think I'm going to do that you're ready to draw your guns?" he asked.

The guards didn't say anything. Cole didn't recognize any of them. It was dark, and they were dressed in black, complete with black hats and sunglasses. Moments later, the first guard came out of the house. He paused at the steps, reluctant, and then he waved Cole up to the front door. Cole gave the two guards flanking him a shrug, and then approached the house.

"You do *anything* I don't like…" The guard got right into Cole's face, nose to nose.

"You'll shoot me?"

"It won't be pretty, let's just say that."

Cole motioned for the guard to move. The guard took a moment, his hand tensed over his firearm, and then he stepped to one side.

"Hello?" Cole stood in the entryway and looked around. From his vantage point, he could see Reynold wasn't suffering financially. The floors were shiny hardwood, and the banister up to the second floor looked like it belonged in some Victorian house. There was fresh paint with vibrant colours on the walls. The kitchen cupboards had see-through doors, and lights inside that made the glasses glisten. Cole didn't expect that many people came into the house. Living like this, when others in the community had trouble affording healthy food, wouldn't look too good. Still, his house was visible from the outside for anybody to see. Maybe people in Wounded Sky thought that since he was successful, he could make the community successful.

Cole slipped his shoes off and put them to the side, against the wall. He took a few steps into the hallway and called out again. "Lucy?"

"In here!"

He followed the sound of her voice to the living room. The focal point of the room was a huge television. For one fleeting moment,

Cole imagined watching some of his favourite movies on it, but stopped himself. *Don't envy this douchebag.* Lucy was sitting on the couch, facing the television screen. There was a bowl of ripple chips on the coffee table in front of the couch, and two glasses filled with Coke and ice.

Cole laughed. "Chips and pop."

"Yeah but, my dad's out, so no chaperone."

"Well there's a bunch of armed chaperones outside, so…" Cole walked around the couch and sat down beside her.

Lucy picked up the remote control, and started to scroll through shows. "What's your pleasure? Comedy? Romance? Romantic comedy?"

"I like anything."

"You like anything," Lucy repeated with an exhausted tone.

"Okay, romantic comedy."

"Better."

"But, you know, I guess we could actually plan for a victory party now. Celebration's back on, from what I've heard."

"Did you join the group text?" Lucy dropped the remote and turned to him with a shocked expression.

"Eva told me."

Lucy picked the remote back up. She kept scrolling. "Boring."

"So is it? Back on?" he asked.

"Oh, it's back on," she said, "but it'll be lame and I don't want to help plan it."

Cole leaned back. He put his feet up on the coffee table, which looked as though it had been made out of a tree trunk and had been varnished so vigorously that it reflected like a mirror. Cole imagined how pissed it would've made Reynold to see Cole's feet resting on his nice furniture.

"When did you find out? About Mrs. Crate?" he asked.

Lucy rolled her eyes. She sunk deep into the couch. "My dad was pretty much dancing around the house. So, I heard *him*, and then I just texted some people."

"And they think he's responsible for her dropping out?" he asked.

Lucy scoffed. "Cole, come on. Of course he is."

"Doesn't that piss you off—that he cheats like that?"

Lucy turned towards Cole. "I think you've misunderstood me. Yes, it sucks that people hate me because they hate him. Yes, parties are lame. Yes, he can be lame, too. Whatever. But he's a winner, Cole. I don't really care how he wins. Not my business."

"Are you serious? You don't care what that means to Anna Crate? Or what having Reynold as Chief might mean to Wounded Sky?"

"Why would I? Why would *you*? What do they have to do to you to turn you off them, Cole? Kill you?"

"You know, I never saw it before, but I do now." Cole stood up from the couch.

"Saw what?"

"How much like your dad you are!"

"Yeah? Maybe I'd know what parent you're more like if they weren't dead!" Lucy stood up, too.

Cole gasped, and he felt a tear form in his eye. He blinked it out. "I'd still have one of them if it weren't for your dad," he breathed out, while more tears fell.

"Sorry? What?" She took a step toward him. Too close.

"That's why I came here tonight, to make sure I was right about your dad."

"Right that my dad killed your parents?"

"My dad," Cole said. Then he said the rest of it, because he found himself already in it, passed the point where he could turn back, "and your mom."

Lucy hit him across the arm with the remote. "Don't you talk about my mom!"

"It's true! Your mom and my dad were having an affair. Your dad found out, and he killed them!" Cole lowered his voice to a whisper. "I know it."

"My mom died in an accident!" Lucy threw the remote control across the room, and it smashed into the television. The screen cracked. Cole jumped from the sound. Then, she sat down on the couch, stared at the broken screen, the distorted movie icons.

"My dad did too. *With* your mom," Cole sat down beside her, "but it wasn't an accident."

"You're full of shit." They were both talking quietly now, like these were secrets that had to be kept. "How could you even know any of this?"

"I'm not full of shit," Cole said. "There were emails on Donald's… my dad's…laptop. He and Vikki were going to run away, and take you, too."

"Shut the hell up. Please."

"I read them. I can show you."

"You could've…you could've written them. That doesn't prove anything."

"What if I can prove it to you?"

"How?"

"Let me look around," Cole said. "If he didn't do anything he has nothing to hide."

Lucy didn't respond. She buried her face into her hands.

"Please," Cole said. "Is there anywhere he'd hide something? Anywhere he'd keep a secret like that?"

Lucy lifted her head. Cole saw tears down her cheeks, too. She turned towards him, mascara dripping from her eyelids. "Yeah," she said, "yeah, okay, fine."

Cole followed Lucy out of the living room, up the stairs with the beautiful railings, down the hallway, and into her dad's bedroom. There was a walk-in closet and in it, a large object was pushed up against the wall and covered under a blanket. Lucy removed the blanket to reveal a chest. A big padlock kept it safely closed. She got on her knees, picked up the lock, and then let it fall back, heavy against the chest.

She looked up at him. "I've never been able to open it."

Cole knelt beside her. He picked up the lock with both hands. He looked at her. "Don't get freaked out."

"From what?"

Cole pulled at the lock as hard as he could. He let out a grunt. The chest scraped across the ground. He held it in place with his knee and kept pulling. Finally, the lock ripped away from the chest, and the latch came with it.

"Holy shit," she said.

Cole tossed the lock onto the ground. He could feel Lucy's eyes on him. He took a deep breath and opened the lid. There was a bundle of cash on top of jewellery and photo albums. He took all these things out and dug deeper.

He pulled out a hazmat suit.

"What's that?" Lucy asked.

"It's a hazmat suit," Cole said, inspecting it. "I saw people wearing them at the facility…"

"Oh, like in that movie *Outbreak*, right? I've seen that."

"Yeah, people wear them around diseases or whatever. Keeps them from breathing in shit, coming into contact with viruses."

"Why would there be—"

"Because of the accident!" Cole said. "It *has* to have something to do with that. He was in there!"

"No," she said.

"Still think he's a winner?"

"He couldn't have…" but she trailed off.

The idea seemed even more likely when he found the folder, sitting there at the bottom of the chest, full of the files Cole had found the week he'd arrived in Wounded Sky. The ones he'd been looking for. The ones Dr. Captain wanted.

"Lucy…" Cole whispered.

"Yeah?"

"Your dad—"

"Her dad's *what?*" Cole dropped the folder, and both he and Lucy sprang to their feet. Reynold was standing at the closet door.

"Mr. McCabe," Cole said.

"Dad," Lucy said.

"To your room, Lucy."

"What am I, seven?" she said.

"This doesn't concern you," Reynold said to her.

"According to Cole it does," Lucy sounded intent on starting shit.

"Oh? Please, enlighten me, Mr. Harper." He took a long look at the chest.

"You should know what I found," Cole said. "It's your chest."

Reynold picked up the folder. "This?"

"Pam was right," Cole said, "a guy like you could look like a monster to a kid. A boogeyman."

"Now, Cole, I don't know what kind of stories you've been reading, but I'm sure you wouldn't judge me for finding a folder."

"You found this? And just decided to lock it in your secret chest with your hazmat suit?"

"That old thing? Tsk-tsk-tsk. I used to work at Mihko Laboratories as a security guard. Every employee had one."

"You worked with my dad and Vikki?" Cole asked.

"That's what this is about?" he asked.

"He thinks you killed his dad, and Mom," Lucy said. "You didn't, right? Dad?"

"Of course I didn't, Lucy." Reynold took a step towards Cole. "Don't try to turn my daughter against me, young man. That's one thing I won't abide."

"What," Cole didn't back down. He took a step towards Reynold, "or you'll kill me, too?"

"Lucy," Reynold said coldly.

"Later, Cole." Lucy left, and Cole listened as she walked down the hallway. A door opened, then shut.

"I'm going to prove you did it," Cole said.

He could feel Reynold's breath against his face, hot and thick.

"You think I'm going to let you leave with this?" Reynold tapped Cole on the head with the folder. "I don't think so."

"I'll find something, and you'll be finished," Cole said.

"You try anything," Reynold said, "against me, against Lucy, you tell her anything about me, and *you'll* be finished."

"I'll be finished with *this*," Cole said, "I know that."

They stood there, staring at each other. Reynold had a smirk on his face, but his eyes were red with fury. Maybe Cole's were, too.

"Let me go," Cole said.

Reynold tilted his head. A curious look came over him, like Cole was a puzzle he couldn't solve. Then he stepped out of the way, and over to his chest. He dropped the folder into it, then folded and replaced the hazmat suit.

Cole moved to the door.

"Careful out there," Reynold said. "There's something crawling around at night."

He slammed the chest shut. Cole heard him pick up the lock and roll it around in his hand.

28

TARGET PRACTICE

THE NEXT DAY, COLE WENT TO THE FIELD by Ashley's trailer, his backpack over his shoulder and Mark's gun shoved into the back of his jeans. He made his way through the tall grass, like he was wading through wet cement. Two large stones stood exactly where Cole remembered them. He sat on one, put his feet up on the other, and fished into his backpack. He took out five empty tin cans then slid off the rock and lined them up biggest to smallest, across both rocks.

It was the exact setup he'd used with Eva and Brady when they were children. They spent a lot of time lining up the cans, nervous to shoot the gun they'd taken from Wayne—stalling, but excited. They did it as a team, like always. Cole placed them on the rocks, one after the other. Brady stood back a foot or two, to make sure they were exactly the same distance apart. Eva kept a lookout for her dad.

Cole left his backpack on the ground by the two stones, and walked away from the rocks like he was in an Old West gun duel. At ten paces out, he turned to face the rocks and drew the gun from his pants. He released the safety, cocked the hammer, and took aim at can number one.

Pop.

Clean miss. He cocked the hammer and aimed again.

Pop.

He felt like it was a closer shot, but there wasn't a way to tell. He still missed.

"Give me a break," he said to himself as he raised the gun again. He breathed in, breathed out. Slowly.

"You're never going to hit the can like that!" Eva was trudging across the field, through the long grass, towards him.

"Got my texts?" he asked.

"I did," she said.

Cole waited until she stood next to him. "Eva, I'm sorry for acting like that, and for pushing you away."

She hugged him, and while he was in her arms she said, "I'm sorry about your dad. If that were me…"

"You've always been there for me, even when you were hundreds of mile away. I want you to know that."

She let go. "Me too, okay? Always."

"We're good?"

She took the gun from Cole and moved him to the side with an "excuse me, please" and a soft hip check. She raised the gun, cocked the hammer, aimed, and fired.

Pop.

The first can launched into the air, and then disappeared behind the rock. She handed the gun back to Cole. "See what I did?"

"Yeah," Cole said, "actually no. Were you picturing my face or something?"

"Shut up. We're good." Eva laughed. "It's your stance and how you're holding it." She walked behind him, put her hand on his right arm and raised it. "Here." She stepped to Cole's side. His right arm was extended. "Now give me your other hand. You watch waaay too many movies." Cole gave Eva his left arm, and she placed his left hand over his right. "There. Now…"

She kicked his left foot forward slightly, then crouched down and chopped lightly at his knees. "Bend them a bit." After this was done, she stood back, looked him over, and then clapped her hands once. "Alright, good to go."

"I was kind of standing like this," he said defensively.

"You weren't standing like this," she said. "This is the Fighting Stance. Dad taught it to me. Now, aim and shoot. Let's go."

Cole aimed down the barrel at can number two. He breathed out, and fired.

Pop.

The second can didn't move.

"Shit." Cole shook his head.

"Try again," Eva said.

Pop.

This time, the can shifted to the side, and then crept off the rock.

"Got it!" she said.

"Hardly," he said.

"Oh Cole, just keep practising," Eva said like she'd heard that tone of voice from Cole too many times. "My dad isn't going to come racing across the field to give us crap. You have time."

"True."

Can number three.

Pop.

The can somersaulted through the air, then landed on the ground. "See?"

Cole lowered the gun, and placed it onto the ground. "Thanks."

"So what's the occasion?"

"Oh," he said, "I'm not sure you really want to know."

She crossed her arms and tilted her head. "Do I get a *choice* to know? None of that, 'I can't tell you,' bullshit?"

"I'm too tired for all that." He looked around and let out a stuttered breath. "Yeah, if you want to know, I'll tell you."

"Anything?" she asked.

"As much as I can," he said.

"You *know* that I want to know everything. You know me."

"I know."

"So, start at the first question: what's the shooting all about?" she asked.

Careful, boy. Choch's voice had never been louder in Cole's mind.

"I'm going back to the research facility tonight. Last time, I didn't get inside because I was chased by that creature. This time, I want to be ready."

Eva stood in silence. She stared at Cole, her mouth slightly open. She uncrossed her arms.

"Yeah," he said, responding to her shock.

"What?" She shook her head like she had water in her ears.

"You wanted to know," Cole said through a breath.

"So what're you going to do? Shoot the thing?"

"If I can hit it."

"Why would you even go back there, if this thing is actually there? Why take that risk?"

"Because I need to prove that Reynold killed my dad, and Lucy's mom."

"Reynold *what?* Cole! You only said you'd found out your dad was cheating on your mom."

"Too much to text."

"Okay, so..." Eva collected herself, "...tell me."

"I think Reynold found out about my dad and Vikki, and—"

"Killed them?"

"I need to find something, some kind of evidence, to prove it," he said, "and I just know it's in the facility."

"And you think that thing is..." Eva struggled to find the right words. "...you saw it? You *actually* saw it?"

"I saw it," Cole said. "I've seen lots of things. I know it's real."

"You've seen lots of things, like what?"

"You don't have to believe me, Eva. It's fine."

"I want to believe you," Eva said. "It's just, show me something, like in my face. I'm an evidence kind of girl. I get it from my dad."

"I see Jayne."

"Jayne? Jayney? Cole, come on. Don't screw around with me. Jayne Flett? Lauren's little sister? Jayne who died in—"

"The fire," he said, sombre. "That Jayne."

Eva turned around, like she was going to walk away, through the field, into the woods. "This is..." she turned back to Cole, standing a foot away from him. "This is *crazy.*"

"I would've thought so, too. I would've thought so a few weeks ago, but I've seen it. All of it. I've seen Jayne, I've seen that creature..."

"This is...Cole...I don't believe any of this...I've never believed *any* of this..."

"She started the fire in the garbage can, not Mark's cigarette butt. She just touched it, and...look," Cole made his fingers twinkle, representing fire, "she is half on fire, all the time. So, she can touch things and make them hot, make them burn..."

"She's half burning, and she can start fires," Eva recited.

"Yes," Cole cupped his hands around his mouth. "Jayney! Jayney, come here!"

"Oh my God, Cole. What are you going to get her to do? Tell me something about me that nobody else could know? Lift a penny?"

"It's daytime so she'll come," Cole said to a very concerned looking Eva. "She's afraid of that thing, too, but she says it only comes out at night." He cupped his hands around his mouth again. "Jayney!"

"Cole stop it," Eva said.

But Jayne appeared beside Cole. She was smiling, almost jumping up and down, happy that Eva was there, too. Cole crouched down beside her.

One snap of my fingers, CB, and Eva and Brady are dead. That's part of the deal. They'll be dead just as they should've been without my help. You cannot—

"She's here," Cole said to Eva. "Hey, Jayney, can you do me a favour?"

"Why aren'tcha pretending about me?" she asked.

"I don't have to right now," he said.

"Cole, you're the worst actor," Eva said.

"Just wait," he said.

"What do ya want me to do, Coley?" Jayne asked.

He leaned forward and whispered into her ear so quiet that Eva couldn't hear. Then, he extended his arm between Eva and Jayne.

"I don't wanna hurt you, Coley," Jayne said.

"It's okay," he said.

Jayne moved around in front of Cole's arm. She placed her burning index finger against his skin. A welt started to form. Eva gasped. Jayne moved her index finger clumsily across his forearm. She took her finger away, and revealed a word spelled into Cole's skin: Jayney.

"Oh...my..." Eva started.

"She's here," Cole said.

"What's happening...?"

"Oh! Tell her I miss her and stuff!" Jayney clapped excitedly.

"She says she misses you," Cole said.

"I miss you, too." Tears poured out of Eva's eyes. She kept looking at Jayne's name on Cole's forearm.

Cole took Eva into his arms. "They're all okay," he whispered. "All of them."

Eva grabbed onto the back of Cole's shirt and squeezed. "Cole..."

"We're okay, too. We'll be okay."

She pushed him away. "I'm going tonight. You're not going to face that thing on your own."

"No, you're not. You can't come with me, not tonight."

"Why?"

"It's too dangerous, that's why!"

"I went with you to the camp, remember?"

"I can't lose you," Cole's voice started to shake.

"I can't lose *you*," Eva said.

"I'll have help," Cole said. "You're not going to lose me."

"Help from who? Jayne?" Eva rubbed her thumb across the name on Cole's skin.

"No, from somebody else."

Cole walked up to a cabin outside of Blackwood Forest, a few hundred meters away from Wounded Sky First Nation's perimeter. There were a handful of houses people had decided to build, and live in, outside of the community. Little one-house suburbs. He paused for a moment at the front door, then knocked. He waited. He heard footsteps. The door opened.

"What?" Victor said.

"Hey, Victor," Cole said.

"Tansi."

"I saw you at the Fish, remember?"

"Before you burned it down?" Victor laughed. "I remember that."

"I didn't do that. I didn't burn anything down. I hate fire."

"I guess you would, wouldn't you?" Victor walked inside the house, and Cole took that to mean he could follow. So he did, all the way across the living room, to the kitchen table, where he sat across from the man. Victor took a sip from his coffee cup. "What are you doin' here? It's not safe. You and I both know that."

"I'm not here to be safe," Cole said.

"Gonna kill lots of people, that thing," Victor said. "Eat 'em up like snacks."

"It's not going to kill anybody, if I have anything to say about it."

"You?" Victor scoffed. "You're just a kid."

"Before, you said you wanted to kill it. Said you knew how to kill it. Is that true?" Cole asked.

Victor sipped his coffee slowly, then nodded. "I wouldn'ta said it if it weren't true, kid."

"Then I could use some help," Cole said. "You in?"

"Damn straight I am."

Cole was on his way to Ashley's trailer when Choch appeared beside him.

"So?" Choch said.

"So what?" Cole replied.

"What do you have to say for yourself?"

"Nothing."

"You *do* remember the rule you were given, don't you? Might I recite that information back to you? Or should I simply end your life, and your friends' lives, right now?"

Cole stopped. "Yes, please, recite that back to me."

Choch's eyes rolled into the back of his head. Choch was nothing if not theatrical. He recited, both in his voice and Cole's:

"Well, I hate to do this, Coley-Boley, but if you insist on telling Brady, the deal is off: do not pass go, do not collect $200."

What difference does it make? I'm here now. I'm still going to do what I can to figure out what happened to Ashley. I'm not leaving.

"No-no-no-NO, you don't understand, my young friend. If you tell anybody about me, or our deal, everybody you saved that night, very—"

"About *you*, or our *deal?*" Cole interrupted.

"Yes, exactly," Choch said.

"I didn't tell Eva either of those things."

"Tomato tom-*AH*-to, CB."

Cole started walking again. Choch followed.

"Sorry, Mr. *Chochinov*. You made the rules, not me. You never said I couldn't tell Eva about Jayne. Jayne was never part of the deal." Cole stopped again. "The deal was that you helped me save Eva and Brady and I would pay you back one day. I didn't tell Eva about that. Or do you want to replay that as well."

Choch kicked some stones along the ground. "Well, no. Not exactly."

"You like playing games so much, well, now I'm playing, too. If you're going to kill us, then kill us. If you're not, then get out of my way and let me do my job."

Cole didn't wait for a response. He just left Choch standing where he was. When he was a fair distance, Choch called out: "Okay, I'll let it slip this one time! But no more secrets pertaining to, uhhh, mystical… forces…to anybody! Or else! That's it!"

"Whatever!"

"I have to say, though, CB, I like this new go-get-em attitude! It suits you! I'll be cheering you on from a very, very safe distance this evening!"

29

HOCKEY NIGHT

COLE PLACED A HAND ON THE TRUNK of the Mustang and ran his fingers over the cool metal. He could hear himself in the trunk at seven years old, nestled up against the back, hiding from Eva, Brady, and Ashley. They always went off into the bush to hide, but Cole always hid in the trunk. And they never found him. Yesterday, he wanted to disappear like that. To hide. Now more than ever, he wanted it over—and not to hide, but to leave, to get out of the trunk and into the driver's seat. He kept his hand against the metal a moment longer, and then he slid his fingertips off the surface.

The trailer, thankfully unlocked, felt different. There was space to move. Too much space. Ashley's wake had been shoulder to shoulder, so packed that it had spilled outside. Cole walked around more than once. He looked at the picture of himself, Ashley, Eva, and Brady. He looked through Ashley's comic collection, a bond that they, and Brady, had shared. Cole sat down on Ashley's futon and stared at the repaired window. And he stared down, where Ashley's blood had stained the floor.

"Are you here?" Cole looked around the room. Beside the futon, Ashley's hockey bag was pushed up against the wall. Ashley was here, and he was not here. Cole knew that. He knew, as well, that Ashley should have never left.

And it was time to make it right.

Cole stood up, and slung the hockey bag over his shoulder. He paused at the door before he left, taking one last look. He heard Michael's voice echo against the walls in the empty room, telling

Cole that he could honour Ashley by playing hockey. He heard himself saying that he would do it, for Ashley. Tonight was Saturday. Hockey Night. Cole took a deep breath in, out. There'd be no hockey for him, but he would still honour his friend.

"I'm doing *this* to honour you," he said. "You, and Alex, and Maggie...Vikki...Donald."

Knock knock.

"Just a second!" Cole finished dressing. He slid Ashley's elbow pads in place, then slipped Ashley's Wounded Sky Thunderbirds jersey over his head. He was almost fully equipped now, minus Ashley's skates, helmet, and gloves.

"Come in," Cole said.

The bedroom door opened. Pam walked in and stopped in the middle of the room when she saw Cole.

"Got your text," she said.

"Thanks for coming," he said.

"What's going on here?" she asked. "In my experience, and I know I just work at the canteen, usually people dress up for hockey at the X, not in their bedroom."

"It's kind of hard to explain," he said.

"Okay," she stayed where she was, "why don't you start with explaining what the hell happened the other night."

"Right," he said. "I was kind of out of my head. I'd just found something out, something kind of horrible."

"So you decided you were going to be horrible to me?" she turned around like she was about to leave, then turned back towards Cole. "I mean, you kissed me, Harper."

"I know," he said.

"Why'd you even say yes to going out with me, if you weren't interested?"

"I was, I am, it's just..." Cole buried his head in his hands "...I'm sorry. I'm confused. I didn't even think you were interested. What's there to like about me?"

Pam walked over to the bed. She sat a reasonable distance away from Cole.

"I'm not going to play the Poor-Cole Game, you know," she said. "I'm the one who got hurt here."

Cole nodded. "I just wanted to say I'm sorry. You've been good to me."

"That's because I'm awesome, and you should recognize that."

"I do."

"Alright, Harper, I forgive you." She inched close enough to give him a punch against his hockey pants. "So, about what's going on here, with the equipment, let me guess: you want to be seven again, when your mom dressed you up for hockey at home, then brought you to the rink?"

"Close," Cole chuckled, "but no."

"Okay, well, that was literally the only guess I had, so care to drop a hint?"

"I, uhh…" Cole started "…I have to do something dangerous."

"This about the boogeyman stuff?"

"Yeah," he said, "it's about the boogeyman stuff."

"Does the boogeyman play hockey?"

"Ha, no. It's just, protection. I was told, somebody told me, that I should wear protection."

"You know this shit is not Kevlar right?"

"I looked at the mall for Kevlar, but…"

"No dice, hey?"

"They said it was coming in next week."

They fell silent. Cole kept fidgeting with his equipment, but he abstained from the urge to adjust Ashley's jock.

"I thought it would be better for you, if I just left you alone," he said. "I ruin things."

"But you didn't leave me alone, Harper. You pushed me away, and you made me feel like crap."

"I know." Cole slid a couple inches closer to Pam. He turned to her, resting one well-equipped leg on the bed. "I like you. I really do. But

I like Eva, too. I don't want to be an asshole. I just want to be straight with you."

Pam crossed her arms. She looked away. "I'm not some problem you have to solve."

"I don't think—"

"I'm not going to beg you to be with me. If you want to be with me, then ask me out for God's sake."

"I'm not…I wasn't trying to…" But he stopped, because whether he was trying to or not, he had been begging.

"If you *don't* want to be with me, then we can just hang out. I'll teach you how to play computer games…*those* kind of games you *can* play with me. You've got a small window here." She demonstrated about an inch of space between her index finger and thumb. "Like, this big. This size of a window."

"That's a pretty small window," he said.

"I'm being generous, Cole. That's me being generous."

"I'll take it," he said.

"Hey," Pam got up from the bed. She crossed the room and stopped in the doorway. "Fill me in on the whole gladiator thing tomorrow, 'kay?"

"I'm sorry I hurt you." Cole stood up. "I won't hurt you again."

"What did we say about sorrys, Harper?"

"I say sorry too much."

"Besides," she said, "it wasn't all that bad. My armour's better than yours."

Victor was waiting for Cole, standing on the path between the X and the Fish's remains, his rifle strapped over his shoulder. The crowd in the X sounded boisterous, their roars shaking the roof. That familiar sound, the muffled excitement of an entire community watching the sport they loved, and the remnants of the Northern Lights Diner, belied the calm the night tried desperately to offer. Portions of walls, parts of the counter, charred and mangled, stubbornly refused to fall.

"You ready?" Victor walked up to Cole, rifle strapped over his shoulder. His game face was most definitely on.

Cole didn't take his eyes off that silhouette. He pulled Mark's handgun from the back of his hockey pants.

"Yeah," Cole said, "I'm ready."

30

HE WHO LIVES ALONE

COLE AND VICTOR WENT THE LONG WAY through Blackwood Forest.

"There might be fewer guards around back," Cole guessed, although he had never looked at the back of the research facility after his failed break-in.

Victor didn't seem to care either way. He said, "Whatever you think," and followed Cole into the woods.

As soon as they'd stepped foot into Blackwood, Victor took the rifle from his shoulder, and had it at the ready. Cole had his gun extended like Eva had shown him. He was holding it properly, but he still worked his way through the trees as though he were in a movie.

"Why the change?" Cole asked Victor, ever closer to the research facility.

"Why what change?" Victor asked.

"From fear to courage, I guess."

"It's not courage," Victor said. "It's something else."

"Okay...what's that?"

"It's seein' your fear, and hearin' it, but not listenin' to it. Like I said, I'm not gonna be ruled by it. So I'm scared, but I'm doin' this."

They pushed deeper into the woods, closer still.

"What about you?" Victor asked. "You're just a kid. You must be shittin' yourself over there."

"Honestly? I'm kind of in the 'screw it' zone right now."

"The 'screw it' zone," Victor repeated. "Humph."

"I'm just so tired of dealing with…everything…that I think I'm almost okay, whatever happens. I know what's there for me, on the other side."

"You got faith."

Faith? Cole thought. Was knowing different than believing? Probably. Was the prospect of dancing up in the northern lights frightening? He hated dancing, but he wasn't scared. He had even forgotten to take a pill today, and his nerves weren't as bad as they should've been.

"I guess I do, yeah," Cole said. "How about you?"

"Me? I dunno, kid. I do and I don't. See somethin' like this thing… I guess if there's somethin' that evil, there's gotta be somethin' that good."

Cole shrugged in agreement.

"Shhhh." Victor put his hand on Cole's shoulder.

Through the thick trees and bush, they could see the electric fence up ahead and, beyond it, the research facility. What Cole didn't see was a guard—not stationed anywhere outside or inside the fence. None marched back and forth, patrolling the area.

"There were a bunch of guards all over before," Cole whispered as they kept moving forward.

"I seen some guards, too, yeah," Victor whispered.

"Maybe it's a trap," Cole said.

Victor was eager, and ahead of Cole now. He was fast, but he moved silently. Years doing the same thing. Hunting out here. Cole just tried to not do anything stupid, like step on a twig, or trip.

"Keep moving," Victor said.

Cole listened. He kept moving.

The closer they got, the more sure they became that there were no guards at all at the back of the facility.

"I know we're not doing the fear thing," Cole said when they were several yards away from the fence, close enough that he could hear the hum emanating from it, "but maybe we should try a different way in. This is way too easy."

Victor stopped, resting his rifle against his shoulder. "Who said anything about going inside this shithole? I'm here for the monster, that's it. If you want to get inside, then get inside. I'll sit out here."

Cole heard a *whoosh* at the same time as low-hanging branches whipped and snapped. It was almost pitch black in Blackwood Forest. Cole and Victor peered into the darkness. Then, a part of that blackness tore off from the rest and charged at them, a piece of night with burning red eyes.

Victor fired his rifle at it, Cole his gun. *Pop, pop, pop, pop.* But it kept coming.

"I can't see what I'm shootin' at!" Victor shouted.

"Get down!" Cole charged forward. He and the creature were on a collision course, and when they met, Cole catapulted backwards, tumbled over the ground and, for a moment, the blackness of the creature was inside him. Cole tried to push himself to his feet, but he couldn't move. The creature roared. He heard it coming at him again with its fast, heavy steps. Then, Cole heard two steps right in front of him. He rolled over onto his side in time to see Victor standing over him, rifle aimed at the creature.

"Astum!" he screamed at the thing when it was only feet away.

Victor fired his rifle. And again. Each time, the creature jerked backwards, but it kept moving until it had Victor in its arms. Victor's rifle dropped to the ground.

"Get outta here kid! Awas!"

Cole struggled to his feet. The thing roared and put its mouth around Victor's neck.

"No!"

Victor was still fighting, trying to gouge the creature's red eyes out. It screamed.

Cole didn't have his gun. He'd dropped it somewhere. He lunged at the creature, but it knocked him over, and Cole was on the ground again.

Victor screamed. Cole could hear his skin and muscles breaking, tearing as the creature bit through Victor's neck, and blood sprayed through the air, all over Cole.

The screaming stopped.

Victor fell to the ground, lifeless. Cole stared at Victor's bloodied body. The creature grunted. Cole looked around frantically, saw his gun. He raced for it and picked it up. The thing was charging at him now. Cole aimed at its chest. He pressed down on the trigger, but the thing was already there. It swiped through the air and knocked the gun away. The gun skipped across the ground and into the dark.

Cole bolted for the gun, but the creature grabbed his ankle and pulled him. Cole was scraping at the ground, digging his fingers into the dirt, against tree roots. Then he was in its grasp, too. Its arms wrapped around his chest. He pushed out with his arms as hard as he could. It tossed him against a tree. Cole's back hit the trunk and he slammed against the ground. The creature roared, and stalked towards him, a hulking shadow.

Cole reached down into his hockey pants, fumbling around in his pocket as the creature came closer and closer. Cole pulled out his phone, turned on the flashlight, and shone it at the thing.

It roared again. "You!"

"Mr. McCabe!"

It was Reynold, but it wasn't. His eyes burned red. His lips were thin and cracked. His fingernails were sharp and long.

"You," it hissed.

"Mr. McCabe, it's Cole! Stop!"

Reynold rushed towards him. Cole got up and raced, again, towards the dark, where the gun had landed. He sifted through the leaves and dirt. Both of Reynold's fists hammered down against his back.

Cole gasped for air.

Reynold had his hands around Cole's waist, pulling him away. Cole fanned through the leaves desperately, palms down, feeling the ground. Then he felt it for a moment. Cool steel against his fingertips. "Jayney! Jayney!" he cried. *Just give me a second to find it again!* She didn't come. He dug his hand into the ground, then the other.

"Diiiieeeeeeee," Reynold hissed.

Cole inched forward. He dug his hand into another area of the ground and pulled harder. He lifted his other hand and reached. His fingers landed on the gun, and he grasped it around the handle. He let go, and it skidded across the ground. Reynold picked him up, tried to lunge for Cole's neck. Cole pressed his scarred palm against Reynold's forearm. Reynold dug his fingernails into Cole's sides. Cole screamed, felt his flesh tearing. He raised the gun, put the nozzle right against Reynold's heart.

Cole pulled the trigger.

Reynold shrieked, and the terrible sound echoed through Blackwood Forest.

Cole fell to the ground. When he looked up, the creature, Reynold, was stumbling away, into the woods.

31

NÓTÁWÍY (MY FATHER)

"EKOSANI." COLE KNELT BESIDE VICTOR'S BODY. He had his hand on Victor's chest. "Ekosani," he whispered again.

Cole picked up Victor's rifle, secured it over his shoulder, and walked to the fence. The gate was padlocked. He put his hand over it and currents pulsed through his body. Steam rose from his hand. He groaned in pain, but snapped the lock off and pushed the gate open. He walked through the opening and crossed the yard to the back entrance. No need for subtlety here. He kicked the door open, and waited again, looking up and down the fenced perimeter into Blackwood Forest, but not one guard came, and no alarm went off.

He took off the hockey equipment and left it on the ground before going inside.

Cole felt a draft. He heard his steps echo through the hallway.

He went to the front of the building where he looked outside, towards Wounded Sky, and even there, no guards stood watch. But really, he thought, what could be worse than Monster Reynold, anyway? He allowed himself a moment to feel good about the fact that he'd shot it. Him. He was sure the wound had been fatal.

Cole looked through every cabinet, every drawer, every pocket in every piece of clothing that had been left behind, but found nothing anywhere, not until he came across a security office. There was no high-tech setup, just two small monitors on a desk. A jacket on the computer chair in front of the desk. A bookshelf full of VHS tapes. Cole went to those tapes, and ran his index finger along the spines. Dates.

Months and months of dated tapes. But only one tape interested Cole, and that tape might still be in the VHS player. He rushed over to it and pressed the eject button, hoping to be right. The machine hesitated a moment, then spat out a tape.

"Yes!"

Cole shoved it back in. The machine whirred as the tape played. The first images that popped up onto the screen were of empty halls, scattered papers. The evacuation had already happened. The scene switched every five seconds to different areas of the building. Fifteen seconds after the tape had started to play, Cole saw Donald and Vikki on the floor. Dead. He fumbled at the controls, and pressed rewind. Cole watched as the scenes played backwards from camera to camera. It felt like slow-motion. Employees started to run backwards, away from the doors, and back into the building.

Then he saw what he was looking for. He stopped the tape and pressed play.

A man in a hazmat suit ran across the floor, past Donald and Vikki. The lights started flashing. An emergency.

The scene changed to another area of the building.

"Shit!"

Cole waited until the scene turned back to Donald and Vikki and the man.

The man turned towards the camera for a moment, but his face was obscured by the suit's visor. He looked down and started doing something out the camera's view. Big, metal doors began to close, trapping Donald and Vikki.

"Look up!" Cole demanded. "Look up!"

Donald and Vikki got up and ran towards the man. Just as the man looked up, the camera switched again.

"No!"

Cole waited. Employees raced for the doors, away from their offices.

The scene came back.

The man stood at the doors. He watched Donald and Vikki try desperately to get out.

The scene switched, and everybody was gone from the whole building. The scene returned to Donald and Vikki.

They were on the floor. Dying. The man waited, then turned to leave.

Cole paused the tape. He leaned forward until his nose was right up against the screen. He finally saw the man's face.

Reynold.

That room. He hadn't seen that room yet. He'd been through the entire first floor.

"A basement," Cole whispered.

Cole ran out of the security office as though he could still save Donald and Vikki, as though the video he watched was in real-time. He found the door to the basement, opened it, and flicked the light switch on. The fluorescent bulbs flickered to life. He followed the stairs down and came to another hallway. The camera that filmed the murder was fixed to the wall just above him, to the right.

He followed the path of the lens to two glass doors framed with metal—the doors that had shut, trapping Donald and Vikki. Through the glass, Cole saw two skeletons on the floor. Face down. They both had lab coats on. Donald and Vikki. Cole ran to the doors and tried to pry them open. Even with his strength, he couldn't move them.

"No!" he screamed.

He turned away from the doors, looked for something, anything, that would help. On the wall to his right, above an intercom, there was a keypad, and above that, a screen. That's what Reynold had been facing when his head was down. The only things on the screen were five dashes: _ _ _ _ _

"It's a code."

He wished Pam was there with him. He even thought about getting her, bringing her back here. It wasn't safe, though. He knew that. And by the time he got back, maybe the guards would be there, and then he wouldn't be able to return. He pulled the keypad away from the wall, and started typing in five-letter words. Any words he could think of.

"Come on!"

He heard his grandmother's voice in his head, from back when they were in Winnipeg, before he'd left for Wounded Sky, before all of this had happened. *Even I know that a name isn't the best password. Especially a three-letter one.*

"Eva," Cole said, thinking about the password to his computer that his grandmother had cracked. But at the same time, his name was four letters long, not five. What could have been as personal? More personal than his name? Then it hit him.

He typed K-I-D-D-O.

The screen turned green, and he heard a loud whirring. The doors pulled apart. Cole ran over to the bodies and fell to his knees. He put his hands on his father's remains, with the short, black hair, messed like it'd been done on purpose. Carefully, slowly, he turned the body over.

"Nótáwíy," he whispered, like he was telling a secret.

"Nótáwíy," he said through tears.

He ran his fingers over his father's skeletal face. Cole covered his mouth, and started to sob uncontrollably.

"I'm sorry," he cried. "I'm sorry."

He checked through his pockets for tobacco, to lay it down for him, to pray for him, but all he found were his pills. He took them out and threw them against the wall.

The bottle shattered. The pills fell across the floor.

Cole leaned forward and touched his forehead against his father's chest. He was seven again, sitting on the couch with his dad. They were watching a cartoon together. *Little Bear*. His dad said, "Isn't this too young for you, son?" but Cole said it didn't matter. It was the only thing on. He just wanted to sit there with his dad, put his head against his chest, and fall asleep.

Click.

Cole looked up to find a gun pointed at his head, the gun held by somebody in a hazmat suit.

He couldn't see who.

Cole reached for his own gun.

Pop.

Cole heard it. He saw the nozzle erupt in flames, felt his head snap back—

And then he heard nothing.

Saw nothing.

Felt.

Nothing.

EPILOGUE

THE CEMETERY GATE CREAKED AS EVA PUSHED IT OPEN. She walked slowly, procrastinating. She hadn't been there since the funeral, if you could call it that. What would you call a service where seven people show up? Lauren Flett, Pam, Mr. Chochinov, her dad (and an accompanying doctor, which Eva didn't count), Cole's kókom, Cole's auntie, and herself. Everybody else thought he was an arsonist. The last straw had been the X burning down. There'd been no question, to the RCMP, that Cole had done that too. After all, his body had been found in the building's ashes. Jerry and Lauren concluded that the building had burned faster than Cole expected, and he couldn't get out in time.

Bullshit.

Eva knew it was bullshit, but nobody listened to her.

She meandered through the cemetery. Walked by almost every grave she could on the way to Cole's. If she didn't see his grave, she could pretend he was alive. But she knew he was dead. She knew, as well, because of what she'd seen, that he was somehow...not. Not alive, not dead. She didn't need a math tutor, she needed an afterlife tutor.

She wanted him to burn his name onto her forearm.

Getting to his grave was inevitable. When she was there, standing in front of it, she saw that she wasn't the only one who'd been there. There were words spray painted and Sharpied all over it. BURN. GOOD RIDDANCE. MONSTER. She would come back again. She would come back and wash it all away, no matter how long it took. And if they came again, wrote words on Cole's grave again, she would wash it all off.

Again.

She reached into her pocket as she stepped forward, and took out a plastic bag full of tobacco. She pulled out a pinch and spread it on the ground. Then she knelt down, knees against the dirt, and touched the grave. It was cold, hard.

She closed her eyes.

"I miss you." She clutched the sweetgrass ring dangling from her neck. "I keep imagining that you're just in Winnipeg again, and you're not calling me. And it's okay that you're not," she started to cry, "I'm not mad that you're not. I just want you to come back. Please come back. I need you back."

"Ahem."

Eva opened her eyes. There was a coyote sitting next to her, looking at her with its head tilted sadly to the side.

She tried to say something to it. She swore that it had just cleared its throat. She stared at it until it looked away from her, and it nodded towards Cole's final resting place.

"You know," the coyote said, "I can help you with that."

To be concluded…

ACKNOWLEDGMENTS

SECOND STORIES IN TRILOGIES ARE TOUGH. There's no beginning, and no end. You're asking the reader to have a lot of faith in you, and the story you're trying to tell. In this way, *Monsters* is the scariest book I've written. The title is *apropos*. I hope the story is scary for you as well, but in a different way.

As always, I want to thank my wife and kids for the sacrifices they make that enable me to do my work. My wife is a true superhero. Keeping it in the family, I want to thank my parents: My mom for her unwavering, decades-long support, and my father, for his wisdom, guidance, and for lending me a couple books on the 'W' word, so I could get it right. As much as this is an Indigenous supernatural mystery, it's imperative I am culturally appropriate and sensitive. In that vein, I want to thank Warren Cariou, my mentor and friend, for reading the book and giving me feedback. I listened to you (mostly). Finally, thanks to my editor, Desirae Warkentin, for the work she put in to ensure my story was the best that it could be. And, you know, as a writer, you never think it's done, so thanks Dee for telling me when to stop.

I want to end by acknowledging somebody out there who might be reading this. At its heart, this book is about the monster of anxiety. I live through it, in my body and my mind. Many do. Sometimes, we think we're alone, that nobody could possibly know what we're going through, and there's nothing we can do to get through it. I've been there. I've found that it helps to know that you are not alone, to share your story, and to hear others' stories. To do things that your anxiety tells you are impossible. Getting out of bed. Writing a book. Even though we might feel weak, we are not.

We are strong.

Ekosani, Dave

THE ADVENTURE CONTINUES IN

GHOSTS

COMING IN 2019

Read on for an advance excerpt

PROLOGUE

"LUCY!"

Reynold had managed to open the front door, but he struggled now. He had one hand pressed against his chest, trying to stem the flow of blood from the bullet wound. His other hand was sliding against the wall, keeping him upright.

"Lucy!"

He finally made it to the living room, then fell forward, tumbling onto the couch. He heard footsteps scrambling above, on the second floor. They rushed down the stairs, as Reynold's vision started to fade.

He gasped for air.

"What the hell happened to the walls?" Lucy ran into the living room just as he felt consciousness slip away. "Dad?"

"UNNNH."

Reynold tried to sit up, but there was too much pain, and his head collapsed onto the couch's armrest. His eyes blinked open to find Lucy perched on the edge of the coffee table, as far away from him as she could possibly sit. She stared at him with grave concern, and something else. Fear. He patted around at his chest and felt it bandaged.

"Thanks, my girl."

She didn't respond. She had her arms crossed and was furiously chewing at a fingernail.

"Cole Harper shot me in the chest, Lucy. If you're wondering—"

"No," Lucy shook her head vigorously, "no, that's not it. Your god-damn blood is blue!"

"My…" Reynold looked at the bandages, and saw splotches of blue seeping through them "…blood?"

Lucy covered her face with both hands, and her body started to shake. Reynold watched her, unsure what to say, unsure what to think. When she'd calmed enough, she lowered her hands. "And it's cold. Your blood, it's…it's like ice." She stood up and backed away, until her calves hit a dining room chair, and sat down there. "Why is it like that?"

"Lucy…"

"Are you sick?" she asked. "Tell me!"

Reynold did sit up now, back against the arm of the couch. *Blue, ice-cold blood*, she'd said. But there was something else. "I'm not sick," he said calmly.

"Then *what*? If I were Cole, I would've shot you too!"

"I'm hungry."

"You're—" Lucy looked ready to vomit, her face drained of colour. Somebody knocked at the front door. She jumped at the sound, almost fell off the chair. Looked at her dad for direction.

She was still his girl, he thought. Even now.

The knock came again.

"Answer it," Reynold said.

"But…" she started to say.

"Do it."

She left the room, almost in a trance. The front door opened. Lucy screamed and ran back into the living room.

"What…the…fu—"

A person in a hazmat suit walked into the living room.

"—what is happening! Who the hell are you?!"

Lucy stumbled backwards against a bookshelf. Reynold was unfazed. The man walked around the couch, then dropped a gun onto the coffee table.

"Lucy," Reynold said, "would you excuse us, please?"

Lucy didn't say a word. She walked away, keeping her eyes on the suited figure. Reynold, staring at the man as well, listened for Lucy's footsteps up the stairs, down the second-floor hallway, and into her bedroom. A door slammed.

Alone now, Reynold's gaze fell to the gun on the coffee table. He picked it up and rested it on his chest.

"Please don't be so dramatic as to damage my furniture," he said.

A thick silence fell over them as they stared at each other.

Finally, Reynold asked, "Is it done?"

"Yeah. It's done."

THE RECKONER TRILOGY

by award-winning author David A. Robertson

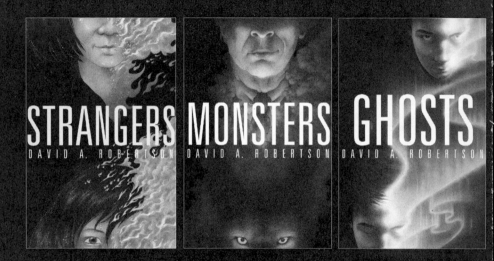

...the tantalizing mystery pulls readers on.

—The Horn Book

...a truly original superhero. Recommended

—School Library Connection